Fay smiled, warm and relieved.

As if getting him to come inside the bed-and-breakfast was some sort of personal victory... Glad he could help her put a check in the win column.

"Thank you," she said. A car drove past, the driver giving them a friendly beep of the horn. She waved without looking away from Zach. "I promise to do everything in my power to make your stay with us pleasant."

He thought again of how pretty she'd looked sitting in the sunshine. How good she smelled. How long it had been since he'd felt a woman's soft skin. How long since a woman had touched him in a nonplatonic, nonmedical or nontherapeutic way.

A long time. A long, long time.

Yeah. Probably not what she meant by making things pleasant.

"I'll just check out the room," he told her, his voice gruffer than he'd intended. Inappropriate thoughts would do that. Especially ones of him rolling around on the front yard of a residential street on a bright, sunny day with a woman who, moments before, had hauled her screaming kid inside. "No promises I'll be staying."

Dear Reader,

I read my first Harlequin romance as a teenager and from that point on, I dreamed of becoming a Harlequin author. Now here I am, releasing my eighteenth book for Superromance, and I couldn't have done it without you. Thank you so much for allowing me to share my stories with you. Here's to many more happy endings!

If you've read my books before, it's probably clear that I'm a big believer in second chances. I believe that if a person sincerely wants to overcome their past, they will—but it won't be easy. A point that was very much brought home in *The Marine's Embrace*.

Fay Lindemuth and Zach Castro are both at turning points in their lives. Fay, who was introduced in the very first In Shady Grove book, *Talk of the Town*, is a single mother struggling with depression trying desperately to overcome past mistakes and move on. Zach comes to Shady Grove to work for his brother so he can figure out what his future holds after losing his arm and leg while serving in the marines. They don't complete each other so much as they help each other heal. Zach gives Fay the strength to see herself as so much more than her illness and her past choices. Fay and her sons accept Zach into their hearts and show him how much brighter his future will be once he includes love and family into his plans.

I can't tell you how much I've enjoyed writing Fay and Zach's story—especially being able to bring Fay's story full circle and give her a well-deserved happy-ever-after. I've loved writing the In Shady Grove series and being able to return to Shady Grove time and again. This series has been very near and dear to my heart—thank you for being a part of it!

For more about future releases and a listing of all my books, please visit my website, www.bethandrews.net, or drop me a line at beth@bethandrews.net. I'd love to hear from you.

Happy reading!

Beth

BETH ANDREWS

The Marine's Embrace

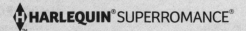

HARLEQUIN® SUPERROMANCE®

Recycling programs
for this product may
not exist in your area.

ISBN-13: 978-0-373-60997-0

The Marine's Embrace

Copyright © 2016 by Beth Burgoon

This edition published by arrangement with Harlequin Books S.A.

For questions and comments about the quality of this book, please contact us at CustomerService@Harlequin.com.

Printed in U.S.A.

During the writing of *The Marine's Embrace*, the eighth book in her popular In Shady Grove series, Romance Writers of America RITA® Award–winner **Beth Andrews** became an empty nester, discovered the joy (and pain) of spin class and was given the best gift of all, a new grandson! When not writing Beth can be found looking at pictures of her grandbaby, printing pictures of her grandbaby or sending other people pictures of her grandbaby—yes, he's that cute. Learn more about Beth and her books by visiting her website, bethandrews.net.

Books by Beth Andrews

HARLEQUIN SUPERROMANCE

In Shady Grove

Talk of the Town
What Happens Between Friends
Caught Up in You
Small-Town Redemption
Charming the Firefighter

The Truth about the Sullivans

Unraveling the Past
On Her Side
In This Town
His Secret Agenda
Do You Take This Cop?
A Marine for Christmas
The Prodigal Son
Feels Like Home

Visit the Author Profile page at Harlequin.com for more titles.

For Andy

CHAPTER ONE

HER PILLOW SMELLED of him.

Caught in that wonderful, hazy time between asleep and fully awake, Fay Lindemuth sighed and pressed her face against the soft fabric. Inhaled the familiar, tantalizing scent of her husband's aftershave. Hugging it close, she wanted nothing more than to hold this perfect moment in her memory forever. To draw it out, make it last as long as possible.

But these perfect moments didn't last. Not for her.

So she had to make the most of it. Happiness, so long sought and even longer fought for, suffused her. She used to dream of having Shane back in her life. They were soul mates, destined to be together, bound by the vows they'd made to each other and the two sons they'd created.

For the past three years, circumstances and their own choices had kept them apart. But never for long. He always came back to her.

He always left her again.

And in those times, when the heartbreak and loneliness threatened to overwhelm her, she turned to her dreams for comfort, to feel close to Shane. It was the only time she was free of pain.

Oh, she was careful. She didn't nap during the day, didn't sleep in until noon or go to bed before 10:00 p.m.—no matter how badly she wanted to. She refused to let the promise of oblivion lure her into backsliding. Into forgetting the progress she'd made.

She was better. Everyone said so.

Maybe, one day, she'd believe it herself.

And this was a step in the right direction. A step closer toward being whole once again. She had Shane back. Everything was how it used to be. How it was meant to be.

Smiling, she reached for her husband…

Only to encounter emptiness.

Her eyes flew open, her fingers curling into the cool sheet as panic reared its ugly head. Whispered to her that he was gone. That she was alone. That she'd always be alone.

Lies, she assured herself, but her fingers went numb with cold, her chest ached. She had her two precious boys and her parents. She had Neil, her older brother. She had Maddie, who, besides being Fay's best friend, was also Neil's girlfriend and the mother of his fourteen-year-old daughter, Breanne. And she had Shane. For good this time.

He'd promised.

Sitting up, she pulled the sheet over her bare

breasts. It took a moment for her eyes to adjust to the darkness, but once they did, she noticed movement by the dresser. Was that a rustling sound?

Someone was in the room with her.

Shane hadn't left her.

Leaning across the bed, she reached for the lamp, the ring she wore on a delicate chain around her neck sliding out from under the loosened sheet. She stopped. The rustling could have been the wind blowing through the trees. The movement a shift of shadows.

After all, she did have a bad habit of letting her imagination get the best of her. Of believing only what she wanted, no matter how solid the proof against her fantasies were.

Face your fears.

That's the advice Dr. Porter always gave during their weekly sessions. The psychiatrist loved spouting platitudes about how Fay was capable of controlling her emotions. Of handling any situation. Strong enough to get through disappointment or heartache. Strong enough to survive.

Which was laughable, but it made him—and her family—feel better, so she went along.

Pretend to be strong and eventually you'll be strong. Act as if—as if you're confident. Clever. In control. Brave.

Act as if, she repeated silently to herself, her

fingers tightening on the lamp's switch. *Act as if...act as if...*

She turned the light on and sagged against the headboard.

Shane was still here.

Thank you, God.

He glanced over his shoulder at her, and she smiled, but he turned back to finish tugging on his jeans.

Her smile fading, she told herself not to read into things. He'd never been big on mornings, had always preferred keeping to himself for the first few hours of the day. Plus, she probably looked awful, the eye shadow and mascara she'd carefully applied last night streaked and smudged, her hair a tangled mess.

Shane liked pretty things. Had always hated when she didn't do her hair or makeup. Said he preferred her all sparkly and shiny.

Act as if...act as if...

She wiped her fingers under her eyes, noted the eyeliner and mascara on her fingertips, before smoothing the sheet and tucking it under her arms. She allowed herself a moment to just take in the sight of her husband. He was so handsome, tall with a lean, wiry build.

And he was all hers.

"Good morning," she whispered, conscious of

their sons sleeping in the room next door. She didn't want to wake them this early.

She wanted a few more minutes alone with her husband. So they could talk. Make plans. Starting with their living arrangements. Since she was manager of Bradford House, the bed-and-breakfast Neil owned, she and the boys were able to live in the third-floor apartment rent free, but she doubted Shane would want to stay here permanently.

Doubted Neil would let him.

They just had a few things to work out. Then they'd wake the boys together, tell them the good news—that they were going to be a family again.

It would be perfect. Just like she'd always dreamed.

Shane sat on the bed next to her, and she leaned forward, reached for him, but he bent over and put on one of his work boots.

Fay frowned. That wasn't right. He was supposed to pull her into his arms. Kiss her. Tell her how much he loved her. Reassure her he was finally coming home for good.

"Are you…are you leaving?" she asked.

He yanked on the second boot, his head down as he tied the laces. "Yeah."

"Did I do something wrong?" She hated how thin and reedy her voice sounded. How pathetic.

Hated how small and stupid she felt for saying anything at all. For worrying.

He shot her a glance, his hazel eyes narrowed,

irritation tightening his expression. "I have a job interview."

He'd told her all about the interview for a position with a heating and cooling contractor in Pittsburgh. It was why he'd come back to their hometown of Shady Grove, Pennsylvania, just forty miles outside the city. Well, the job *plus* her and the boys, of course.

"But it's not even five thirty," she said, shifting onto her knees. She rubbed his bare shoulders, trailed her fingers through the soft strands of his dark blond hair. He'd grown it out this past year, the ends now brushing his collar. She preferred it shorter. Not quite so shaggy. Or young looking.

Contrite at the traitorous thought, she kissed the back of his neck. It was only hair. He could wear it however he liked. "You don't *really* have to leave right now, do you?" she asked.

She could wake the boys, fix them all a quick breakfast. Elijah and Mitchell had been asleep when Shane arrived late last night, and she was sure they'd want to see him.

Even if a change in plans meant her having to deal with a couple of cranky little boys the rest of the day.

Shaking his head, Shane stood. "Sorry, babe, but I need to prepare for this interview. You want me to get the job, right?"

She sat back on her heels, hands in her lap, duly chastised by his words, trying not to let his gruff tone bother her. Everyone said she was too sensitive. Always taking things others said too personally.

"Of course I want you to get the job. And you will."

He was smart and had lots of experience, having worked the past two years for a company that installed heating and air-conditioning units in large office buildings, schools, hospitals and prisons. But that job had meant traveling across not only Pennsylvania but also into Maryland and New Jersey. Taking him away from her and the boys.

And while others might think Shane had been running from them, running from his responsibilities and the promises he'd made, she knew the truth. He'd been lost.

She could relate.

Which was why she could also forgive.

After untangling herself from the sheets, she got to her feet and crossed to him. He was checking his phone, so she wrapped her arms around his waist from behind and laid her cheek against his shoulder blade, hoping the feel of her naked body would entice him to at least turn around. "Come back after the interview. You can see the boys and we'll celebrate you getting the job."

"Not sure I can," he said, stepping forward, forcing her to let go. He pulled on his shirt then checked his reflection in the dresser mirror, smoothing his hair before facing her. "I'm already down to half a tank of gas and I don't know how long it'll be before my last paycheck catches up to me."

"I have money," she assured him quickly, reaching for her robe on the end of the bed. "In my purse in the living roo—"

"I'll get it." He stepped toward her and she lifted her arms in relief—only to lower them when he brushed past her to pick up his wallet from the nightstand. "I'll call you."

He left, without a goodbye kiss or a backward glance. Without the words she needed to hear—that he loved her.

That he needed her.

Like she needed him.

He just...walked away. Walked out on her like he had so many times before.

Feeling more exposed than she could ever remember, she started shivering violently. From the chill in the air, she was sure. The chill and her nudity. But when she put on her robe, the tremors continued. She sat on the corner of the bed and rocked back and forth. Back and forth.

Her eyes stung, but she fought the tears. She wouldn't cry. Not today. Today was a good day. A turning point in her life.

Today she got back everything she'd lost.

She wouldn't speculate about what Shane hadn't said or why he'd acted so distant. He was stressed, focused on acing the interview so he could come home for good, that was all.

But…oh, God…what if it wasn't? She leaped to her feet, began pacing as she chewed on her pinkie nail. What if he was mad at her? She'd been clingy. Needy. What if…what if she'd said something she shouldn't have? What if she'd upset him or…or disappointed him in some way? What if he'd found her lacking last night?

No, everything was fine. *She* was fine.

Except she didn't feel fine. She felt anxious, as if her skin was too tight. Wound up and terrified, her heart pounding, her stomach churning.

She had to talk to him. Apologize for whatever she'd done. Promise to do better, be more adventurous in bed, give him more space. To give him whatever he needed. Whatever he wanted.

She burst out into the short hallway, peeked in on the boys—still asleep, *thank God*—then hurried down the stairs, her fingers trailing over the banister, the wood steps cool beneath her bare feet.

Hurry, hurry, hurry, she chanted silently. She had to get to him in time, had to apologize for overreacting.

She hit the second floor and slowed. Tried to quiet her breathing. Only two of the guest rooms were occupied and their doors were shut, the entire floor silent. She rounded the corner and took the back stairway down to the kitchen. Why did she have to upset Shane? She was so stupid. She should have been more understanding. Should have kept quiet and just let him go with a smile and a kiss.

She'd make it up to him. First with her apology and then, when he came back tonight, with her body. She'd go downtown that afternoon, pick up some slinky lingerie. Reaching the kitchen, she raced across the tile floor to the back door and whipped it open.

"He's gone," a deep, male voice said from behind her.

She whirled around, her hand at her throat. "Damien," she breathed, noticing Bradford House's chef at the six-burner stove on the other side of the room. It was a testament to her focus on getting to Shane that she hadn't seen Damien. Huge, bald and heavily tattooed, the man had presence.

Not to mention his yellow do-rag and matching T-shirt were bright enough to rival the rising sun.

She glanced out at the small parking lot, but Shane's truck was nowhere to be seen. She was too late. She'd pushed him away.

Again.

The darkness inside her head grew, pressed against her skull, thick and insistent, tempting her to give in to it. A sense of sadness, of hopelessness overcame her so swiftly, so sharply, it took her breath. She wanted to collapse right there on the cold floor, lay her head on her knees and weep.

But she couldn't. She wouldn't. She no longer gave in to the thoughts whispering in her mind, telling her she was useless, that no one loved her. They were horrible, terrifying lies, and she refused to listen to them.

Most of the time.

Swallowing the despair rising in her throat, she shut the door, knowing Damien watched her, ready to catch her if she fell. Ready to tell Neil if she slid into one of her *moods*—as her mother had deemed them when Fay had barely been ten and would slip into quietness, curl into herself.

When she'd all but disappear.

"You okay?" Damien asked.

She hung her head for a moment then inhaled deeply. Forced a light laugh as she faced him. "Yes. You just…surprised me."

"I'm sorry."

His gentle tone and the sympathy in his dark eyes told her he was sorry for a lot more than nearly giving her a heart attack. He was sorry for her. Because she couldn't hold on to the man she loved. Because she was weak. Damaged.

Curling her fingers into her palms, she pulled her shoulders back and pasted a smile on her face. "It was my fault. I wasn't paying attention."

Everything was her fault. Her fault Shane left. Her fault her family treated her with kid gloves. Her fault she couldn't get rid of the dark feelings. Couldn't live in the light. Couldn't be whole.

Suddenly exhausted, her legs heavy, her body aching, she shuffled toward the stairs, wanting only to go back to bed. To sleep and sleep and sleep.

Small steps count.

She frowned. How did Dr. Porter's voice always know when to pop into her head? It was disconcerting, to say the least.

Small steps count, the voice repeated stubbornly. *Take enough of them and you get where you're going. Win enough small victories and you'll eventually win the war.*

Well, the man did make sense. And while she wasn't sure she'd ever be completely cured, she could get better. Dr. Porter told her all the time that she was smart enough, strong enough to take her life in a new direction. She just needed to work harder at living up to his confidence in her. To making it true.

And she'd start today. Right now.

It took willpower—surely more than it should have—but she turned to the right instead of heading upstairs, then skirted around the huge center island and crossed over to the coffeepot next to the industrial-sized stainless steel fridge.

"Honey," Damien said softly, "what are you doing?"

Winning the battle.

"Getting a cup of coffee." She poured some into a mug, added a small amount of cream and sipped it before grabbing a napkin and helping herself to one of the cranberry–white chocolate scones cooling on a wire rack.

Even small victories deserved to be celebrated.

"No, I mean what are you doing with Shane?"

"I have no idea what you're talking about," she said, all faux serenity and innocence, popping a bite of scone into her mouth.

Damien frowned, which, for some reason, brought out his dimples. "You're not fooling me. I know a walk of shame when I see one."

It was then she realized that she was still in her robe and hadn't even bothered to wash her face or brush her hair.

Heat washed up her neck and into her cheeks. With her fair skin, there was no way Damien could miss her blush. Hoping she could ride it out—at least until she wasn't glowing red—she ducked her head, pretended great interest in pouring more coffee into her already almost-full cup, adding a drop of cream and stirring.

Damien inhaled deeply then heaved a long, drawn-out sigh—as if sucking in patience before huffing out the weariness that came along with dealing with her.

Her mother often did the same thing. It was a wonder they didn't hyperventilate.

"Ignoring me won't work," he said as he took eggs out of the fridge. "Neither will pretending you don't know what I'm talking about."

"I'm not ignoring anything." But it took a moment before she was able to meet his eyes. "And I'm not on a walk of shame—I have nothing to be ashamed of."

She and Shane were husband and wife.

Sort of.

Even if they weren't technically married at the moment, being with him could never be wrong.

Damien shook his head. "He left you. He *divorced* you."

Though his voice wasn't unkind, the words still had the power to make her head snap back.

"Thank you," she managed, but had to stop and clear her throat before continuing. "But I don't need to be reminded of those facts."

If she did, she'd only have to ask Maddie. Lord knew her best friend had never held back when it came to listing Fay's mistakes or telling her how she should live her life. She loved to remind Fay what Shane had done.

As if Fay didn't remember the pain each and every day.

"Then why did you sleep with him?" Damien asked, taking a large ceramic bowl down from an open shelf.

She broke off a corner of the scone, raised it to her mouth, only to set it down again. "Things are different now. Between me and Shane. He's changed."

Damien cracked an egg into the bowl, then another. "If he's so different, why did I catch him sneaking out—"

"He wasn't sneaking out." But she couldn't help but think of how she'd discovered him getting dressed in the dark, as if he was going to leave without waking her. Without saying goodbye. Like a one-night stand eager to escape.

"It's barely daylight," Damien said, adding another egg to the bowl. "And *you* were running after him." He nodded sharply as if he'd just cracked the case along with his eggs. He grabbed a large whisk from the crock next to the stove and pointed it at her. "He snuck out."

"We said our goodbyes upstairs. And the only reason he left so early is because he has a job interview."

"Before 6:00 a.m.?"

At her friend's incredulous look, Fay stared into her coffee, wishing she could somehow dive in there and swim away from this conversation. "He had to go back to his hotel. Shower and change and...and prepare for it."

Another sigh, this one of the you-poor-thing variety. "Honey, he crept out of here like a thief. You should've seen the look on his face when he came down and realized he wasn't alone."

"I'm sure he was just surprised to find anyone awake so early. Anyway, we're getting back together," she continued, though why the words came out so quickly, why she sounded so tentative, she wasn't sure.

She licked her lips. Linked her hands together at her waist. It was only a matter of time before people knew she was seeing Shane again. They'd need to understand that Shane was back in her life for good.

"Shane and I are back together."

There. That was better. Direct and to the point. A statement of fact and not some wishy-washy hope.

Damien stared at her, narrow eyed, mouth tight. "What?"

"He wants us back—me and the boys. He wants us to be a family again."

"Uh-huh. I see. And did he say this before or after you had sex?"

"I don't see why that matters."

"Before? Or after?"

She squirmed. Forcing her body to remain motionless, she said, "Before."

Damien looked at her as if she was some brainless idiot. "Don't you see? He just said that to get what he wanted."

"It wasn't like that." Damien hadn't been there last night. He didn't see how Shane looked at her. "He meant it this time."

"I know you want to believe that, but he's using you. It's the same thing every time. He calls in the middle of the night—"

"It wasn't that late."

"No? What time was it?"

Well, she'd set herself up for that one. "A little before midnight. He missed me and didn't want to wait until morning to see me."

"He didn't think to call you earlier? To let you know he was coming to town?"

She blinked rapidly. "He…he probably wanted to surprise me."

"He wanted what he always wants," Damien muttered.

"He wanted to see me," she insisted, hugging her arms around herself.

She wouldn't let Damien or anyone else tarnish what had happened between her and Shane last night. Wouldn't let them take away her happiness. Not when she was already terrified of it slipping away.

"It's the same thing, time after time. Shane just happens to be in town—a spur-of-the-moment trip—and calls in the middle of the night, telling you how much he misses you, how much he wants to see you. He shows up, a little or a lot drunk, says what you want to hear, gets you in bed then takes off before the sun comes up."

"He wasn't drunk." Yes, maybe she'd tasted beer when Shane kissed her, but his movements had been steady, his gaze clear. And last night wasn't like those other times. Last night was different.

It had to be.

Damien set the whisk down and rounded the island to take both her hands in his large ones. Squeezed gently. "You can't keep sleeping with him. You're going to get hurt."

She tugged free of his hold. Told herself he was only trying to help her. That he didn't mean to be cruel. But she was tired of giving everyone the benefit of the doubt when they were all so quick to doubt her intelligence, to judge her decisions.

"You don't understand." No one did. They couldn't comprehend what the past three years had been like for her. How hard she'd had to pretend that she was fine without Shane in her life.

"I understand he's a user and a liar and that he cheated on you—left you for a nineteen-year-old."

"He made a mistake," she said hoarsely. "One he regrets. I've forgiven him."

She clutched the ring hanging from the chain around her neck. Her wedding ring. She had to wear it under her clothes like some secret, like a personal sin. But soon, soon she'd put it back on her finger for the world to see. Then they'd all know she wasn't some fool, hoping and wishing for a fantasy to come true. They'd all see how wrong they were about Shane.

How wrong they were about her.

Damien shook his head sadly. "I know you think you need him, but you don't. The sooner you realize that, the sooner you start to believe in yourself and put yourself first, the better off you'll be."

Fay's bottom lip trembled. She bit down on it. Hard. There was nothing more to say and certainly nothing more she wanted to hear, so she swept past him and went up the stairs. As much as she'd like to believe she did so as calmly and as regally as a queen, by the time she reached her apartment she was sweating and out of breath, having raced up the two flights like a teenage girl in the throes of a major pity party.

In her bedroom, she shut the door and leaned back against it. Damien was wrong. They were all wrong. She did need Shane.

She didn't know who she was without him.

CHAPTER TWO

HE WAS LOST.

In Shady Grove, Pennsylvania.

How the hell was that even possible?

Not lost, Zach Castro amended. He knew where he was. At the corner of Main and Kennedy Streets, downtown Shady Grove, surrounded directly by squat buildings, most of which looked to be one hundred years old, the outer area nothing but rolling green hills. The sun warmed his head, but the cool breeze ruffling the empty right sleeve of his T-shirt reminded him that though it was late April, this small town was a world away from Houston in more ways than one.

Yeah, he knew exactly where he was. He just didn't know where he was going.

Story of his freaking life.

The cab driver had dropped him off, insisting this exact spot was the address Zach had given him. Lying bastard.

He pulled out his phone, opened the maps app and typed in *O'Riley's*. Two blocks away. He could do that.

He hoped.

He shifted his weight onto his left leg, but the ache in his right thigh remained and would no doubt grow in intensity. Pain was his new normal. There was nothing he could do about it except grit his teeth and bear it.

His right leg had stiffened up during the plane ride from Houston to Pittsburgh and had only gotten worse in the forty-minute cab ride that had brought him here. Moving would help. Eventually. But first, he knew, it was going to hurt like a son of a bitch.

New normal, he reminded himself. Bending at the waist, he grabbed his duffel from where the cabbie had dropped it at the curb and slung the strap over his left shoulder. Following the directions on his phone he turned—slowly and carefully—to the east and began walking.

Pain shot from just above his knee up to his hip. Sweat formed on his upper lip. He breathed through his mouth, fighting the nausea rising in his throat, and kept going, his stride awkward, his limp heavy, his gaze straight ahead. He felt people staring at him, scurrying out of his way, watching him as they passed. Wondering who he was. What he was doing there.

Their curiosity rolled off him, but their sympathy—and worse, their pity—grated. He didn't want it. Didn't need anyone feeling sorry for him, for what he'd lost. He was getting through it, wasn't he? He'd already made progress, had gotten himself out of that wheelchair and on to a prosthetic leg. The surgeries, the grueling physical therapy, learning how to walk again had all been worth it. Each step he took, no matter how small, was a victory.

One that would be easier to celebrate if it didn't hurt so goddamn much.

He passed a hardware store with a row of colorful, decorative flags waving in the breeze, then a bookstore's bright and cheerful window display. At the corner he turned right. Halfway there, he told himself, squinting against the sun.

By the time he reached the next corner, his shirt was damp and sticking to him and his breaths were coming in gasps. He leaned against a street lamp and looked across the street at O'Riley's.

It wasn't what he'd expected at all.

Thank Christ.

Knowing the bar was owned by Kane Bartasavich, of the Houston Bartasaviches, Zach had pictured an upscale place, all sleek lines and plenty of glass. A place where the country-club set went to drink their lunch or stopped by after work for a fancy cocktail that cost as much as a decent meal.

He hadn't pictured a two-story gray building that seemed to list to one side, a parking lot that needed repaving and neon beer signs in the windows.

It wasn't the first time he'd been wrong. Wouldn't be the last.

Unlike certain members of his family—namely his father and eldest brother—he didn't get bent out of shape when things didn't go his way. Didn't carry the illusion that he had all the answers. He liked to think the arrogance that ran in his bloodline, the huge egos that had been handed down generation to generation, had somehow skipped him, but the truth was, he'd worked damned hard to be as different from them as possible.

He had spent his entire life pushing them away. Keeping them all at a distance.

Now, here he was—not quite broken, but a far cry from being whole—and who was the only person he could think to turn to?

A Bartasavich.

Fate was a coldhearted bitch with a twisted sense of humor.

Readjusting his duffel bag, he crossed the street, then made his way past a number of vehicles in the parking lot. Something else he hadn't counted on or, to be honest, considered when he'd decided to come here—that there would be people inside a small-town bar in the middle of a Wednesday afternoon.

All there to witness his humiliation.

He'd faced worse, he reminded himself as he stopped in front of the door, the muted sounds of music and conversation floating through the wood. Had faced much worse than public embarrassment and survived. Was still surviving it.

That wasn't to say he looked forward to what he had to do. He was just realistic enough to know he didn't have many other choices.

Jaw tight, shoulders back, he reached out to open the door—only to realize he was lifting his right arm to do so. He quickly dropped it. His arm, like his right leg from above the knee down, wasn't there anymore, but unless he consciously thought about an action—opening a door, brushing his teeth, signing his name—his brain still wanted to use it. Call it habit, instinct or just the fact that he'd been right-handed his entire life—whatever the reason, it wasn't that big a deal.

Just a reminder that even the simplest tasks were now anything but simple.

He grabbed the handle with his left hand, swung it open and stepped inside before he changed his mind. Beggars couldn't be choosers and all that bullshit.

And that's what he was. A freaking beggar, come to plead for scraps.

He rolled his head a few times, trying to ease the tightness in his shoulders, then moved forward. The bar was like any other dive he'd ever been in. Dimly lit with wooden floors that needed refinishing, tables and chairs that had seen better days and walls decorated with more of those neon beer signs. The scents of grilled meat and barbecue sauce filled the air. People occupied a few of the tables and the booths lining the walls, eating a late lunch or getting an early start on their evening drinking. There was a pool table in the back along with a dartboard, and the bar ran the length of the room to the left.

A waitress with a neck tattoo, her dark hair cut in a weird, uneven style, wove her way through the tables, delivering drinks and food. And behind the bar pulling a beer was none other than the owner himself. Kane Bartasavich, second son of Clinton Bartasavich Sr.

One of Zach's three older half brothers. And the man Zach had come to see.

He made his way to the bar and noted how Kane momentarily stilled when he caught sight of him, saw the surprise in his brother's eyes. But by the time Zach reached him, Kane's expression was clear, his posture relaxed.

"What's this?" he asked, shutting off the beer tap. "Slumming?"

"Looks like." He nodded at the beer Kane set on a tray next to a soda. "I'll take one of those."

The waitress came, picked up the tray as Kane got a clean glass. Drew Zach's beer.

Older than Zach by more than five years, Kane still looked like the hell-raiser he'd once been, in faded jeans and a black T-shirt, his dark blond hair pulled back in a ponytail, the edges of his tattoos visible just below both shirtsleeves.

His leg aching, Zach shifted, but that didn't take enough weight off it. He eyed the empty stool next to him, feeling as if he was going into battle once again. He should have sat at a table or a booth, let Kane come to him. Too late now. There was no easy—or smooth—way to do it, but he'd be damned if he wouldn't try. He dropped his bag at his feet, laid his left hand on the bar and lifted with his arm while he pushed off the floor with his left leg.

His ass hit the edge of the seat and he slid off, coming within an inch of knocking a few teeth loose against the bar before catching his balance. Kane reached toward him, but Zach shook his head and Kane eased back. There wasn't anything he could do from the other side of the bar, anyway.

And Zach was already there to ask for a favor. He wasn't about to add insult to injury by having his brother help him do something as simple as sitting down.

Zach glared at the stool. He didn't need to look around to know he'd attracted attention. He could continue standing there, pretend nothing had happened, act as if he'd rather drink his beer and have the upcoming conversation with Kane on his own two feet—one real, one not. He could give up. Could give in and take the easy way out, just this once.

But he was afraid that like any temptation, one time wouldn't be enough.

He took hold of the bar again, bent his left knee

and hopped onto the stool, wiggling fully onto the seat.

Breathing heavily, he shut his eyes for a moment. It might not have been pretty, and yeah, he'd just made a fool of himself in front of at least thirty strangers, but he'd done it.

Best of all? He'd done it all on his own.

Kane set his beer in front of him, and Zach grabbed it. He was pathetically grateful when Kane's expression didn't change in the least, even though Zach was sure his brother had noticed how badly Zach's hand was shaking.

Hard not to, since he'd slopped beer over the shiny bar.

Kane wiped up the spill then tossed the towel over his shoulder. "You're a long way from home."

Sipping his beer, Zach grunted. He wanted to down the entire glass and ask for another. When he'd first been injured, he hadn't touched any alcohol, had known that it would have been all too easy to rely on it to ease the pain. As the months passed, as he'd survived surgeries and physical therapy, he'd continued to stay away, wanting to be able to say he'd recovered on his own, by his own strength and nothing else.

Now, every once in a while, he allowed himself a drink. Just to prove to himself that he could stop at one.

Kane's gaze flicked to Zach's empty sleeve, his mouth a grim line. Zach's fingers tightened on his glass. He slowly lowered the beer, waiting for Kane to say something. To offer him sympathy or ask him something idiotic like how was he feeling.

"Get you something to eat?" Kane asked, his tone almost bored.

Zach could have kissed him.

Instead, he settled on shaking his head. Took another sip of beer before setting it down again.

He hated this. Hated what he'd been reduced to.

But he wouldn't hide from it. Would do what he'd done with every obstacle, every hard time or unpleasant task he'd encountered in his life.

He'd face it head-on.

"I need a job," he said, his quiet tone still somehow defiant. Belligerent.

Pissed off.

If Kane was surprised, he didn't show it. Then again, the man had been a ranger. Not in league with the marines, of course, but he could at least be respected. Zach had come to Shady Grove and sought Kane out due to that shared connection of serving in the military.

He held Kane's gaze while the other man studied him, trying, he knew, to read Zach's thoughts. To gauge what was really going on inside his head.

Hell, over the past eight months, Zach had been poked and prodded by dozens of doctors, analyzed and questioned by shrinks, therapists and counselors. Let Kane look. He wouldn't see anything Zach didn't want him to see.

"You ever tend bar before?" Kane asked.

Zach's mouth thinned. "No."

"Wait tables?"

"I joined up right after high school." Which Kane damned well knew. "Not sure how the army works," he continued, "but the Marine Corps is too busy teaching us how to win wars to focus on mixing drinks and carrying plates."

Kane took the towel off his shoulder with a snap then put it over his other one. "No summer jobs working in food service?"

He shook his head. He'd spent three summers working on building sites. Had even considered, those few times he'd thought about his future outside the corps, pursuing a career in construction. Maybe running his own business.

Back when he'd thought he'd leave whole.

"I can clean," he said softly, hating that he had to beg for the most meager of jobs. Especially from a Bartasavich. He cleared his throat. Leaned forward. "I can stock the bar, wash dishes—" Probably. "Or if you know of any local business that could use someone…"

Someone. Right. More like a one-armed, one-legged man who suffered from headaches, flashbacks and PTSD. Christ, there were probably tons of job opportunities out there just waiting for him.

Maybe coming here was a mistake, but he hadn't known where else to go.

All he'd known was that he couldn't stay in Houston.

Kane pursed his lips. "I could always use an extra set of hands around here."

Zach raised his eyebrows. Lifted his empty sleeve. "Will half a set work?"

Kane's wince was so slight, Zach doubted most people would have noticed it. "Poor choice of words. You want an apology?"

"If you give me one, I'm going to lose what little respect I have for you."

"Wouldn't want that," Kane said so drily Zach was surprised a puff of dust didn't come out of his mouth. "You can start tomorrow."

Zach finished his beer, hoping to wash away the sudden tightness in his throat. "I appreciate it."

"Tough getting those words out, huh?"

"Only when saying them to a Bartasavich."

Kane's grin was sharp and appreciative and not the least bit insulted. Best of all? He didn't point out that Zach was a Bartasavich, too—in blood if not in name.

"You know, the apartment upstairs is empty," Kane said. "If you need a place to stay."

"I'll pass."

"You could bunk with us," Kane suggested. "We have a guest room on the first floor."

His brother obviously thought Zach was refusing due to the apartment being on the second level. That wasn't it. He could handle a few steps. It might even be good for his recovery, climbing up and down a bunch of stairs each day.

But he didn't want to owe Kane for anything more than the job.

"Does Charlotte know you go around collecting strays?" Zach asked of Kane's wife.

Kane lifted a shoulder. "You're not a stray. You're family." As if reading Zach's mind, he quietly added, "Whether you like it or not."

He didn't like it, but that wasn't news. "I don't need a handout. I make my own way."

"It's a place to sleep, not the account number to my trust fund. It doesn't have to mean you like me or that you suddenly want to change your name to Bartasavich and come over for Christmas dinner."

"I'll find a place. On my own."

Maybe.

The only other time he'd been to Shady Grove, he'd stayed at a Holiday Inn off the highway, but that had to be at least five miles away. And he didn't think there was any public transportation in town. Not exactly a great setup for a man who needed to relearn how to drive.

"King's Crossing has rooms," Kane said, writing something on the back of a cocktail napkin. "But it's on the other side of town. Bradford House is closer. It's a bed-and-breakfast, though, not a real hotel." He handed Zach the napkin. "I put my cell number on there, too. On the off chance you can't find a room tonight and would rather ask for help than sleep on the street."

Easy for Kane to say. He had this place, his pretty little wife, probably a house with a white picket fence. He had Estelle, his eighteen-year-old daughter and the only Bartasavich Zach actually cared about.

He had everything.

The only thing Zach had was his pride. And he'd choked down enough of it today.

Zach had to lay the napkin on the bar to fold it with his one hand. When he was done, he stood—getting off the stool was considerably easier than getting on the damned thing—and dug his wallet from his front left pocket.

"How much for the beer?" he asked, putting the napkin in with his money.

"On the house."

"Don't," Zach said, holding Kane's gaze. "Don't make me regret coming here."

"Yeah, I get it. You make your way," Kane said mildly, pulling another beer. "It's one beer. You going to insist I work you twelve hours a day? Pay you minimum wage and not one cent more?"

"How. Much?"

Kane served his customer then wiped his hands on the towel. "Ten should cover it."

Zach narrowed his eyes. "Ten bucks for a draft? What'd you do, lace it with gold?"

"The drink was four dollars, but I figured you'd want to leave your friendly bartender a nice tip."

He handed him a five. "You figured wrong. What time should I come in tomorrow?"

"I'll be here at noon."

"Noon? What's the matter? Need your beauty sleep?"

"That's why I'm the fairest of us all," Kane said, pouring tequila into a blender.

Zach scratched the scar at his right temple. Had to admit what Kane said was true.

Especially now.

"I can be here earlier. I don't need special treatment. I'll put in a full day's work."

"I come in at noon," Kane said, slicing a lime, "because I'm behind this bar most nights until 2:00 a.m. then I spend another half an hour cleaning up. I'll need you to come in when we open for lunch, so you'll work the early shift, 10:00 a.m. to 6:00 p.m., Monday through Thursday, and 7:00 p.m. to 3:00 a.m. either Friday or Saturday night. I know math has never been your strong suit, so I'll save you from having to count on your fingers. Each shift is eight hours."

"Hard to count to eight," Zach said, waving the fingers of his left hand at Kane, "when you only have enough for five."

Kane sent him a bland look, not the least bit of

sympathy in his gaze. "Take off your shoe, then, and use your toes."

Apparently Kane wasn't going to coddle him like a child.

Or worse, treat him like an invalid.

Zach bent and picked up his duffel bag. Put it over his shoulder. "I'll see you tomorrow then."

"I don't suppose you want me to drive you to a hotel?"

"Nope."

"Right. If you change your mind—"

"I won't." He wouldn't. Not about anything.

He turned and skirted the stool, his leg hurting worse now than when he'd first come in, but he kept going. His entire focus on taking the next step. Then another.

He'd just passed the end of the bar when Kane's voice reached him.

"Hey," his brother called. Zach stopped but didn't turn around. Couldn't. It took all he had just to remain upright, and would take extra effort to get him out the door. No way was he risking falling on his face in front of all these people by trying something as fancy as a turn without anything to hold on to.

"Before you come in tomorrow," Kane continued, "do me—and the world in general—a favor and see about getting that stick dislodged from your ass."

Several customers laughed; a few watched him

to catch his reaction. Nope. No special treatment on Kane's end.

Guess he shouldn't have been worried about that.

Zach's answer was to walk away—arm raised, middle finger extended.

He didn't smile until he stepped outside, the door shutting behind him.

Maybe coming here hadn't been a mistake after all.

CHAPTER THREE

"MAMA?"

Checking her phone on the bottom porch step outside Bradford House, Fay didn't even glance up. She heard the words *Mom*, *Mommy* and *Mama* at least a thousand times a day. Both of her sons seemed to start every single sentence with one of them. They were like the background music to her life.

"Hmm?" she asked, closing out her text messages to check her emails.

Mitchell, her three-and-a-half-year-old, crouched in front of her, peered up into her face. "Mama?" He shook her free arm. Repeatedly. And hard enough to have her head wobbling along. "Mama? Mama?"

With a half laugh, half sigh, she smiled at him. "What-a? What-a? What-a?"

"Mama, are you mad at me?"

"What? No. Of course not. Why would you think that?"

He shrugged. Rubbed her arm, his hand warm and clammy and covered in potting soil—which now streaked her skin from elbow to wrist. "I asked if I could plant the daisies and you didn't answer me."

She flushed. Guilt, so easily induced, twisted in her stomach. "I'm sorry, baby. I didn't hear you. I was checking my phone." Standing, she put her phone in her pocket. Took hold of her son's hand. "Of course you can plant the daisies. We'll put some in here," she continued, picking up a sunny yellow ceramic pot and carrying it out to the grass. "Why don't you pick out the colors while I open another bag of soil?"

"Okay!" He raced over to the flat of colorful gerbera daisies and knelt down, studying them intently.

She dragged the potting soil into the sunshine, the grass thick and green under her sneakers, then used a pair of scissors to open the bag. Knowing how much Mitchell liked to "help," she waited for him to bring the flowers over so he could fill the pot.

"Mama," he said, running back to her to tug on her jeans. "How many?"

"Let's start with three and go from there."

He nodded, then hurried back to the flowers.

Her baby didn't like to venture too far from her. Every few minutes he'd come back to her side, touch her leg or arm, make sure he had her attention, that she was still there, and then wander off again.

Elijah would have just yelled at her, as if he was

a half a block away instead of across the brick sidewalk that bisected the yard. Then again, Elijah was more likely to take off down the street than stand still long enough to pick out daises, let alone plant them. That boy had energy to spare.

While she so often felt as if she had none.

But not today. Today she'd taken control. As much as she'd wanted to curl into a ball after her conversation with Damien, she hadn't. She'd showered, dressed, put on fresh makeup and straightened her naturally curly hair.

Just as Shane liked it.

She'd gotten the boys up, cooked pancakes in their tiny kitchen while they got dressed, then sent Elijah off to school before greeting her guests downstairs. She'd put in a few hours in her office, letting Mitch watch TV before heading to WISC, an upscale clothing boutique downtown. It had taken her close to an hour, but she'd finally chosen a deep purple lace chemise and matching panties for tonight. Mitch had been so patient and well behaved, she'd taken him to Panoli's for lunch. After pizza, they'd stopped at the garden center on the way home.

She eyed the flats of flowers—over a dozen perennials and annuals of all shapes, sizes and colors littered the space between the driveway and sidewalk, plus two azalea bushes, a rosebush and three different kinds of decorative grass.

She chewed on her pinkie nail. Perhaps she'd

gotten a tad bit carried away, but there was nothing better than tending a garden, caring for it so it flourished. Bloomed. Cullen's Greenhouse had just received a new shipment, and she'd had a hard time reining in her enthusiasm.

And, it seemed, her business credit card.

Not that Neil would complain. Or even question the purchase. He never did. Her brother trusted her to run Bradford House as she saw fit, and encouraged her to make every decision, from what sort of linens to use to whom to hire. Whatever she wanted, he made sure she got.

But sometimes she wondered if his being unable to refuse her anything had less to do with trust and more to do with him thinking if he denied her something she'd break into a million pieces. Pieces he'd be unable to put back together.

"I got three, Mama," Mitch said, his little arms around three plastic containers as he headed toward her. "See?"

"I do see," she said, crossing the short distance to take two of the flowers from him. "These will look very pretty together."

"Yeah. I got yellow 'cuz it's your favorite color and red 'cuz it's mine and orange for 'Lijah. It's for all of us. They'll be a family like we are."

She hated that he didn't remember a time when they'd been a real family. That he'd never had his father in his life full time.

She brushed his hair back. The once almost-white strands were now darker, with a definite reddish tint, but it was still baby fine and stick straight. "You know," she said, wanting to ease Mitchell into getting used to having Shane around, "Daddy's favorite color is red, too. Just like you."

Mitch seemed more curious by the idea than happy over it. Then again, he was shy around strangers, especially men. And that his father was a stranger broke Fay's heart.

Thank God all of that was about to change.

"It is?" he asked.

She nodded. "So maybe these flowers could be for all of us. You and me and your brother and your daddy."

"Do you want them to be?"

She knew what she should say. That she wanted him to make that decision. That he didn't have to include Shane in anything he did, not after Mitch had spent only a handful of days with Shane since he was a baby.

But that wasn't all Shane's fault. She bore some responsibility for the problems in their marriage. For not being strong enough to weather the tough times. For wanting too much. For needing too much.

"I do want that," she said, unable to hide what was in her heart. "Very, very much."

"Okay," he said reluctantly.

"Thank you. That's very sweet of you."

He grinned, so eager to please. So thrilled to

be praised. Even when it was obvious he was only doing it to make someone else happy.

Just like she did.

"Can I put the dirt in?" he asked.

She couldn't speak, her throat was too tight, so she nodded. Worried now that she'd made a mistake in speaking the truth. That she'd somehow tainted him with her fears.

"But not too full, right?" he asked, hopping from foot to foot, either in excitement or because he had to pee. "'Cuz there has to be room for the flowers' roots. Right?"

"Right." But the word came out a whisper, so she cleared her throat. Tried again. "That's right."

He dived at the bag of potting soil, using his hands to scoop some out. Most of it drifted to the ground before it reached the pot, and even more clung to his pants and shirt, covered his arms.

She was surprised he didn't climb into the bag and just dig it out like a dog.

He stopped jiggling, which meant his little dance had been excitement. Best of all, he was smiling, talking cheerfully, a running commentary about what he was doing. He was, in this moment, happy.

Maybe she wasn't ruining him after all.

Still, she only had so many bags of potting soil, and at this rate, more than half of it was going to feed the yard.

"Wow, great job. If you want," she said, as if

just coming up with the idea, offering to do him a huge favor, "I could finish filling it. Then you can dig the holes for the flowers."

She held out a small garden shovel. His eyebrows drew together into an adorable frown, as if he wasn't sure whether this new development was to his advantage. She could almost see him weighing his options: play in the dirt or get to use the potentially lethal tool.

He grabbed the shovel. Lethal it was.

Using an empty flower container, she scooped the soil into the pot. "There you go."

"Three holes, right?" he asked, his pudgy hand gripping the shovel tight. His tongue sticking out, he stabbed the pointed edge of the shovel into the pot then flung it up in an explosion of dirt that showered his hair and clothes.

"Yes. But maybe not quite so hard?"

He nodded. And showered himself with even more dirt.

Oh, well. No harm in getting dirty. Clothes— and little boys—were washable. Though she might have to hose him off before getting him into the tub.

"Look! I did it," he said. "I made a hole."

"Yes, you did. Good job. Two more to go."

She thought she felt her phone buzz in her pocket. Covered it with her hand, holding her breath. Yes, that was a vibration. Wasn't it? She pulled it out and exhaled heavily at the blank screen. She quickly unlocked it just to double-check. But there were no texts, no emails, no missed calls.

Where was Shane? Why hadn't he called her? Or better yet, stopped by?

She'd practiced her apology to him in the shower, had it memorized and perfected only to have her call—all five of them—go straight to voice mail. Which was understandable. She was sure he'd been busy preparing for his interview, showering and shaving and getting dressed. So she'd texted him, had poured her heart out to him, told him how sorry she was, let him know how much last night had meant to her. How excited she was for the future.

That had been hours ago. It was now past two and she hadn't heard from him yet. She just didn't understand what she'd done wrong. If he'd tell her, she could fix it. She could change.

"Mama, are you sad?"

She looked down to find Mitch frowning up at her. He was so like her—from his coloring to his blue eyes to the shape of his mouth. They both hated peas, burned easily in the sun and hummed constantly. He'd inherited her sensitivity, too. Was always wondering how others were feeling. Worried if they were sad or upset or angry with him. Needed to be told constantly that the people in his life would always be there. That they loved him—would always love him.

She didn't know whether to hug him tight and

reassure him that everything was fine or demand that he snap out of it. That he not be like her.

She wanted him to be stronger than she was. More confident, capable of facing challenges. Able to live without constantly worrying.

All good life skills. She wished someone would teach them to her someday.

Crouching, she smiled at him. "I'm very happy. It's a beautiful day, I'm planting flowers with my best helper and after we pick up your brother from school, we're going to stop at City Creamery."

Eyes wide, he started doing his happy dance again. "We're getting ice cream? Can I get two scoops?"

City Creamery was known not only for its home-made ice cream but also its huge portions. "You can have whatever you want, baby."

So what if he'd be full before he finished one scoop? There was no harm in making sure he was happy.

He pumped his fist—a move he'd picked up from Elijah—then gave her a hug. "I love you, Mama."

She squeezed him carefully, knowing she had a tendency to hold on too tight. "Love you, too, baby."

When he let go to finish digging his holes, she straightened. Brushed at the dirt on her shirt. She hadn't lied. Not really. She was happy. It was just that she'd be happier if Shane was there.

She was sure of it.

What if he stopped by while she and the boys were out? She hadn't planned on going to City Creamery after getting Elijah, but she'd wanted to do something for Mitch, to prove to him that she was fine.

She'd better call Shane. So he wouldn't come over and be disappointed they weren't here.

It went directly to voice mail. Again. "Hi. It's me. I hope the interview went well. I mean… I'm sure it did. I'm sure you were great." She stopped. Inhaled deeply then blew it out as quietly as possible, strolling to the other side of the yard. "I wasn't sure what time you planned on coming over, but the boys and I are going to City Creamery after school. Why don't you meet us there? The boys would love to see you. You can call me back if you get time or just meet us. Whichever is easier. Okay? 'Bye."

She clicked off before realizing he might not know what time Elijah got out of school. Ugh. She lowered herself to the ground and sat cross-legged, holding her head in both hands. Should she call him back? Send him a text?

No. She'd bothered him enough. He hated it when she was too persistent. When she didn't give him enough space. He'd call her back or show up here. So she'd wait.

She'd waited for him for three years. She could wait a few more hours.

This time she and Shane were going to work. They'd both made mistakes, yes, but they'd also grown and learned from those mistakes.

After making sure Mitch was still occupied, she shifted around to kneel on the grass. The sun warmed her face and arms, and she shut her eyes. Focused on that warmth, that light. Imagined absorbing it into her skin, her body glowing as the rays shot out of her fingers and toes.

She smiled at the fanciful thought. Pressed her palms against her jeans, her body relaxing. Her mind quiet, if only for a moment.

A shadow briefly blocked the sun. Her scalp prickled with apprehension. She was being watched.

Guess that moment was up.

She turned her head to the side as she opened her eyes but Mitchell was still happily occupied, his back to her. She caught movement to her right and noticed a man walking up the sidewalk, the sun behind him, his features undistinguishable from her vantage point.

Scrambling to her feet, she ducked her head to hide her blush, pretending great interest in slapping at the soil on her clothes.

Though they weren't expecting any guests today, they did, at times, get a walk-in, so she lifted her head and smiled as he approached, then felt that smile slipping.

Dark. That was her first impression. Dark jeans and a black T-shirt clung to broad shoulders, a wide chest. Dark hair that reached his collar, the ends lifting in the breeze. A dark, full beard, just beyond the point of trimmed and heading into scraggly. Dark eyes surrounded by thick, sooty lashes, the lids heavy.

Eyes she couldn't look away from. Eyes that seemed to assess—and dismiss—her before he even blinked.

She shivered. Hugged herself.

Dangerous.

Not exactly the most reassuring—or kind— assessment, but there it was, born of some inner knowledge she hadn't even realized she possessed.

Which was ridiculous. She could hardly claim to know whether he was dangerous or not based on being in his company for a few seconds. Just because he had a hard expression, hooded eyes and was in serious need of some professional grooming didn't mean he wasn't a perfectly nice man.

And no matter how hard she tried to convince herself of that, some primitive, maternal instinct had her glancing at her son to make sure he was safe. Had her edging to the side, putting her body between Mitchell and the stranger coming toward her.

The man turned, too, his hard gaze flicking behind her to see who she was protecting. Beneath the beard his face was lean, almost gaunt, his complexion sallow, as if he'd recently been sick.

It was then she noticed the scars, pink and angry looking, along his temple and high on his cheek.

It was then that she noticed the empty sleeve on his right side.

She jerked her gaze back up to his face as he reached her. Cursed the fairness of her skin, knowing her blush was not only visible but probably neon bright.

"Hello," she said, trying that smile again. He nodded. She waited a moment, but that gesture seemed to be his response, so she forged ahead. "May I help you?"

"Is this Bradford House?" he asked.

"It is."

"I'm looking for a room." He paused, his expression tightening. "One that's accessible."

She stared at him blankly, trying to figure out why his deep voice tugged at her subconscious, the cadence and the way he said Brad-*ferd* instead of Brad-*ford* strangely familiar. "They're all accessible."

How else would people get in and out of them?

He looked at her sharply, as if she was a few petals short of a full bloom. But it wasn't until he set a large duffel bag on the sidewalk, the movement causing him to wince and fight to remain balanced, that realization dawned.

She really was as dim as everyone thought.

He hadn't just lost an arm and suffered injuries to his face, he'd hurt his leg, as well.

"You mean handicap accessible?" she blurted out.

Another nod, this one short and sharp. "Do you have one available?"

His words were clipped. A challenge. As if she'd refuse him.

She wanted to. She wanted to tell him they were fully booked, recommend King's Crossing or the Holiday Inn.

The thought shook her. Shamed her. Refusing to rent him a room was illegal. Not to mention immoral and hateful.

But her wanting to turn him away had nothing to do with his physical disabilities and everything to do with her instincts. They were shouting at her, begging her to please, for once, listen to them. To trust them. To believe them when they said that while the man before her might not be a con artist, thief or murderer, she still had to protect herself from him.

Dangerous.

Thank goodness she always followed her heart and not her gut. Or her head.

The breeze picked up, blew her hair into her face. A strand stuck to the gloss on her lips and she hooked it with her pinkie, pulled it aside. "We have a room on the first floor that should work for you."

It had been her idea, she thought with no little amount of pride, to add a handicapped-accessible room off the library. And just in time, it seemed, as the addition had been completed only a few weeks ago.

"Mama!" Mitchell called, racing over to her, his hands black with dirt, his clothes covered in it. He grabbed her hand, started tugging. "Mama, come look. I'm done!"

She stumbled, caught herself. How someone so small could be so strong was beyond her. "Just a minute, honey. Mama's talking to someone right now."

Mitch sidled closer and wrapped his arm around her leg above her knee. Then he lifted his head to take in the stranger.

And burst into tears.

HE'D FLOWN HALFWAY across the country, almost fell on his ass in front of a bar full of people, humiliated himself by begging for a job and made a kid cry.

Yeah. He'd say his day was now complete.

Zach scratched the underside of his jaw. The beard itched like hell, but at least it hid the scars scattered across the side of his neck and jaw. Not that he'd grown it for vanity. He just hadn't mastered using a razor with his left hand, and as much as his life might suck, he wasn't so bad off that the idea of slicing his own neck held any appeal.

The kid sent up a high-pitched wail that probably had every dog in the neighborhood cowering. He pressed his face against the woman's leg, his little body shaking.

Christ.

The woman knelt, said something to the kid— her son, if the resemblance was anything to go by—who quieted for a moment. Until he glanced at Zach again and cried louder than before. Kid had some pipes, Zach would give him that.

"Maybe I should go," Zach said.

Color washed up the woman's neck into her face, the red contrasting with her strawberry blond hair. "No, no. Please. I'm really sorry for this. Just…give me a moment." She picked up the boy. Zach was surprised she could lift him when it looked like a stiff breeze would knock her over.

"It's okay," the blonde murmured, and he could have sworn she was talking to him as well as the kid. "Everything will be all right."

The thought irritated him. He didn't need her reassurance, didn't need anyone spouting off about how he should look on the bright side and be hopeful for the future. He needed a damn room.

And she wasn't doing her kid any favors, either, lying to him. How did she know everything would be all right?

She pressed a kiss against the side of the boy's head and jiggled him the same way he'd seen his aunts, cousins, mom and grandmother do with the countless babies and kids in his family. As if bouncing the hell out of them would impart some comfort or maybe shake some sense into someone who couldn't even tie their own shoes.

Then again, he was having some difficulty with that task himself. Maybe his mother was right about not casting stones.

The kid clung to the woman, his pudgy arms around her neck, all but squeezing the life from her. At least the jiggling and murmuring were working. His cries quieted. Though they didn't stop.

She sent Zach a tight, embarrassed smile over the kid's head as she rubbed the child's back. "I'm so sorry. Really. Let me just get him settled down," she continued, walking backward. "It'll only take a minute. You can wait in the entryway if you'd like." She turned, took a step then paused long enough to look at Zach over her shoulder. "Sorry."

And she took off, speed walking down the sidewalk then jogging up the porch steps before disappearing into the house—hotel...bed-and-breakfast...whatever—leaving the door open behind her.

Leaving him standing alone on the sidewalk, wondering what the hell he was supposed to do now.

He started to rock back on his heels only to remember that wasn't such a good idea given the pain in his leg, the unsteadiness of his muscles. The walk from O'Riley's to here hadn't helped, nor had carrying his duffel, which all went back to not having a choice.

His current life motto.

There used to be a time when he could run for miles at top speed in full combat gear with fifty pounds of supplies, weapons and ammunition on his back.

Now he could barely make it a mile carrying what little clothes he owned, his toothbrush and a few personal items.

New normal.

Leaning to the left, he picked up his duffel. His head swam. Ached. Nausea rose, but he swallowed it down. Headaches were just one of the lingering effects of the severe concussion he'd suffered during the blast that had taken his arm and leg.

He needed to sit down, preferably someplace dark and quiet. He stared at the doorway. No sign of the blonde. She expected him to follow her, to wait while she tried to convince her kid Zach wasn't some monster. *Good luck with that.*

He turned slowly, started back toward the street. Tidy houses with lush, thick lawns lined the road. Birds chirped. A dog barked.

He never should have come up the walk, never should have spoken to the blonde. As soon as he'd seen Bradford House, he'd known it wasn't for him. The Victorian was too cute, with its tall windows, huge wraparound front porch and neatly trimmed lawn.

A place where couples came for romantic weekend getaways. Where groups of women stayed when they ditched the men in their lives. Somewhere for people who wanted to be charmed by the manager, who wanted to sit with other travelers, chat, learn about their lives.

It was not a place for someone who spent most nights wide awake, watching TV or limping around his room, avoiding sleep and the nightmares that came with it. Someone who only wanted to be left alone.

Bradford House wasn't for him.

The kid had known that right off.

He'd noticed the boy first—hard to miss that beacon of bright hair. The kid had been digging in a pot of dirt, flowers at his feet, his hands filthy, his clothes stained as he talked a mile a minute to no one, his joy obvious.

Then Zach had caught sight of the woman and he'd just...stopped. Froze right there on the sidewalk, his heart slamming in his chest, his mind hazy. She'd sat back on her heels, her hands tucked primly on her bent knees, her head turned up to the sun, a small smile playing on her mouth.

That dreamy smile had captured him. She'd seemed so peaceful, the bright sun catching the fiery strands of gold in her hair, her expression soft. She seemed to glow, to have been lit from inside, her pale skin almost translucent. He'd started moving toward her before he'd even fully realized his intent, drawn to that warmth, that sense of serenity. Longing for a way to somehow bask with her in that peace.

Except when he moved, he'd blocked her light, casting her in shadow. Touching her with darkness. She'd frowned, but that had been nothing compared to the unease in her eyes when she'd first seen him. The vulnerability.

Or the flinch when she'd noticed his empty sleeve.

He gave an irritable shrug, felt like he had an itch he couldn't reach between his shoulder blades, even if he'd still had two hands. No, Bradford House was definitely not for him.

Feeling as if he'd just lost something he'd never even had, he turned onto the main sidewalk, heading back toward town.

"Wait!" a female voice called, followed by the sound of running feet. "Wait!"

He kept walking. Not that it mattered. It took her ten seconds to catch up with him.

"Where are you going?" she asked breathlessly from beside him.

"I hear there's a Holiday Inn off the highway."

He could buy a car, hire someone to drive him everywhere, to drop him off at O'Riley's, take him to whatever restaurant he wanted to eat at. Hell, he didn't even have to work—he could buy a house somewhere, anywhere, sit there day in and day out. He had money. More than he'd ever be able to spend in two lifetimes.

But he hadn't earned it. Had been given it because he was Clinton Bartasavich Sr.'s bastard son.

He hadn't earned it, so he wouldn't use it.

She scooted in front of him, forcing him to stop. Her cheeks were pink. Whether she was still embarrassed or if it was from her quick jog, he wasn't sure. "Why would you go there?"

"For that room I mentioned?"

Her eyebrows drew together in a confused frown. She lifted her pinkie to her mouth only to drop it and link that hand with her other one. "But…but we have an available room here. It's on the first floor. It's very nice."

She spoke slowly, her tone calm and clear. As if she'd somehow figured out he'd suffered a head injury. Then again, some people did that. Saw you were missing a piece of yourself and automatically went into nurturer mode, wanting to take care of you, offering their endless patience and sympathy.

And wouldn't that be fun, being exposed to that every day? "I figured you wouldn't want me hanging around. Traumatizing your kid."

The color that had been fading from her face came back with a vengeance. "I'm so, so sorry about that," she breathed. "I…I don't know what got into him."

"I scared him."

"No. I mean…it wasn't you. Really. Mitchell's very, very shy. He's not comfortable around any strangers."

Zach snorted softly. Yeah, that was the kid's problem. Shyness. "It's probably best for both of us if I go somewhere else."

"Oh, no, please, come in. Just for a few minutes. I'll go over our amenities and rates and you can look at the room. See if it suits your needs."

How the hell was he supposed to refuse when she was looking at him so expectantly? When she stood so close he could smell the soil dusting her clothes, and under it something sweet and light and flowery? He wanted to close the distance between them, breathe in that sweetness.

Yeah, staying here, even long enough for her to give her sales pitch, was a bad idea.

Seemed to be his day for those.

"Lead the way," he said.

CHAPTER FOUR

AT HIS ACQUIESCENCE, she smiled, full and warm and relieved, as if getting him to come inside was a personal victory.

Glad he could help her put a check in the win column.

"Thank you," she said. A car drove past, the driver giving them a friendly beep of the horn. She waved without looking away from Zach. "I promise to do everything in my power to make your stay pleasant."

He thought again of how pretty she'd looked sitting in the sunshine. How good she smelled. How long it had been since he'd felt a woman's soft skin. Since a woman had touched him in a nonplatonic, nonmedical or nontherapeutic way.

A long time. A long, long time.

Probably not what she meant by making things pleasant.

"I'm just checking out the room," he told her, his voice gruffer than he'd intended. Inappropriate sexual fantasies would do that. Especially ones of him rolling around in the front yard on a bright, sunny day with a woman who, moments before, had hauled her screaming kid inside. "No promises I'll be staying."

"Of course. But I think once you see the room, you'll want to."

Right now all he wanted was to sit down. Or at least get out of the sun. His head was starting to ache, a pounding to match the throbbing in his leg. He shifted to the side, gestured for her to go ahead.

She brushed past him, then waited at the end of the walkway. When he reached her, she moved onto the grass and walked with him toward the house. Took tiny, slow steps so as not to outpace him.

"Bradford House has a long and rich history in Shady Grove," she said. Seemed this tour came with a guide. "Built over one hundred years ago by local timber baron Reginald Bradford, it was a gift to his third wife, Marjorie, a socialite from Boston thirty years his junior."

She went on. And on. And on some more. Reginald died of a heart attack in a hooker's bed… Marjorie passed the house down to their only child, a daughter, who married some guy with a gambling habit…yada, yada, yada…the house was lost in a high-stakes poker game and turned into an orphanage…

He didn't give a rat's ass about the house's history or its past inhabitants, but he let her talk. It helped knowing she was occupied with giving her spiel and not focused on trying to catch him should he fall. Plus, he liked the soft lilt of her voice, the way she spoke so slowly, carefully, as if reciting a memorized piece for school.

"The house stood empty for over five years," she said when they finally reached the porch, "at which point NHL star Neil Pettit purchased the house and property."

Neil Pettit. Zach had never heard of him. Then again, he didn't follow hockey, preferred watching baseball or basketball rather than a bunch of guys on skates. But he was curious—not about the house or its current owner. About her.

"Is that your husband?" he asked as they reached the porch.

She started, as if shaken out of her tour-guide trance. Glanced around, doing a full spin. "Where?"

He looked around, too, but they were the only two people out there. "Neil Pettit."

"Oh. No." She checked the street again, then her phone before looking Zach's way. "Neil's my brother."

"You and he are partners?"

"Partners?"

He nodded toward the house. "Business partners."

Something crossed her face, a flash of resentment gone so quickly he might have imagined it. "I'm not an owner." Now her eyes widened. "I can't believe I didn't introduce myself," she said, obviously horrified by her oversight. "I'm so sorry. I'm Bradford House's manager, Fay Lindemuth."

And she held out her right hand.

Hell.

He shrugged the duffel bag's strap off his shoulder. As it hit the ground with a dull thud, she seemed to realize what she was doing and started lowering her arm, her eyes wide and distressed. He stabbed his left hand out, took hold of hers in an awkward, upside-down squeeze. "Zach Castro."

He held on for a beat. Then two. Longer than necessary, but it was nice, having her warm, soft palm against his. When she started pulling away, he immediately let go. But could still feel it, that warmth. Softness.

He curled his fingers, tried to hold on to both for as long as possible.

Her hands fluttered, touching her chest again, then brushing at her hair before floating down to her sides. "It's nice to meet you, Mr. Castro."

"Zach," he grumbled. *Mr. Castro*. Like he was her elder when, if he had to guess, she was around his age—thirty.

Another smile. She had an ample supply of them. "Well, let's get you that tour, Zach."

The sound of his name in that soft voice blew through him. He should have let her stick with Mr. Castro.

He eyed the four porch steps. Wide and deep, he'd be able to step up, get his balance before moving on to the next. But there was no handrail to hold on to.

And he had to climb them all under the watchful eye of the pretty woman next to him.

Resigned, he leaned to the side for his duffel.

"Oh, I can take that," she said, reaching down across his body. The back of her hand brushed his knee, and he froze for a moment, her hair tickling his chin, the scent wrapping around him, while she tugged at the bag's strap.

"I've got it," he said tightly and felt her look at him, her face close enough that her soft exhale warmed his cheek.

He kept his gaze down, on the sight of their hands wrapped around that worn, rough strap, her fingers long and narrow with shiny pink nails. Her skin pale next to his, the bones of her hand delicate. He raised his eyes to hers, felt a pull of something—interest, attraction or, hell, plain old lust—deep in his stomach. Any of them would be understandable, he told himself. All of them were natural reactions. She was a pretty woman with her bright hair and clear blue eyes. Sweet with her many smiles, easy blushes and that hint of vulnerability. And he was just a man. A man who hadn't had sex in over eight months.

Didn't mean he had to act on those feelings. Didn't mean he wanted to.

But he did want her to leave him with some self-respect.

"Let. Go."

At his quiet, rough command, she jerked upright. Blinked rapidly. "I'm sorry. I didn't mean…" Those pretty hands were back to flapping uselessly, her throat working as she swallowed.

He jutted his chin toward the porch. "After you."

No way was he going first and having her hovering behind him, waiting to catch him if he fell.

She went up the stairs, crossed the wide porch to the front door, her movements quick. Easy.

Envy pinched him, but he pushed it aside. He wasn't about to start feeling sorry for himself now. He'd get back to 100 percent. Eventually. It would take time, patience and hard work. He had plenty of the first, not nearly enough of the second. And the third? He embraced it. He wasn't afraid to push himself, was actually looking forward to it. To proving he was more than his perceived limitations. To overcoming the odds and living a normal life—whatever that new normal turned out to be.

He climbed the steps slowly, carefully, leaning to the right to compensate for the weight of his duffel bag on his left. It couldn't have taken him more than fifteen seconds to reach the top, but it felt like an eternity. Especially knowing Fay watched him, cataloging his every move, nervous and on edge that any moment he might tumble to the ground.

Used to be a time, before his injuries, when women checked him out as he went by, the look in their eyes appreciative. Interested.

Now they either looked at him with pity or their gazes skittered over him, as if it was too painful for them to see him.

He crossed the porch, didn't miss how pleased and relieved Fay looked, as if he'd successfully scaled Everest instead of conquering a few porch steps.

He reached past her and pulled open the door.

"Thank you," she murmured, stepping inside. He followed, closing the door behind him.

The foyer was large, bright and airy with a high ceiling, a curving wooden staircase to his left and a set of French doors leading to what looked like a den to his right. The woodwork gleamed, dark and ornate, and wide planks of aged oak covered the floor. Some sort of antique stand with drawers and carved scrolls in the wood was against the far wall, a glass bowl of chocolates on it along with a Welcome to Bradford House sign. He caught sight of his reflection in the mirror. It still took some getting used to—the missing arm, the long hair. The beard.

He rubbed his chin. He really needed to work on his shaving skills.

"You can leave your bag here," Fay said, indicating the corner under the stairs. "Or you can bring it," she continued quickly, as if wanting to cover all her bases. "If you'd like."

He left it. Then followed her down a short hallway that opened up into a sitting room on the right—more French doors—and a library to the left. "Through here is the dining room and kitchen," she said, gesturing ahead of them. "We serve breakfast each weekday from seven until ten, weekends from eight to eleven."

She turned into the library, a huge room with floor-to-ceiling windows and three walls of built-in shelves housing what had to be thousands of books. Cozy, plump chairs were tucked into corners, and a few round tables were scattered throughout. "We offer snacks in the library every afternoon and wine and cheese in the den in the evenings," she continued, leading him through the room and down another short but wide hall-way, this one bright with open glass on one side overlooking a patio, a handrail on the other. "We offer basic laundry services, dry cleaning drop-off and pickup, cable television and free Wi-Fi in each room."

She stopped at the end of the hall, pulled a key—an actual key, not a swipe card—from her pocket and unlocked the door, the width enough for a wheelchair to get through. She went in, flipped on the light, then stepped aside so he could enter.

The room, and the hall, had obviously been built at some point recently, or at least redone, if the lingering scent of paint was anything to go by. But they blended seamlessly with the rest of the building, the floors new but still hardwood, the ceilings high, the windows long and narrow.

It didn't look like any hotel room he'd ever stayed in, or how he'd expected a room at a charming B&B to look. It had vaulted ceilings and a large four-poster king bed, again, with enough space for a wheelchair to get around. The walls were neutral, with pencil sketches of Shady Grove hanging in thick frames, the color scheme deep greens and pale creams with some gold thrown in.

Other than the bed, there was a flat-screen TV on the wall, a large dresser, a small writing desk and chair under one window and a fat armchair next to the other window. It was a decent blend of masculine and feminine, traditional and contemporary.

She showed him the closet before opening the door to the bathroom. Spacious, with a tile floor and double vanity, there were handrails in both the walk-in shower and jetted tub, and also next to the toilet.

"This is the only guest room with its own external entrance," she said, leading him out to the French doors—they must have gotten a deal on them—that opened up to a small patio accessible by either stairs or a ramp. To the right there was another ramp, this one longer and wooden, leading to a back entrance of the building.

"We'll put an awning up in a few weeks," Fay said, "and set a table and chairs out here, maybe a seating area?" He had no idea if she was telling him her plans or asking for his permission. "Anyway, this room is not only our largest, but it also affords the most privacy."

It would definitely work, and having his own private entrance would be a hell of a lot better than having to traipse through the entire building every time he came or went.

"Does Shady Grove have a YMCA?" he asked.

"A YM—" She shook her head. "Oh, I'm sorry, do you want to stay at the Y? Because I don't believe they have rooms anymore. Not the one here, anyway."

"I don't want to sleep there. I need a place to work out."

"Work out?" Her gaze flicked to his empty sleeve. "The Y is at least three miles from here, near the river. But if you want to...to exercise, we have a fitness room in the basement." She crossed to the desk, picked up a brochure and flipped it open. "It's actually much nicer than anything the Y has," she said, sounding almost apologetic. "Being a professional athlete, Neil made sure it was top-notch. He even designed it. It doesn't get much use, though. Most of our guests prefer to relax rather than lift weights while they're here."

She handed him the brochure. It listed not only the amenities of Bradford House but also local tourist attractions and restaurants. And the picture she pointed at was of a state-of-the-art gym, complete with everything he'd need to get back in shape.

To get his life back.

He set the brochure down. "I'll take it."

FAY'S FACE HURT from smiling so much.

The cost of always proving to everyone around her that she was mentally and emotionally healthy and just so darn happy. All. The. Time.

She couldn't let that smile slip, not one bit. Not now.

I'll take it.

Mr. Castro, of the dark eyes, grim mouth and deep, flat voice, was going to rent a room here. All because she'd chased him down and given him her best sales pitch.

Oh, Lord, what had she done?

"That's...wonderful," she managed, cheeks aching, lips stretched wide. And it *was* wonderful. They were in the business of renting rooms, after all, and they weren't booked full until the July Fourth weekend. "We'll go to my office and get you registered."

As much as she wanted to let him go ahead of her, she knew better. She'd tried that outside and it hadn't worked so well for her. And despite what Neil and Maddie thought, she really could *learn a lesson*.

It was just that sometimes it took six or seven times for that lesson to stick.

Not today, she assured herself.

She led him back the way they'd come, sensing him behind her like a dark, limping ghost, silent except for the heavy fall of his footsteps. The sound of his soft breathing.

He'd unnerved her—more than once, actually. Which in and of itself wasn't unusual. She was often jittery and anxious, especially around strangers. Too often more concerned about what they were thinking about her than what they were saying. Too worried about making sure they liked her.

It was exhausting. Unfortunately, she had no idea how to stop.

But her nervousness around Zach was…different. More acute. As if her skin was too tight and itchy. Her stomach knotted. She didn't like how he seemed to see right through all her smiles and cheerful chatter. She'd almost stayed in the kitchen when she'd left Mitchell there with Damien. She'd wanted to hide. All because her inner voice had continued screaming at her to let Zach walk away and find another place to stay.

But her heart had overridden it.

She really needed to start listening to her instincts.

"Here we go," she said, gesturing for him to

enter her office. Following him inside, she shut the door.

And realized her error immediately, as the room seemed to shrink. He had a presence that took up a lot of space. He made her feel small and slight in comparison. It was because he was so broad. Wide through the shoulders and chest. So dark and intense and unsmiling.

Nothing at all like her tall, rangy, golden husband.

She pushed Shane from her mind even as her fingers twitched to check her phone again. For some reason, she didn't want to think about him now. Didn't want him arriving and finding her in this cramped space with another man. This man.

And she really, really didn't want to delve too deeply into why that was.

She certainly didn't want to remember that weird jump in her belly when she'd tried to take Zach's bag and he'd lifted his head, their faces inches apart. Or how, for a moment, her breath had caught in her throat and she'd had the strangest sensation of…longing.

Only she had no idea what for.

Didn't matter. Soon, she'd have everything she wanted. Now she had a job to do.

She shifted, only to realize there was no way to get around Zach. Everywhere she turned, she risked brushing against him. And that would not do. She considered leaping over her desk, but good sense prevailed, forcing her to do a shuffling side step around him, making sure to leave a good six inches between them.

"Have a seat," she blurted out, practically jumping into her own chair behind her tiny desk. She watched, motionless, while he eased himself into one of the two chairs facing her, grimacing slightly, noticeably favoring his right leg.

"Breathe," he commanded softly and for a moment, she thought he was talking to himself.

Until her lungs burned and she realized she was the one holding her breath.

And he'd noticed.

Exhaling as quietly as possible, she pretended to be very, very busy booting up her computer. But her face was hot—again. And though she was, indeed, taking in oxygen, the air seemed heated. Stifling. As if he was using it all.

Selfish of him, really.

Ridiculous, she told herself as she opened a new registration form on her computer. There was plenty of air in the room. Air tinged with the scent of sunshine and spring and something spicy—his aftershave? She sneaked a glance at his face, most of it hidden by either his shaggy hair or his beard. Okay. Not his aftershave. And he didn't seem like the type to use cologne. Whatever it was, it was… nice. Clean and masculine.

And she had absolutely no right to be thinking about the man's scent. Or liking it. She was a married woman.

She touched her wedding ring, the slight bump of it under her shirt reassuring. She *would* be a married woman again soon.

Clearing her throat, she forced a smile. "Let's get you registered." She bit back a grimace. Well, that had come out quite...enthusiastically. And loudly.

She tried again, softening both her tone and expression. "Is it Zachary?" At his nod, she typed it in, followed by his last name. "Address?"

He hesitated and shifted in his seat. Both actions so subtle, done so quickly, that as he gave her an address in Houston, she wondered if she'd imagined his unease.

"How many nights will you be staying with us?" she asked.

"How many nights are available?"

She felt her brows drawing together at the odd question. Smoothed her expression as she checked future reservations. "That room is open until mid-May."

"That'll work."

Her hands stilled. "You want to stay here for four weeks?"

"Is that a problem?"

She wasn't sure. "No problem at all."

But it was strange. Most guests booked Friday to Sunday with the occasional weekday visit thrown in by a rare business traveler or day-trippers wanting to immerse themselves in the local flavor.

Unless…

Unless he wasn't looking for a place to stay. He was looking for a place to live, for however long he could get it.

He was homeless. That had to be it. And the reason he'd been so uncomfortable when she'd asked for his address was because he didn't have one. So he'd made one up.

Her heart went out to him. How had he gotten here? What had happened to him? She was curious, as anyone would be, about how he'd gotten those scars and lost his arm. Had it happened a while ago, long enough for him to be used to his limitations? For acceptance?

Maybe it had happened recently and he was still railing against the unfairness of it all. Did he curse his fate? Or blame himself for the choices he'd made that had led to that one moment when his entire world had changed?

Like she blamed herself for her choices. For her world imploding.

Whatever had happened to him, he was here now. Giving her the opportunity to help him try to put that world back together.

Or at least give him a place to stay.

It would be nice to give back. To be the person giving help instead of needing it. To be someone

else's strength. Maybe then she'd be able to figure out how to be her own.

"I'll need to see photo ID," she said, adjusting
the room's rate on the form to give him a significant discount. Bradford House wasn't the most
expensive place to stay in Shady Grove, but even
their reasonable rates would stretch someone of
limited resources.

He handed her a Texas driver's license along
with a second card.

She frowned at it. "What's this?"

He lifted his eyebrows. "A credit card." When
she stared at him blankly, he added, "To pay for
the room."

She typed in the card information and printed
out the form for him to sign. He had a credit card?
How was that possible? Where would the bill be
sent? Confused, she did what she did best: second-
guessed herself.

Maybe she'd been wrong. Maybe he wasn't
some homeless drifter in need of help. The address on the driver's license was different from the
one he'd given. And while the man in the photo
had dark hair, it was short, the face clean shaven,
showing an angular jaw and sharp cheekbones.
So different from the man in front of her now.

What if her instincts had been right and he really was dangerous? A criminal on the run or a
con man out to fleece his next victims, or an iden-
tity thief, using Zach Castro's license and credit

card for his own gain? What if he was a serial killer, here to murder them all as they slept?

Control your thoughts. Don't let them control you.

Dr. Porter's voice was so loud in her head, Fay glanced around the cramped room, just to make sure he hadn't somehow appeared out of thin air, his ever-present notepad in hand.

Fay sighed. *Control your thoughts. Control your thoughts.*

Easier said than done, Dr. Porter. Much easier said than done. But she'd give it a go.

"This is wrong," Zach said, his low voice dragging her back to the present before she could put the whole controlling-her-thoughts theory into practice.

"Excuse me?"

He pointed to the paper she'd printed out, specifically, the room rate. "This isn't the price listed in the brochure."

Caught. She hadn't realized he'd checked out the prices when she'd shown him the pictures of the fitness area.

"Oh. Yes, well, that's…that's a special we're running."

"Is that so?" he murmured, his quiet voice doing odd things to her nerves. To her pulse rate.

She nodded. Swallowed. "April is slow—not much going on around here this month, what with skiing season being over—and May isn't much better, so we decided to offer a discount." She waved her hand in what she'd wanted to be a casual gesture but ended up being more of a frantic, flopping motion. "To draw in more guests."

He studied her and she squirmed. Rolled up the corner of an invoice she had to pay. Unrolled it. Rolled it again. She didn't like to be the center of attention, didn't like to be singled out or watched with such…intensity.

And she really didn't like how this particular man watched her. As if seeing through her was no challenge at all.

Finally, thankfully, he shifted forward, and she thought he was going to sign the agreement, only to slowly, deliberately crumple it in his hand. "I'll pay full price."

She opened her mouth and immediately wished she hadn't when she made a squeaking sound, like a mouse caught in a trap. "But…the sale…"

Her words trailed off as he leaned forward to lay the crumpled paper in front of her. "Full price."

Embarrassment swept through her, a wave of heat that flowed from her toes to the top of her head. Honestly, she might as well just stay red, as often as she blushed in front of this man.

Her own fault, she was sure. But part of her wondered if he couldn't accept some of the blame, as well.

She fixed the room rate and printed out a new form. Handed it to him wordlessly.

He read it then took a pen from the ceramic holder on her desk, his grip on it awkward. "You're not very good," he said, head down as if having to concentrate on signing his own name.

Her first instinct was to apologize for...well... whatever it was she'd done wrong. To beg for another chance.

But something held her back, kept the words stuck in her throat. Something that, if she didn't know better, she would claim was irritation.

Maybe even the slightest bit of anger.

She pushed it aside. She had no right to be angry. Hadn't she thought the same thing herself, many, many times? That she wasn't good enough. Not smart enough. Not strong enough. *Never enough.*

Which was exactly why she didn't need him pointing it out. She did an excellent job of questioning her abilities on her own.

She tried to flatten the corner of the invoice she'd rolled. Smoothed it and smoothed it and smoothed it with her thumb. "You'll find a guest survey in your room." She sounded a bit...put out...so she softened her tone. Forced her hands to still. "You can fill it out and let us know if you're unhappy with any aspect of your stay here— including my job performance."

He lifted his head, eyebrows raised. "I'm not unhappy with your job performance."

"You said I wasn't very good at it," she reminded him, working to keep the hurt, the offense, from her voice.

He put the pen back. "I wasn't talking about your job."

She frowned. *Don't ask*, she told herself. *What other people think about you is none of your business. It's what you think of yourself that matters.*

Not true. It did matter what others thought, how they felt about you. If they liked you. If they loved you. If they were going to stay with you, be by your side no matter what.

It was all that mattered.

"What were you talking about then?" she asked, telling herself the only reason she did so was to prove she was strong enough to handle the truth. Brave enough to ask for criticism. Even as she braced for both.

He hesitated, but then he lifted his right shoulder, shrugging his hesitancy off. "I was talking about you not being a very good liar."

She frowned. And what was wrong with that? Shouldn't she want to be known as someone honest and trustworthy?

So why did his words sting?

"I didn't lie," she told him, keeping her voice calm as she took the paper from him. "I just hadn't…advertised the discounted room rates yet."

She checked his signature. It didn't match the one on the back of his credit card. Not even close.

What should she do?

Neil would know. He'd do whatever he needed to get to the truth. His competitive nature wouldn't settle for anything less than getting his own way.

Maddie wouldn't question her instincts or the proof before her. She'd be laying into Zach, pestering him until she got answers.

Fay was sure there was a simple explanation for it all—the change in address, the different signatures, the differences between him in real life and the picture on his license.

And it was her job as Bradford House's manager to find that explanation. She had to protect her employees and the other guests. Had to protect her sons.

She couldn't let them down. Couldn't make a mistake.

"Your address is different," she rushed out, her words loud in the quiet room, shocking her and, if the slight widening of his eyes was anything to go by, surprising him, as well. To hide her nerves, she stood, the height advantage giving her the ability to look down at him.

"On your license?" she continued, hating that she'd made it sound like a question. Like she was begging for his response. "The picture on it doesn't look like you, either. I mean, not exactly like you… And your signature doesn't match. On your credit card." She licked her lips. "If…if it is your credit card."

He stood, wobbling a bit and having to lay his

hand on her desk to catch his balance, making her think once again that he'd hurt his leg. "The address is different," he said, "because I recently moved and, as I'm not sure exactly where I'm going to be, I didn't bother changing it with the DMV. The picture was taken over three years ago—" He gestured to his hair, his beard. "Long before either of these grew."

It made sense. It all made perfect, logical sense. But there was still one thing that felt off... "And the signature?"

"I used to be right-handed," he said simply.

Used to be...

She shut her eyes on an inner groan. Oh, God, she was such a complete ninny, scared of her own shadow. Wasn't Dr. Porter always saying Fay had the ability to choose her thoughts? Her reactions?

She could have chosen to believe the best in the man in front of her. Instead of giving in to her fears.

He wasn't even the only person to want to rent a room for longer than a few days. Just last summer Clinton Bartasavich Jr. had stayed here for over a week and returned every weekend while trying to convince Ivy—then working as Bradford House's chef and pregnant with his baby—to give him a chance.

Fay blinked several times as her brain worked, things clicking into place.

C. J. Bartasavich, of the extremely wealthy Bartasavich family of Houston, had succeeded. He and Ivy were now married and living in his Houston penthouse, raising their infant son together. C. J. Bartasavich, whose brother Kane owned a bar right here in Shady Grove. Another brother, Oakes, had spent a weekend at Bradford House just this past Christmas while in town for Kane's wedding to local ER nurse Charlotte Ellison.

But she now remembered that there was another brother, the youngest, who hadn't attended that wedding, who'd been unable to come due to being injured in Iraq while serving in the marines.

Her gaze flew to the man watching her silently. A brother who'd lost his arm and his leg. A brother named...Zach.

"You're a Bartasavich."

His response to her blurted statement? The slightest wrinkling of his brow. No denial. No affirmation.

The man sure knew how to do the whole not-all-that-tall-but-still-dark-and-very-silent thing. She envied him—at least the last part. Silence made her nervous. Made her feel as if she had to do her best to fill it. As if she'd said or done something wrong to cause it.

"I mean, you're not a murderer."

She winced. Wished the words back, but if there was one thing she knew for sure, it was that all the wishing in the world couldn't turn back time. Couldn't erase your mistakes.

"I'm sorry," she continued. "I...I have a wild imagination. My mom says I have a tendency of letting it get the best of me." Before she could make this entire scene worse, she took his room key from her pocket and held it out to him along with his credit card and driver's license. "I hope you find your stay with us enjoyable. If there's anything you need, please don't hesitate to contact me or anyone on staff."

Not her usual happy welcome-to-Bradford-House spiel, but right now, she didn't want to be polite—she just wanted to send him on his way and forget this entire humiliating episode ever happened.

She wanted to get back to her life. To waiting for Shane.

Whom, she realized with a jolt, she'd rarely thought about since the man in front of her walked into the yard.

Zach took the items and she quickly pulled her hand back before their fingers had a chance to brush. "Thanks."

Touching her necklace, reminding herself of her ultimate goal, she sidled past him to the door and opened it.

"Oh," she said to the very beautiful, very pregnant, very *young* woman who stood on the other side, her hand raised as though she'd just been about to knock.

She was stunning, her short cap of dark glossy hair accentuating her long neck and high cheekbones, her full mouth slicked red, her eyes a dark green. She wore black leggings, high-heeled black ankle boots and a knit light gray sweater that molded to her breasts and bulging belly. Her dangling silver earrings swayed as she tipped her head and raked her gaze over Fay before giving Fay a tight, mean smile, like a cat about to pounce.

Unease prickled Fay's scalp. Had her wanting to take a step back—but Zach was there, behind her, close enough to sense. To touch if she moved more than a few inches.

"Hello," she said, using her most professional, warmly welcoming innkeeper tone. "May I help you?"

"That depends," the younger woman said, her low, husky tone a soft purr. She set her hand on her bulging belly, a small, plain diamond ring winking on her ring finger. The move should have been maternal. But somehow it came across as less protective and more arrogant. As if she'd done something singular and spectacular that no other woman in the history of the world had ever accomplished. "Are you Fay?"

"Yes," Fay said slowly, wondering at her own hesitancy.

"Then you can definitely help me. You can help

me," she repeated, her eyes gleaming with what could only be described as malice, "by not screwing my fiancé anymore."

CHAPTER FIVE

ZACH RAISED HIS EYEBROWS. Glanced at Fay—who, for all her blushing earlier, had gone completely white.

It was like he'd walked onto the set of one of Abuelita's stories, the Mexican soap operas she watched religiously every afternoon. The ones he might have caught a glimpse of once or twice while recovering from his injuries at his mother's house. Enough of a glance to know they were filled with beautiful people and intrigue, and pregnancies, infidelities and secrets reigned supreme.

Enough to recognize the lead-up to a hair-pulling, face-slapping catfight when he had a front-row seat. Looked like more fun on TV.

Fay shook her head, her hair swishing against her shoulders, the sweet scent of her shampoo releasing into the air. "You have the wrong idea," she rushed out, eager, it seemed, to state her case. "I'm not…" She gestured between herself and Zach. "We're not having an affair. We just met."

Upgraded from the front row to smack-dab in the middle, Zach thought.

"Not me," he said, but if Fay's frown was anything to go by, she wasn't getting it. "I'm not her fiancé. I'm not in the habit of proposing to teenagers. Or getting them pregnant."

That would be following a little too closely in his old man's footsteps.

The brunette's eyes narrowed to slits. "I'm twenty-one."

Zach smirked. "Not even if you showed me a birth certificate."

She crossed her arms. "I'm *almost* twenty-one."

Right. Like his younger sister, Daphne, had been *almost* twenty-one when he'd found out she'd been bar hopping as a college sophomore.

Nineteen and a half wasn't almost twenty-one no matter how you did the math.

"Who…who is your fiancé?" Fay asked the brunette, her voice unsteady. Her expression made it clear she was not only lost in this little unfolding drama, floundering for a way back to somewhere safe, but that she was out of her element, too. Uncomfortable with confrontation.

Unable to stand up for herself.

The brunette snorted out a laugh. "What's the matter? Are you screwing so many engaged men you can't keep track?"

"I'm not…sleeping with any man. With any *engaged* man," she added, her voice getting stronger.

"You're a liar." The brunette raised her chin. "And a slut." She edged forward and Fay shrank back. "I know he was here last night. Don't bother denying it. He admitted the whole thing. How you called him, begging him to come over. How you threw yourself at him. Well, I'm here to tell you that Shane is mine."

At the name, Fay's head snapped back and she seemed to crumple into herself. "You're not… Shane's not your…he's not getting married."

Zach's eyebrows rose. A new twist to this drama. But one thing was clear. Shane—whoever he was—was a lying, cheating bastard.

"This ring," the brunette said, holding her hand up to show off what had to be the smallest diamond in history, "and the fact that I'm carrying his baby, say otherwise. You need to stay away from him."

"No," Fay repeated louder. "You're lying."

The brunette rolled her eyes. "Yes, because I don't have anything better to do than track down my fiancé's ex-wives and pretend to be engaged."

Zach ducked his head to hide his grimace. Mystery solved. Shane was Fay's ex-husband. And she didn't want to let him go.

"I'm Shane's wife," Fay said, and Zach was surprised to hear a bit of steel in her voice. "His only wife."

"You're forgetting the *ex* part. The part that leaves him free to move on with his life. With me." The brunette patted her stomach. "With us.

So quit calling him. Stop chasing him. And for God's sake, stop being so freaking pathetic."

The brunette whirled on her high heels and walked away, shoulders back, head high, belly leading the way.

Leaving him and Fay once again alone in the too-small room.

Fay covered her face with her hands, murmuring under her breath. Zach glanced at the door. At his escape. Wished like hell he could take it.

But he'd never been good at walking away when someone was in trouble.

He really needed to work on that.

"Are you all right?" he asked, harsher than he'd intended, but damn it, he'd thought his superhero complex had died in that blast in Iraq, along with his arm and leg.

Looked like he was putting the cape on once again.

"I'm sorry…" Fay gasped from behind her hands, and he waited for the rest of her apology. Waited for her to say she was sorry for the drama. Hell, she apologized so much, he wouldn't be surprised if she took the blame for global warming, the price of gas and his injuries.

"I'm really sorry, but…I can't…" She lifted her head, her gaze terrified. "I can't seem to breathe…"

Shit.

Her hair was damp at the temples, her face pale, her body trembling. She was at the start of a panic attack. He should know—he'd had more than a few since waking up in the military hospital in Germany three days after the explosion. Times when the fear was so real, he wanted to run, if only to escape his own thoughts.

But he wouldn't leave her. Couldn't.

She needed him.

He gestured to the chair. "Sit down."

She remained rooted to her spot, her eyes wide, her body rocking slightly, her fingers curled into her palms.

"I…I'm not…feeling…well…" She wheezed and his own chest seized, his breath burning his lungs. "I'm…going to…pass…out…"

"No," he snapped, "you're not." He did a few neck rolls. Blew out a heavy breath and tried again, softening his tone. "You are not going to pass out," he told her. If she did, he wouldn't be able to catch her. And the last thing he needed was for someone to find them in this cramped room, her a crumpled mess on the floor. He edged closer, keeping his eyes on hers. "You are going to sit in this chair, catch your breath and calm down. You are not going to let some mouthy teenager push you into losing control. You hear me?"

Eyes wide, she nodded, like a puppet on a string. But color was returning to her face and her breathing was evening out.

"Sit," he repeated, then walked out of the room, not waiting to see if she obeyed him.

He had a feeling she did. Had a feeling she always did as she was told. It was probably the root of all her troubles.

Not his problem, he told himself as he crossed the empty dining area to the beverage service set up in front of the windows. It didn't matter to him whether she got knocked down by the slightest breeze or had a backbone made of steel. He was here to get his life back in order. To figure out his future. Not to save her.

He was afraid he couldn't even if he wanted to.

But he wouldn't leave her like this. What if she'd been his sister? Not that Daphne would ever let someone get the better of her, but if Daphne were in trouble, he'd want someone to help her get through a difficult time.

He grabbed a bottle of chilled water and went back to the office to find Fay perched on the edge of the chair, her expression confused, as if unsure how she'd gotten there.

He shoved the water at her. "Hold this."

She fumbled the bottle, almost dropping it before recovering and holding it in both hands. He twisted the cap but she held the bottle too loosely and the entire thing turned.

"A little help here," he said gruffly.

Straightening, she tightened her hold and he opened it.

"Drink," he said when she just frowned at it.

He watched her take a hesitant sip. Then another. "Better?"

"Yes." She cleared her throat. Met his eyes briefly before her gaze dropped to her lap. "Thank you. I'm feeling much better now."

She really did suck at lying. "Yeah?"

"I'm fine. Really."

"Do you want me to call someone?" Someone better equipped to deal with the situation. Someone who knew her better.

"No!" She inhaled sharply. Licked her lips. "I mean...thank you...but that's not necessary. There's no need to worry anyone. I apologize for all...that." She waved her hand vaguely as if to encompass both the scene with the pregnant brunette and her resulting mini breakdown. "I can assure you that sort of thing does not happen regularly at Bradford House. I'm just sorry you had to witness that...unpleasantness."

"You need to stop doing that."

She blinked, looked confused. "Stop being yelled at by strangers?"

"Stop apologizing. You do it too much."

It made her weak. Made her vulnerable, an easy target for people like the brunette.

Fay's eyes welled, her lower lip trembled. As if this day hadn't been shitty enough, she had to go and turn on the waterworks. Tears didn't freak him out. He just didn't have the time or patience to deal with them. Not today.

"Suck those back," he growled lowly.

She flinched. "Ex-excuse me?"

He hardened his heart against the sight of tears in her eyes. She didn't need someone to coddle her. She needed to grow a goddamn backbone. "Crying isn't going to help."

"I'm sor—"

He cut off her apology with the swipe of his hand. "You're letting them win."

She shook her head. Sniffed. "Letting who win?"

"The brunette." He paused, watched her expression carefully. "And your ex."

"He's not my ex," she rushed out. Twisted her fingers together. "I mean, he is, but we're getting back together."

Not according to the brunette. And why Fay would even want the asshole back was beyond Zach. Beyond him and none of his damned business.

"Do you need me to escort you to your room?" she asked.

He almost smiled. He was being dismissed. Politely, but it was a dismissal all the same.

Good for her. Maybe she wasn't as fragile as he thought. Maybe she just needed someone to help her see that.

"I've got it." He crossed to the door and told himself to keep walking. And not look back. It wasn't his problem if she got pushed around.

Wasn't his concern whether or not she was so trusting she believed her ex even when the proof of his faithlessness showed up on her doorstep. Literally.

She wasn't his to worry about. He had his own issues—plenty of them.

He crossed the threshold only to stop. Hang his head. And curse himself inwardly as he turned to face her.

"Life isn't fair."

He winced at that bit of freaking wisdom coming out of his mouth. Next thing he knew he'd be telling her that the sun would come out tomorrow and to look on the bright side.

"I'm well aware of that," she said, her tone soft and somber, and he wondered what had put that weariness in her eyes. The sadness.

He shifted, felt uncomfortable and itchy, but he'd come this far—he might as well say his peace. "Tears don't help." He should know. His mom and sister had cried for him, over him, many, many times, but their tears hadn't stopped his stepfather from whaling on him. Hadn't stopped the pain or the beatings when he was a kid. Hadn't helped his injuries now heal faster. "When someone pushes you, push back."

She laughed, but the sound held no humor. "If you knew me," she said, wrapping her arms around her waist as if holding herself together, "you'd know I've never been much for pushing back."

He could tell. Every thought, every emotion was clear on her face, in the way she held herself. She was sweet and vulnerable and delicate.

God help her.

"You'd better get used to being flat on your ass, then," he told her, "because you're going to spend your entire life getting knocked down."

She lifted her chin, held his gaze. "Then I guess it's a good thing I'm good at picking myself back up."

There it was again, that unexpected flash of defiance. Of strength. "I guess it is. And maybe," he continued quietly, sincerely, "the next time you're getting back on your feet, you'll give yourself some credit for doing so. Because staying down is the easy way out. It takes guts to take a hit and go back for more. Don't ever forget that."

IT TAKES GUTS to take a hit and go back for more. Don't ever forget that.

Fay couldn't move, couldn't speak as Zach's words played over in her mind. She certainly couldn't stop him from leaving, so she stood there, like an idiot, eyes bulging, jaw hanging, while he walked away.

Well, that was…different.

The whole experience had been surreal, from the pregnant brunette laying into her, claiming to be carrying Shane's child, to Zach's reaction to her almost but not quite breakdown.

He hadn't been nice. Or compassionate. When she'd first started hyperventilating, she'd expected him to help. Had thought he'd offer sympathy. Support. The least he could have done was try to calm her down and tell her everything was going to be okay.

Not simply demand she snap out of it.

She closed the door then leaned back against it. Okay, so he hadn't done that in so many words, but the end result was the same. He'd been gruff and bossy. Almost like a bully, she thought.

That it had worked and she'd somehow managed not to fall completely apart wasn't the point.

The point was he hadn't been very kind.

And she, like the infamous Blanche DuBois, had always depended on the kindness of others—strangers or otherwise. Maybe it was time she stopped doing that.

Because while he hadn't exactly been nice, he had helped her, with his brusque tone and quiet insistence that she control herself. He had, it seemed, understood her.

And she couldn't help but wonder if that wasn't its own sort of kindness.

That she'd managed to stay in control was a point of pride. One she would hold on to for all she was worth. And she had Zach Castro to thank for it.

She'd humiliated herself several times in front of him, all within the span of twenty minutes, and yet he hadn't looked at her like everyone else did—with pity. As if she was crazy. She'd often thought they were right.

But now, remembering Zach's words, the confidence in his tone, how he'd looked at her as if she was someone who could handle herself, who could stand up for herself, she wondered, for the first time, if she could prove the rest of them wrong.

Hands shaking, she pulled out her phone, dialed Shane's number. It went to voice mail.

She hung up without leaving a message. It wasn't as if she could say, *Hey, your pregnant, teenage fiancée showed up at my door and was mean to me.* What did she expect him to do? Ground the brunette?

For one thing, that would only make it seem as if Fay believed the other woman. And she didn't. Shane would never be with someone so young. She began to pace the small space, the energy zipping through her a welcome change from the usual numbness.

Yes, Shane *had* been with someone that young, had cheated on Fay with a nineteen-year-old when they'd still been married. Had left Fay and the boys for her, demanding a divorce so he could be with her.

Only to come back to Fay time and time again.

But that was all in the past. He'd apologized. Sworn he'd changed. They'd all moved on.

She flashed back to the brunette's ring finger, to that tiny diamond, to her pregnant belly.

No. She wouldn't jump to conclusions. Shane loved Fay. He did. Hadn't he told her last night?

Maybe he hadn't said it in so many words, but he'd made love to her, had stayed with her until morning. That meant something. And he'd told her that once he got a few things figured out, they'd be together again.

She clutched the ring around her neck. She believed him. Trusted him. Forgave him. Because she loved him, she assured herself even as doubt tried to creep in. She loved him. But more than that, more importantly, she needed him.

She didn't know who she was without him.

CHAPTER SIX

THAT HADN'T EXACTLY gone according to plan.

Sitting behind the wheel of Shane's pickup, Josie Hutchingson glanced at her belly. Then again, quite a few things hadn't gone according to plan the last year or so.

Which just sucked the big one.

"No offense," she murmured to the baby girl inside her. The baby continued using Josie's bladder like a trampoline, so she figured all was forgiven.

Still, Josie wished she could go back—if not an entire year then at least one hour ago, when she'd decided to confront Shane's ex-wife.

She'd gone to that bed-and-breakfast sure she was in the right. That she was the one who'd been mistreated. She'd expected to feel vindicated, getting in Fay Lindemuth's face that way. She'd had every right to lay into the other woman, she assured herself. She'd let Fay know she wouldn't put up with her trying to steal Shane. When she'd left, Fay had been pale and shaking and obviously scared. Josie should feel triumphant. Powerful.

Instead she just felt mean. And small.

Like she'd kicked a sick puppy.

Fay wasn't anything like Josie had pictured her. Oh, sure, Shane had told her Fay wasn't a threat. That she was meek. That she was trying to win him back by making up excuses as to why he needed to come over—one of the boys was sick or she needed help changing a lightbulb. He'd promised Josie up and down and three ways to Sunday that what had happened last night had been a onetime thing. That he wanted to be with Josie, wanted to be a father to their daughter.

And Josie had bought it. Had been so pathetically needy, so eager to believe she'd made the right choice in being with him, she'd eaten it up like it was her favorite ice cream and asked for seconds.

She lowered her head, tapped her forehead against the steering wheel—once, twice, three times. She was a freaking idiot.

Because one thing had become crystal clear during her little visit to Bradford House: Fay had no idea that Shane was involved with someone else. Or that he'd gotten another woman pregnant.

She'd been stunned. No woman, however good an actress, could have faked that reaction. Meaning Shane had lied. To both of them.

"What are we supposed to do now?" she whispered, rubbing her stomach.

The baby had no answers, just a hard kick that seemed to tell Josie to suck it up and deal.

Story of her life.

Well, one thing was for sure, she needed a plan. And, she thought as the baby rolled, a bathroom. Not necessarily in that order.

She climbed out of the truck. It was a beautiful spring day—clear blue sky, light breeze, moderate temperature. Beautiful if you didn't mind being stuck in some no-name town in Pennsylvania far from the Jersey shore.

Her eyes stung. Stupid hormones, making her an emotional mess over nothing. And every-thing. But the truth was, she missed her home. She missed Callie, her little sister.

She even missed her mom.

And she really, really missed her old life.

The baby kicked again. Hard. Josie rubbed her stomach. "Yeah, yeah, no use crying over spilled milk," she murmured, ignoring the raised eye-brow look she got from the old lady passing her. "I know."

Or in this case, no use crying over the train wreck that had become her life.

She'd gotten herself into this mess. She'd get herself out.

Spying a diner two doors down, she quickened her pace. The inside was decent—old but clean, the narrow space done up in reds and creams, the floor tiled, the booths lining the walls well used. Square tables filled the rest of the space, and the air smelled of grilled meat and something sweet and cinnamony. After using the restroom, she slid into a booth in the back corner. Her phone buzzed. She checked and saw a text from Shane.

Where r u?

She rolled her eyes. Seriously? The man was thirty-two years old. You'd think he could spell out simple words like *are* and *you*.

Sometimes she wondered which of them was the adult in this relationship.

She considered texting him back, tried to tell herself he was worried about her—and the well-being of their baby.

But while she'd always been fairly good at lying to herself, she seemed to be losing that skill. He wasn't worried. He wanted his truck back. The truck she'd taken without permission to confront the woman he'd spent last night with.

Josie held down the button on her phone with more than the necessary force, shutting it off. Guess he'd just have to wait. And wonder what she was doing. Who she was with.

Like he'd left her waiting and wondering at their hotel room last night while he'd been screwing some other woman. As soon as he'd returned to their room early this morning, his hair mussed, his clothes smelling like perfume, she'd known what he'd been doing, and she'd laid into him but good. Not that they'd had a fight. Shane didn't fight. He got quiet. Cold.

Leaving her to yell and scream and feel like an absolute idiot for losing control.

And what did he do while she was losing her mind, her heart breaking? He'd lain down on the bed and fallen asleep.

She'd wanted to smother him with a pillow.

Luckily, good sense had prevailed and she'd told herself that they would talk through their problems once he woke up. She'd drifted off only to wake up shortly before noon to find him leaving. *Again.*

She was starting to think it was what he did best.

He'd left her to go hang out with a couple of old high school buddies. He hadn't even introduced her to his friends, hadn't invited her to go along, had just told her he'd be back later then walked out of the room. She'd watched through the dingy window as he'd climbed into a gray SUV.

Bastard. Cheating, lying, no-good, scum-sucking bastard.

"Hey." A deep male voice startled her right out of her internal tirade.

He had her thinking, hoping, that Shane had found her. That he'd cared enough to actually look for her.

Until she glanced up at the guy standing next to the booth. Not Shane, but a waiter. A cute waiter setting a menu in front of her.

He leaned over the table to pour ice water into

a glass, and when he glanced at her, his face only inches away, she forgot how to breathe.

Instinct took over and she inhaled sharply, had him giving her a curious look, but...whatever.

Make that a seriously cute waiter. He must have been over six feet with broad shoulders and long legs. Blue eyes surrounded by thick lashes, dark, mussed hair that curled up at the ends and tanned skin.

He looked around her age, which—the guy at the bed-and-breakfast had pegged right, *damn him*—was nineteen.

The waiter straightened and gave her a slow once-over, which she felt from the top of her head to the soles of her feet. Interest lit his eyes and his body language changed from just-doing-my-job to what-do-I-have-to-say-to-do-*you*?

Of course, that was only because he hadn't caught sight of her stomach yet.

"How's it going?" he asked.

"Hi," she said, intending to tell him that it was going great, that life was one big, fabulous party, but what came out of her mouth was a pathetic whine. "It actually sucks right now."

His eyebrows rose. Well, that was her. Surprising people left and right, keeping them on their toes. "Yeah? Sorry to hear that. Anything I can do to help?"

The funniest part? He actually managed to

sound like he meant it. Guys who looked like him always had game, though.

But just the fact that he asked brought her up short. And made her want to cry. It had been a long time since someone was nice to her.

And she didn't want to think about how long it had been since she'd been nice in return.

Nice didn't get a girl anything but a broken heart.

"I *could* use someone to talk to," she said, putting a pout and a plea in her tone. She even batted her eyelashes before giving him a beseeching look. "I don't suppose you'd want to maybe—" she twisted a lock of her hair around her finger, letting her tone go breathless and flirty "—talk?"

He blinked, seemed a bit stunned by his good fortune but recovered quickly. "Uh…sure," he squeaked, his voice going up an octave. He cleared his throat. "I'm…uh…actually due to take my break in fifteen minutes."

She smiled. "Perfect."

And then she twisted toward him, waited until his gaze dropped to take in…well…all of her. It took a moment, but she saw the moment when any interest he had in her—on a male-female level—rolled over and died. His eyes widened; the grip he had on his little order tablet tightened. "Uh…"

"Problem?"

"No. No problem." But he'd paled and had a definite *oh shit* look about him.

She almost felt bad for him. Almost. But he was a guy, and they weren't her favorite people at the moment.

And she was too busy feeling sorry for herself to have any leftover sympathy.

"Don't tell me," she said, unable to keep the bite from her tone, "you suddenly remembered something important you have to do during your break."

He frowned. Held her gaze. "No. I'm free. That is, if you still want to talk."

Well. Guess it was her turn to be surprised.

Not that he meant it. He was probably already making plans to sneak out the back. Guys did not want to sit around and listen while some girl complained about her lot in life. If a guy wasn't getting laid or didn't have the possibility of getting laid in the very near future, they moved on.

She tried not to take it personally.

"Yeah, well, that's probably not the best idea," Josie said, then scanned the menu, well aware of his eyes on her. Studying her. Probably trying to figure her out.

Ha. Good luck with that. She hadn't even figured herself out yet.

"I'll have a chocolate milkshake," she told him, handing him the menu. "And an order of French fries."

"You want whipped cream on your shake?"

"Am I alive and breathing?"

He grinned, and her heart did a weird flipping thing. Which was stupid. Just because he had a killer smile did not mean her insides were turning to mush. She didn't get mushy over guys.

"You'd be surprised," he said, still grinning, as if he knew the effect that smile had on females. Bastard. "I never understand it, though. It's like, you're sucking at least five hundred calories through a straw as it is. Saying no to whipped cream at that point is useless."

Five hundred calories? The waistband of her pants grew tighter just hearing it. Oh, well. Like she'd said, she'd had a bad day. And honestly, she was as big as a house already, so what did five hundred more calories matter? "It's a definite yes to the whipped cream. The more on the milkshake, the merrier I'll be."

He nodded, and she watched him walk away before shifting to stare out the window to her right. Not much of a view, just a wide alley between buildings. A stray cat with matted gray fur cleaned itself next to a trash can. In the booth across from her, a group of high school girls giggled and tossed their hair, putting on a show for the boys in the booth behind them.

She was only one year removed from that, and yet it felt like a freaking lifetime.

She remained lost in her thoughts until the waiter returned five minutes later.

"Here you go," he said, setting a tall milkshake

with a mound of whipped cream and two cherries in front of her along with a plate filled with French fries.

"That was fast."

This time his grin was almost shy. "I had them put a rush on it. Far be it from me to keep a pregnant lady from her ice cream and fries."

Pregnant lady. Huh. And he hadn't even flinched when he said it.

"Ketchup?" he asked. She nodded and he was off again.

She wanted to call him back.

Stupid, she thought, scooping up a huge spoonful of whipped cream and shoving it in her mouth, just in case the words decided to come out of their own accord. She wasn't some sweet, innocent coed looking for a boyfriend. A) She'd never be considered sweet. B) She was already pregnant, which left out the innocent part. And C) she already had a boyfriend. She was in a committed, adult relationship with the father of her unborn baby.

Who just happened to be a lying, cheating scumbag. And that he was her best option at the moment really bit the big one.

She tossed the maraschino cherries aside then stirred a bit of whipped cream into the shake before taking a sip. She was reaching for a fry when the waiter returned, a bottle of ketchup in one hand, an iced tea in the other.

And sat across from her.

She froze, her hand hovering over the hot fries. "What are you doing?"

"Bringing you ketchup." He slid the bottle toward her then sipped his tea, leaning back in the booth, making himself right at home.

She narrowed her eyes. "You don't need to sit to do that."

He shrugged. "No, but I thought it would be easier for us to talk this way."

What game was he playing? "You don't want to talk."

"I don't?"

She leaned forward, caught the scent of the fries and picked one up, and wagged it at him. "Look, we both know what happened. You were hoping to get into my pants. Until you noticed the bun baking in my oven. Then you were just hoping to get away without catching my pregnant cooties."

To end what she considered a none-too-shabby mini set-down, she bit viciously into the fry, but her moan of pleasure at its hot, greasy, salty goodness made her sound less victorious and more creepy.

She really needed to stop skipping breakfast.

He nodded slowly, his gaze never leaving hers. "You're partially right. I did want to…get to know you—"

She snorted. "Is that what you call it?"

"—and that hasn't changed."

"Right," she said, drawing the word out. "So you get off on pregnant chicks?"

He flushed. "I'm not here to hit on you. I thought you could use someone to talk to."

"I have nothing to talk about," she said quickly. Because she did. She so wanted to tell him everything. To unburden herself with this too-handsome boy, this stranger who wouldn't judge or criticize her or give her his unsolicited opinion. But she needed to keep some things hidden. She couldn't even admit them to herself.

Such as what a mistake she'd made being with Shane.

"Are you sure?" he asked. "Because if you ask me, you look kind of..."

She held her breath, waiting for him to say she looked pathetic, just another pregnant teenager, adding to the statistics.

"Alone."

Alone. The word, said so softly, so...sympathetically...swept through her.

Tears clogged her throat. Oh, hell, no. She was not going to cry. She wasn't some bawl baby, whining when things didn't go her way. Crying over the fact that her boyfriend was sleeping around, that she hadn't talked to her sister in five months and that she'd been disowned by her mother.

Tears were a waste of time and wouldn't change her circumstances.

She ate more fries, keeping her eyes downcast until she was sure any weepiness wasn't visible. When she raised her head, she found him watching her again in that way that was a combination of patience and understanding and just…acceptance.

"I'm not alone," she told him, flashing the almost-invisible diamond on her finger. "I have a fiancé."

Okay, so that wasn't exactly the entire truth, but since lightning didn't strike her dead, she figured whoever was running things upstairs wasn't going to quibble over it. In truth, Shane had bought her the ring after the huge blowup they'd had last month in Baltimore. It'd been his way of keeping her happy—and shutting her up.

But it hadn't come with a formal marriage proposal.

"Yeah?" the waiter asked. "That's good."

She bit into a fry. He sounded sincere enough, as if he couldn't care less that she was already taken.

"What's your deal?" she asked.

He helped himself to a fry but didn't eat it. "No deal. Just trying to make a new friend."

"Why?"

He pursed his lips thoughtfully then bit into the fry, a frown wrinkling his forehead as he chewed. "Because you were right," he finally said. "I was freaked out when I realized you're pregnant and I'm trying to be less of a douche. Plus, it's pretty clear you could use a friend." He nodded toward her half-empty glass. "If only to keep you in chocolate milkshakes."

A friend, huh? She hadn't had one of those in a long time, maybe since high school, and even then she could count the number on one hand. Her best friend had always been her younger sister, Callie.

Until their mom had tossed Josie out of her house and forbidden seventeen-year-old Callie from having anything to do with her.

"I'm not sure how long I'm going to be in town," she heard herself saying. Even more surprising? That she was seriously considering accepting his offer and becoming milkshake buddies.

Pregnancy really messed with a woman's brain.

"So if we do this whole…friend thing," she continued, "don't get too attached to me."

He nodded solemnly. "It'll be tough, but I'll do my best."

She rolled her eyes at his dry tone. "Hilarious. Just don't blame me when you're moping around because you miss me."

Not that he would miss her. No one did.

"I have heeded your warning. Why don't we start off slow?"

Tipping her glass to get to the milkshake at the bottom, she dipped a fry in it. Ate it. "You mean like a probationary period?"

"Sure. Or maybe we could call it a trial run? That way I don't feel like a criminal."

Whatever. The end result was the same. They'd chat a bit today, exchange cell phone numbers and maybe text a few times before he got bored or found some other girl to be "friends" with.

Some other girl who wasn't pregnant. *And almost engaged*, her inner voice reminded her.

Yeah, that, too.

"If we're going to be friends on a trial run," she said, "we should probably exchange names." She offered him her hand across the table. "I'm Josie."

When his hand closed around hers, big and warm and a bit callused, her heart did that annoying flip-flop thing again. "Drew Freeman."

She slid her hand free as quickly as possible and settled it over her stomach. The baby moved. As if making sure Josie remembered she was still in there.

A reminder that Josie was in a completely different phase of life than her new buddy, and possibly a hint that she and Drew had nothing in common. And even if they did, she shouldn't trust some random guy just because he seemed decent.

Just because he was being nice to her.

All valid points. Ones she should listen to. But she didn't want to. Not now. All she wanted was to sit across from a cute boy and forget what a mess her life was.

And how afraid she was that it would only get worse.

CHAPTER SEVEN

WHEN FAY WAS ten years old, Maddie Montesano had approached her one day during recess and announced they were going to be best friends.

If only Fay had stayed home sick from school that day.

The wistful thought brought on a pang of guilt followed by contrition. She didn't regret her friendship with Maddie. She just didn't want to be standing in her apartment, getting the third degree from her.

Of course, she could have avoided this entire scene if she hadn't been so anxious to see Shane. But with her parents out of town until next weekend, she'd asked her fourteen-year-old niece, Bree, to come and watch the boys while she went out for a few hours.

She should have realized Maddie wouldn't just drop off her daughter and go on her way. No, she'd come up to Fay's apartment with Bree. Because she'd missed Fay and the boys, Maddie had insisted.

If only Fay could lie as well as that.

"I told you," Fay said in answer to Maddie's

question about what, exactly, she was doing that required her needing a sitter. "I have a few errands to run."

While she wasn't all that skilled with outright lies, she had learned how to hide certain parts of the truth.

Maddie crossed her arms, feet wide, gaze narrowed. In faded jeans, scuffed work boots and a grungy white T-shirt that clung to her ample curves, she was a suspicious goddess, digging for the truth—and blocking the door.

At their next session, Fay would ask Dr. Porter to give her some tips on making a graceful, and forceful, exit.

"Is that right? What kind of errands?" Maddie asked, as if simply curious.

Fay didn't buy it for a minute.

Maddie only used that mild tone when she was trying to lull someone into complacency. Well, Fay was not going to fall for it. She wasn't doing anything wrong. Nothing could be more right than putting her family back together, so there was no reason to feel like a criminal trying to dig her way out of prison.

She smiled and knew Maddie would see right through it, but kept grinning, anyway. She considered adding an innocent bat of her eyelashes, but she was smart enough—contrary to what her best friend might think—not to push it. "The usual kinds."

"Really?" Maddie asked, cocking her hip, her long dark ponytail sliding over her shoulder. "Are you going to Pineview?"

"Yes," she said, though she had no plans to visit the grocery store on the other side of town from where she was really going.

"Then you won't mind picking up a few items for me," Maddie said, casual as you please. "I'd go myself, but I want to have the Cochrans' estimate finished before the game starts."

Maddie worked for her family's contracting company, Montesano Construction, along with her father and two of her older brothers. The job suited her and gave her a sense of purpose and pride.

Fay envied her that.

But not as much as she envied Maddie and Neil's relationship, their second chance. They'd been high school sweethearts, but when Maddie got pregnant with Bree at the age of sixteen, Neil had left Shady Grove—and Maddie—for his shot in the NHL. It'd been almost three years since they'd reunited, and they were making it work despite Neil traveling so often. At least he'd gotten the trade he wanted, leaving the Seattle Knights for the Columbus Blue Jackets, who played only a three-hour drive from Shady Grove.

Neil was currently on a six-day West Coast road trip, which meant the games he played weren't broadcast here until at least 10:00 p.m., but Maddie would stay up and watch every minute of them. Including tonight's game against Los Angeles.

"I'd be happy to," Fay said, plowing ahead with her lie.

"Great. We need milk—organic, of course—"

"Of course," Fay said, and immediately felt ashamed of her dry tone, though Maddie didn't seem put off by it.

Then again, Fay had never been very good at being sarcastic. Not when it might hurt someone's feelings.

"Bananas," Maddie continued, counting items off on her fingers, "a pound of their house-made vanilla granola and a loaf of their oatmeal honey bread, please."

This was why Fay didn't lie. She was horrible at it. She either got caught outright or, in this case, ended up stuck doing something she'd had no intention of doing.

And Maddie had chosen items that weren't available anywhere else.

Fay could claim they'd been out of granola and bread, but she wouldn't give Maddie the satisfaction. Not because of any false sense of pride, but because she'd heard enough *I told you so*s to last a lifetime.

"Milk, bananas, granola and bread," she repeated, typing the list in the notes app on her phone. She felt quite defiant, taking her little white lie this far. Guess she wasn't so sweet and fearful after all.

Staying down is the easy way out.

Zach Castro's voice filled her head. Great. Any more people in there and she really would be certifiable.

She wasn't staying down. This wasn't about someone treating her badly. This was her choice. She was in control. She was being smart and resourceful and…and…

And she was as much of a coward as she was a liar.

There she was, wasting time taking down Maddie's shopping list, making plans to drive out of her way to pick up the items her friend wanted just so Fay wouldn't have to tell her the truth.

So she wouldn't disappoint Maddie.

She was always afraid of saying the wrong thing. Of making the wrong choice. Of upsetting someone else.

And she was getting so very tired of it.

"I'm not a coward," she whispered to her toes.

"What?" Maddie asked.

If she were a coward, she wouldn't be heading out to see Shane. She'd wait for him to come to her. She'd continue to believe in him. Trust him.

She wouldn't be about to ask him if he'd gotten another woman pregnant.

Part of her didn't want to. A big, huge part wanted to forget she'd ever seen the brunette, but even she wasn't that delusional. She had to know the truth—even if she wasn't sure she could handle it.

Act as if...act as if...act as if...

"I'm not going to Pineview," she said, her voice not much louder than her previous whisper.

"No? I'm shocked."

She wasn't. That was clear from Maddie's snide tone.

Fay had always hated that tone.

She opened her mouth with the intention of letting Maddie know she was going to see her husband only to decide against it when she saw the expression on Maddie's face—the one telling Fay she already knew.

"You heard Shane is in town."

Fay wasn't sure where the words came from, or how she managed to say them so calmly, but once they were out, she was glad. If only because of the shock on Maddie's face.

Maddie's arms dropped back to her sides. "So you are going to see him?"

Fay accepted the thread of surprise in her tone. Welcomed it. Because Maddie wasn't surprised Fay wanted to see the man who'd hurt her so badly in the past—she was surprised that Fay had been brave enough to admit it.

Yes, well, the day had been full of surprising events and revelations. Might as well embrace the trend.

Still, it took some deep-down, previously unknown courage for Fay to nod. "Did Damien call you?"

"Damien? Why would he call me?"

Fay slung her purse over her shoulder. Sent Damien a silent apology for thinking he'd sold her out. "He mentioned to me that he saw Shane."

Not a lie. He'd told her just that morning that he'd seen Shane…leaving Bradford House.

"Was that when you lost your mind and decided to search him out?"

"My mind is fine," Fay said, stung.

She knew what people thought. Had heard the gossip, the nasty whispers. They thought she was incapable of making rational decisions. That she was crazy.

Knew her parents, her brother and her best friend agreed with them.

"Obviously it's not," Maddie said, a hint of remorse in her tone. A silent apology that Fay had no choice but to accept. She hated confrontation and didn't have it in her to hold on to anger.

Didn't have the right. Not after what she'd done.

"You're making this into a big deal," Fay said. *Making it into your business.* "Shane and I have things to discuss, that's all."

Things such as the promises he'd made to her just last night, his finding work closer to Shady Grove and oh, yes, the angry pregnant girl who'd showed up on Fay's doorstep. She clutched her purse strap, her nails digging into her palm.

The angry, beautiful, oh-so-very-young, *lying* pregnant girl.

Please, please, let her be lying.

Was it really so wrong to want to hold on to her hope? To keep believing in the man she loved no matter what her own heart was trying to tell her?

"You don't have to search Shane out," Maddie said, reaching up to take the band from her hair. Pacing, she scooped her fingers through her hair, pulling it back into a ponytail with so much force Fay's own scalp ached. "If you have something to say to him, your attorney can contact his attorney."

When Maddie reached the end of the couch, Fay began to edge her way toward the door. "This isn't a legal matter."

"I can't believe this," Maddie muttered, shaking her head. "I cannot believe we're having this discussion after everything that man has done to you. After the way he's lied to you and hurt you again and again. I can't believe that you stood there and lied to me," she continued, her voice rising, "and that you had the nerve to ask *my* daughter to watch the boys so you could run off and be with a man who continues to use you and toss you aside. Well, guess what? I won't stand by and watch you get hurt again." She crossed the room toward the short hallway, her long, angry strides eating up the distance.

"What are you doing?" Fay asked, hurrying after her.

Maddie whirled around, her ponytail arcing behind her. "I'm getting Bree and going home. I am through enabling you."

Fay could only gape. *Enabling* her? As if she was some rebellious teenager, trying to sneak out to see a boy from the wrong side of the tracks. Making Fay the powerless, disobedient child to Maddie's all-controlling, all-knowing mother figure.

Was this really what their friendship had become? Or had it been this way all these years and Fay just hadn't wanted to see it?

"Fine," Fay said, her chin lifted. "I'll take the boys with me."

"And won't Shane love that?"

He wouldn't. Oh, he loved the boys. But he wasn't used to being around them and had some trouble dealing with their constant chatter, their endless energy.

And if she brought the boys, Shane would use them as an excuse to blow off her questions about the brunette. To delay discussing their reconciliation.

But Maddie wasn't giving her a choice. She was taking away what little power Fay had.

Fay could almost hate her for it.

"The boys and I really need to leave," Fay said, pushing the words through the tightness of her throat, "so you should get Bree now." She bit back the urge to add a *please* or *if you don't mind*.

Maddie's eyes narrowed. "Are you kicking me out?"

"I'm trying to," Fay admitted, refusing to back down. "But you're not cooperating."

Which was just like Maddie. Couldn't she take a page from Fay's book and do what someone asked her to do?

"No, I guess I'm not," Maddie murmured thoughtfully, staring at Fay as if she'd never seen her before. "Then again, you're not exactly cooperating with me, either."

True. It was a small piece of pride she clung to.

"Would you really still go if I take Bree home?" Maddie asked.

"Yes." But it came out soft. Questioning. As if asking for Maddie's permission to go against her wishes. "Yes, I have to." That sense of pride grew, warmed her. Until she heard herself say, "Don't be mad."

And, oh, how she hated the plea in her tone. The fear.

Maddie sighed. "I'm not mad. I'm…"

Fay tensed, waited for Maddie to tell her how disappointed she was in Fay's lack of self-respect.

"…worried."

And that was even worse. Worried meant Maddie felt entitled to share her thoughts on each and every one of Fay's choices. Because she loved her.

There was no sense assuring her Fay knew exactly what she was doing. Maddie would never believe it. Not with Fay's track record, so she kept quiet.

It was only a matter of time before Maddie filled the silence, anyway.

Which she did with a sigh so drawn out, Fay was surprised she didn't faint from lack of oxygen. "I suppose Bree could stay if this really is *that* important."

"It is," Fay said, irritation pricking. Why would Maddie even say that, and in that long-suffering maternal way? She should know by now what was most important to Fay.

Why couldn't she, just once, be on Fay's side?

Maddie nodded, jailer to prisoner, granting a reprieve. "All right. She can stay."

"Thank you," Fay added, wondering why it was so hard to get those words out. She was used to thanking others for their time, their understanding. Their love. This should be no different.

But it was. Because while she was grateful she didn't have to take her boys with her, she also felt…resentful. Which gave her something to worry about later. And one more thing to feel guilty about right now.

"But I meant what I said. I can't do this. Not anymore," Maddie said.

Fay rubbed the strap of her purse, unable to still her hands. "What do you mean?"

Maddie's hesitation was unlike her. She always plowed forward, saying whatever came to mind, doing what she thought was right without worrying about the consequences. Without constantly fretting over her choices. Her words.

"I can't continue to stand by and watch you make the same horrible decisions time and again," Maddie finally said. "Until you're finally ready to put the past behind you and embrace the future, I…" She paused. Inhaled deeply, her words quiet. Final. "I can't be a part of your life. And after tonight, I can't let Bree be, either."

The words rocked Fay back on her heels. Just as Maddie had intended, Fay was sure. For her to be so frightened of losing her best friend and niece that she'd do whatever Maddie wanted.

When someone pushes you, push back. She couldn't. No matter how much she might like to. But she could stand her ground. Could refuse to be knocked down.

"I'm sorry you feel that way," she said, proud that despite the way her heart raced, her voice was steady.

Maddie didn't mean what she said, anyway. It was just her notorious temper getting the better of her. She wouldn't toss aside twenty years of friendship.

She wouldn't abandon Fay.

"That's it?" Maddie asked in pure disbelief. "That's all you have to say?"

"What else is there?"

Maddie started pacing again, her hands gesturing wildly as she spoke, her words shooting out like bullets. "You can say you won't do this to yourself again. That you're ready to let Shane go."

"It would be so easy for me to do that," Fay said, the realization like ice water tossed in her face—a cold wake-up call. "So easy for me to agree. To just say what you want to hear. I've always said what everyone else wants to hear. Made promises I had no intention of keeping because I thought you all knew best. Better, certainly, than I did." She met Maddie's gaze, held it. "But what if you don't? What if I'm not as clueless, as weak as you all think I am?"

Maddie went white, and when she spoke, her voice shook. "No one thinks you're clueless."

"Just weak." But in this moment she didn't feel weak. She felt…well, not strong, exactly, just… right.

"I won't stay away from Shane," she continued. "He is my husband—"

"Ex-husband."

"—and the father of my children. I love him."

But what should have been a heartfelt declaration came out passionless.

"You're just going to pretend he never cheated

on you?" Maddie asked. "Or have you forgotten how he left you for some girl barely out of high school?"

A vision of the pregnant brunette flashed in Fay's mind and a bubble of hysterical laughter rose in her throat. She gamely swallowed it down... down, down, down...where it could mix with everything else she needed to keep hidden—her thoughts and feelings, her fears and guilt. "It's not about pretending or forgetting. It's about forgiveness."

"Shane doesn't deserve your forgiveness."

"Everyone deserves forgiveness," Fay said quietly, praying it was true.

Maddie stared at her as if she'd never seen her before. Nodded toward the door. "Go on then. Go running back to him. But I won't be here when you get back. And I won't be around to pick up the pieces when he breaks your heart again."

Fay wanted to insist that Shane wasn't going to break her heart. That she believed in him, but the words were twisted and tangled inside her. She stared at the door all the way across the room, wishing she could storm over to it, head held high. But doubts were creeping in, weakening her resolve. Laughing at her pitiful attempts at defiance, at running her own life. Reminding her of all the many times before when she'd been such a fool.

The darkness nudged at her heart, her mind, trying to find a way in. To take control. Oh, how she wished she could let it. She wanted to open her arms and embrace it, let it swallow her whole until there was nothing left. No thoughts. No pain.

No more Fay.

Shaken at the thought, she forced her feet to move, silently counting her steps, each one a small victory.

One...two...three...four...

On the ninth step, she reached the door. Opened it. And found her words after all.

"I never wanted you to pick up the pieces," she told Maddie as she faced her. Her fingers tightened on the door handle, her voice thickened with unshed tears. "All I've ever wanted was for you to just be my friend."

Maddie flinched. She reached out as she stepped forward. "Fay..."

But Maddie had already made up her mind. It was time for Fay to do the same. She shook her head and walked away, shutting the door behind her.

"ALL I'M SAYING is that you're a good ten years past the socially accepted age for a man to run away from home."

Sitting in the armchair looking out through the French doors at the sun setting behind the rolling hills, Zach sighed, leaned his head against the back of the chair and stared up at the ceiling, his legs outstretched. He would have pinched the bridge of his nose, but as he was holding his phone, he'd run out of hands. Too bad, because his sister was giving him one hell of a headache. "I didn't run away. I left."

"Fine," she said in the way women did that made it clear things were anything but. "Let me rephrase—"

"Rephrase," he muttered. "Jesus. You sound like a lawyer. You need to cut back on the time you spend with Oakes."

And thinking of his baby half sister with his older half brother did nothing to improve his mood. They'd been a couple for almost four months and Zach still wasn't used to it—never wanted to get used to it.

Though Daphne and Oakes weren't related— Zach and Daphne shared a mother while he and Oakes had the same father—them being together was just too weird.

As usual when it came to his advice about Oakes, she ignored him and continued on. "You're too old to be trying to find yourself."

"I moved," he said, seriously regretting even answering the phone. Then again, it had been the fourth time she'd called since he'd left Houston that morning. If he hadn't answered, she probably would have called the police to check on him. Or worse—Kane. "Stop making it into something that needs to be psychoanalyzed. You want to practice running a counseling session, do it with Oakes."

"Yes," she said drily, "because out of all the Bartasaviches, Oakes is the one most in need of a good dose of therapy."

She had a point. Oakes had turned out surprisingly well-adjusted, but that was probably because after his mom divorced Clinton Sr. she'd married a respectable judge and had two more sons. Giving Oakes what most people would consider a normal upbringing. Plus, Zach's most easygoing brother had never felt the weight of responsibility of being a Bartasavich, not like C.J., who'd followed in Senior's shoes and was now running Bartasavich Enterprises, a multimillion-dollar corporation. Or Kane, who, as a teenager, had turned to drugs and alcohol as a way to rebel against their father's control.

While Zach had spent his entire life pretending he wasn't a Bartasavich.

He tucked the phone between his shoulder and ear and rubbed at the cramped muscle in his right thigh. "Stop worrying about me."

"Sir! Yes, sir! And so you have a visual, I want you to know that I'm saluting you."

"Giving me the middle finger isn't a military salute. Though I like the *sir* part."

"I bet you do, but we're not talking about your deep-seated need to be seen and treated as an authority figure, we're talking about you leaving everyone and everything you know behind."

"I left everyone and everything behind when

I was eighteen and joined the corps." He wasn't touching her other comment. He didn't need to be seen or treated like an authority figure. That was his father. Or had been, before a debilitating stroke two years ago left Senior unable to speak or even feed himself, let alone demand people give him the adulation he thought he deserved.

"But you were doing so well here," Daphne said. "I don't understand why you had to move halfway across the country. What about your physical therapy? And your counseling?"

He'd stopped going to counseling weeks ago. He'd had enough of people trying to get inside his head. What did it matter how he'd felt when he'd lost his arm? When he'd learned his leg couldn't be saved? No amount of bitching, crying or being pissed could bring them back. Would make him whole.

The only way to really move forward was to take that first step. And keep going.

"They have physical therapists in Pennsylvania," he said. "Maybe even one or two on this side of the state."

"Ha-ha. So glad your hilarious—" she drew the word out so he knew she meant the opposite "—sense of humor is as sharp as ever."

The back door to the bed-and-breakfast opened, and Fay stepped out. She stood there, her hair like a beacon catching the fading rays of the sunset, her face in shadows, neither leaving nor going back inside. As if waiting for something.

Or someone.

He thought of the pregnant teenager. Of her accusations about Fay sleeping with her fiancé. Was she waiting for him?

And if so, why the hell did that piss Zach off so much?

"Are you even listening to me?" Daphne asked, exasperated.

"Yeah."

Fay finally shut the door and walked across the yard to a small paved parking lot. Only to turn around and walk back again.

What the hell?

"Is that so? Then what did I just say?"

He had no idea. But he wasn't dumb enough to admit it and have his ass handed to him by his too-smart sister with her college degree and sharp tongue. "Daphne," he said, his quiet tone serious. Honest. "I'm okay. Really."

There was a beat of silence on the other end. "You're not. If you were, you wouldn't have left."

Fay turned again, and this time headlights flashed as she approached a dark minivan— she must have pressed a key fob. He watched her move, her shoulders bent, her steps slow and heavy, as if she had a rope tied around her waist and was being pulled backward.

I've never been much for pushing back.

Maybe not, but she was obviously fighting an internal battle, one that kept her from getting into her vehicle.

"Tell me what's going on," Daphne continued.

He couldn't, because nothing was going on. He couldn't explain his reasons for coming here because he didn't fully understand them himself. His instincts had told him it was time to leave Houston. That in order to move on with his life he needed a fresh start.

Simple as that. He hadn't done any soul searching trying to figure out why he needed to go. Hadn't wasted any time mulling over the pros and cons.

He saw Fay open the minivan's door, look up at the house, then shut it. She opened it again but didn't get in.

Not everything needed to be overthought.

But that's what Daphne wanted. She wanted to burrow into Zach's head until she knew his every thought and feeling. Damn it, he had a right to keep those to himself. A right to make his own decisions.

"Do you trust me?" he asked, getting to his feet and stepping closer to the door.

"What does that have to do—"

"Do you trust me?"

Daphne sighed. "Of course."

"Good. Then there's nothing else to say."

"Oh, sure. Throw trust in my face. That's a dirty trick and you know it."

"Whatever works."

"Now if I ask you what's really going on inside that thick head of yours it'll seem like I don't believe you're capable enough or strong enough to make your own decisions. So, that's great. Thanks a lot."

"Like I said, I'm okay. Stop worrying."

"Hooray," she deadpanned. "You're okay and, I might add, thirteen hundred miles away from home, so excuse me if I don't do a happy dance over your mental well-being."

He grinned. She drove him bat-shit crazy, but he loved her. "I'm going to miss you, too, brat."

"Yes. You will. But I'm not hanging up until you promise you'll call if there's ever a point where you're not okay."

Once again, Fay walked away from the minivan. Once again, she turned right around and went back to it.

"You do realize I can end this call with the push of a button?" he asked, frowning at the scene outside.

"Like you'd ever hang up on me."

"First time for everything."

"Uh-huh. The way I see it, you can either promise or we can continue our lovely chat. Oh, did I ever tell you about the first time Oakes kissed me? I mean, really kissed me, not just a brotherly peck on the cheek? It happened right there in Shady Grove. It was so romantic. We were walking downtown and—"

"I promise," he grumbled. The last thing he wanted was to have an emotional tell-all conversation with his sister.

"Great," she said, sounding smug. "And I have absolute faith that you'll keep that promise. Seeing as how I trust you so much. Good night, Zach. I love you."

She hung up, getting in the last word after laying on a preemptive guilt trip should he even consider breaking his word.

He almost felt sorry for Oakes.

Zach tossed his phone onto the bed. When Fay did her whole come-and-go routine yet again, he found himself reaching for the door. He drew his hand back. The last thing he needed was to go out there.

He had no reason to. He didn't know her. Wasn't invested in her life, in any way, shape or form.

But he'd thought of her. She'd sneaked into his thoughts over and over again the past few hours. Her bright hair and sweet scent. Her wary eyes and broken smile. Her vulnerability intrigued him, but it had been that burst of inner strength after her encounter with the pregnant teen that enticed him.

Made him want to do what he hated others doing to him—dig deeper.

Stupid. There was no reason for him to insert himself into her life. No reason for him to want to help her. They weren't friends. Any relationship between him and Fay Lindemuth was going to remain strictly professional and temporary.

But when she finally climbed behind the wheel of her minivan and sat there for a good five minutes, not even bothering to turn on the engine, he couldn't resist opening the door and stepping out into the cool night. He couldn't resist helping her.

Damn it all to hell and back.

CHAPTER EIGHT

ZACH MADE HIS way slowly across the yard, the sky above the hills streaked with orange and red. When he reached Fay, she had her head lowered, her hands covering her face.

Shit. He never should have come out here, but when he made to move away with stealthy grace, she raised her head.

Looked like the ninja skills he'd developed in the marines had disappeared along with his leg and arm.

She blinked at him several times from behind the window. And kept right on blinking. He wondered if she was trying to convince herself that he was a figment of her imagination. It must not have worked, because she turned on the ignition and rolled the window down. "Mr. Castro…hello," she said, her smile nowhere in sight.

He nodded.

"Was there something you needed?" she asked after a moment.

He shook his head.

She rubbed at her temple. "Is your room satisfactory?"

He nodded again, felt like an idiot for thinking he could… Hell, he didn't even know why he'd come out. But she'd seemed so lost, the way she'd gone back and forth, back and forth. Like she needed someone to tell her which direction to go.

Her hand dropped. "If you need extra towels or…toiletries…"

"I don't." He shifted like a teenager talking to a girl for the first time. Forced himself to remain still. "You're going out?"

"Yes." She pulled her shoulders back, wiggling in her seat to sit up taller, her hands gripping the steering wheel. "Yes. I have some…errands to run."

"Are you sure?"

Her gaze flew to his. Surprised. Wary. "Wha-what do you mean?"

"Just that you seem…undecided. About those errands."

Even in the twilight, he could make out the blush staining her cheeks. She opened her mouth, but before she could speak, something behind him caught her attention. Her lips pressed together. He turned, followed her gaze to Bradford House, where a tall brunette in jeans and a T-shirt watched from the doorway, hands on her hips.

"I'm not."

At Fay's blurted words, he faced her. "You're not what?"

Her blush deepened and she lifted her pinkie to her mouth, only to curl her fingers into her palm and lower her hand. "I'm not undecided. I'm definitely going."

The last bit was said louder, as she looked over his shoulder at the woman.

He followed her gaze, saw the brunette shake her head in obvious disgust.

"Friend of yours?" he asked.

"Yes. No." She ran her palms up and down the steering wheel. "I guess our relationship is currently...*undecided*."

His lips twitched, but since he didn't think she'd appreciate him finding her amusing at this point in time, he bit it back. "I take it you and the bombshell had a fight."

"Bombshell," Fay said with a short laugh. "Well, I suppose that's one word to describe her. She can be quite...explosive. But Maddie and I don't *fight*."

He raised his eyebrows at the vehemence in her tone. "An argument."

"We don't argue, either. I don't like to argue," she muttered, sounding pissed by that fact. "Dr. Porter says it's because I'm not comfortable being emotionally uncomfortable."

He'd seen enough shrinks to know one of their quotes when he heard one.

Enjoying this interaction more than he would have thought, he nodded toward the bombshell. "Your friend doesn't have that problem."

Even from this distance, he felt the heat of the brunette's glare. She seemed more than content to stand there all night, one hip cocked, waiting for Fay to make up her mind.

Fay tipped her head back against the seat. "Nothing makes Maddie uncomfortable."

"Don't let her chase you away."

"Excuse me?"

He shoved his hand into his pocket. Shrugged. "This is your place, right? Don't let her run you off."

"She didn't run me off. I'm…" Fay swallowed. He watched as she dragged her thumbnail across the top of the steering wheel then curled her fingers around it and met his eyes. "I'm pushing back."

When someone pushes you, push back.

I've never been much for pushing back.

And there it was. That spark. That hint of hidden strength that had intrigued him so.

"Yeah?" he asked gruffly. "Good for you."

"It's not easy," she rushed out. "This pushing thing."

"Easier for some than others."

"I bet it's easy for you."

"Yes," he said, ignoring the accusation in her tone, the resentment. "It's easy for me."

But it hadn't always been. When he was a kid and his stepfather had hit him, he'd dreamed of fighting back, but he'd been too little. Always smaller, slower, weaker than Michael Lynch.

"How do I do it?" she asked, her tone soft, her eyes pleading.

"No."

She frowned. Agitation showing in the set of her shoulders. The tilt of her chin. And he was messed up enough that he found it sexy as hell.

Damn concussion was really screwing with his head.

"That wasn't actually a yes or no question," she said.

"Maybe not, but my answer's the same. I'm not going to tell you what to do."

"I didn't ask you to tell me what to do. I know what I'm going to do. I just need you to tell me how to make doing it easier."

While she didn't raise her voice, the tone of it changed, became distressed.

A subtlety the bombshell, Maddie, noticed. She started toward them, aggressive and protective, a watchdog racing over to protect her charge.

Zach shifted, standing in front of Fay's window, blocking her view of her friend. If Fay saw her, the other woman could sway her decision.

"I think what you want," he told Fay, "is for me to tell you that you're doing the right thing."

"That would be a nice change of pace."

He could feel the friend getting closer, bearing down on them. He leaned forward, resting his arm on the window. "How about, for a change of pace, you decide what's right for you?"

"I don't know if I can," she whispered.

"You can. Either you go. Or you stay. It's as simple as that."

Her gaze held his. Something sad in the blue depths. Something broken that he had the strongest urge to fix. "My life hasn't been that simple in a long, long time."

"Then change it."

No, he couldn't fix her, but he could help her see she didn't need him to. She just needed to believe she could fix herself.

"Is everything okay here?" Maddie asked, trying to nudge Zach aside.

He planted his feet—real and artificial—and kept his eyes on Fay. "Change it," he repeated. "Make a decision and just do it." Her gaze flicked to the friend and he shifted, blocking her view.

"You did not just do that," Maddie muttered, practically breathing fire down the back of his neck.

"If it's the wrong choice," he continued to Fay, "you'll get through it. No one has died from being uncomfortable."

"Fay," her friend called, going around to the passenger side. "What's going on?" She tapped the window. "Is this guy bothering you?"

"What if the right choice," Fay said to him, ignoring Maddie, "means losing something I'm not sure I can live without?"

"You'd be surprised what you can learn to live without," he said, stepping back so she could see him fully. He raised what was left of his right arm, and she blanched. But he didn't want her sympathy or guilt. He wanted her to see, to understand.

Losing something didn't have to break you. It could make you stronger.

"Come on, Fay," Maddie said with more window tapping. "Turn off the car and come inside and we'll talk this through. It's obvious you don't want to do this."

Fay's knuckles turned white on the steering wheel. "Yes, I do," she said, but she wasn't speaking to her friend. She was looking at Zach.

He stepped back as she shifted into Drive and pulled away.

Her friend leaped back with a curse. "What the hell was that?" she asked as Fay braked at the end of the driveway then turned right and sped off. "I've stepped into an alternate reality. That's the only excuse…" She turned, narrowed her gaze on him. "This is your fault." She stormed over to him, not stopping until they were inches apart and eye to eye. "What did you say to her? Did you tell her to go see Shane? Are you a friend of his or something?"

Shane?

Zach wiped his hand over his face. He'd just

convinced Fay to take charge of her life, to take control of her choices by going to see her ex, the bastard who'd gotten a teenager pregnant. Shit.

"I'm not a friend of Shane's," he said.

Maddie tossed her hands in the air, almost clipping him on the chin. "Then what were you thinking, encouraging her to go after him that way?"

As much as it pinched his pride, he stepped back. Better bruised pride than to lose a tooth. "I didn't encourage her to do anything. She's capable of making her own decisions."

"Of course she is. She's not an idiot!"

"Then why did you treat her like one?"

She blinked, her mouth working soundlessly for a moment. "Did she...did she say that?"

"She didn't have to."

Maddie tipped her head back. Blew out a heavy breath. "Ca-rap." When she lowered her head, she skewered him with a heated gaze. "You still should have stopped her. You have no idea what Shane's like—"

"He's hurt her?" Zach asked, taking a step forward, his hand clenching.

Maddie frowned. Dropped her arms. "Wha—"

"Does he hit her?" Zach's stomach turned with the thought of Shane putting his hands on Fay, marking her pale skin, causing her pain.

"No. No," Maddie repeated, her tone gentling the slightest. "He's not physically abusive, he's just an asshole. A manipulative, lying, cheating asshole who won't stay out of Fay's life."

"They have a kid," he said. "Seems that'd be a good reason for him to be around."

Maddie sent him a sharp, indecipherable look. "They have two kids, but believe me, those boys are not the reason Shane comes sniffing around. He couldn't care less about being a father. But does Fay see that? No. All she sees is the boy she fell in love with a hundred years ago. All she can think about is getting that boy back, but he is long, long gone. Which is why I don't want her seeing him."

"It's not your choice to make."

"I'm trying to protect her."

"She's a big girl. She doesn't need protection."

"You don't know her. At all. You've been in town, what? Less than twelve hours, have probably spoken to her a few minutes, and you think you know who she is or what she needs?"

"How do you know how long I've been in town?"

"I'm a carpenter. And the only people in a small town who hear more gossip than carpenters are hairstylists, bartenders and anyone who works at the hospital. And seeing as how your brother is a bartender and your sister-in-law a nurse, you've more than got your bases covered. You're Zach Castro, one of Kane Bartasavich's brothers. You came here to find yourself—"

"Why the hell does everyone think I'm trying to find myself?"

"After losing your arm and leg in Afghanistan—"

"Iraq."

She waved the distinction away. "Which happened when the vehicle you were in drove over a bomb—"

"IED," he said, pinching the bridge of his nose. Yep. His headache was back.

"Thank you, by the way, for your service and sacrifice." She edged forward, jabbed a finger at his chest, stopping before making contact. "Now, since you're probably only in town for a short time and you don't know Fay, her history or the current situation, I think it'd be a swell idea if you stay out of her personal life."

Her arrogance bugged him; her pushiness pissed him off. But she was right. He didn't know Fay. And maybe he should have kept his opinions to himself, but he hated bullies, and from what he could see, that's what the woman before him was. "What I think is that you pushed away your friend by trying to control her when you should have been supporting her. And that instead of building her up, trying to help her figure things out and find her voice, you keep her quiet and small so you can act like her savior."

Maddie visibly shook, her glare telling him she wanted him dead on the spot. "Like you don't know Fay, you also don't know me. Or anything about my and Fay's friendship. Our history."

"Maybe not, but I know she was terrified of leaving here. And it wasn't just because of her ex."

"Fay is not scared of me," Maddie said, her lips barely moving.

He gave a shrug, and wanting the conversation over and done, he just walked away.

Which had Maddie the small-town carpenter chasing after him.

"You think I don't know what this is really about?" she asked, easily catching up to his uneven gait, passing him and walking backward. "You come to our humble little town for a few weeks and one of the first people you meet just happens to be a very pretty, very sweet, very naive single woman."

They reached the small patio and, still facing him, she hopped up onto the pavers, never releasing his gaze.

Freaking show-off.

"So you," she continued, "in the misguided, testosterone-filled, idiotic way males have, decide she'll be a fun little distraction during your stay here."

She stopped in front of the door, immovable and irritating. "Distraction?" he asked. "Is that code for something?"

"Yes," she said, tone dry. "It's code for whist partner. Because you look like the type of guy who loves quiet evenings sitting by a cozy fire playing card games."

He scratched the scar under his right jaw. "Actually, I'm more of a gin rummy man."

"The last thing Fay needs is another man screwing with her head. Especially one who has his own set of problems. No offense."

"Lady, everything you say is offensive."

She lifted her shoulders. "I've never wanted to be Miss Congeniality. Look, we both know a well-adjusted person doesn't leave their home, travel halfway across the country, move into a bed-and-breakfast and work at his brother's bar if he has his life figured out. Fay doesn't need some lost soul sniffing around, pretending to be on her side, getting her to trust him and playing on her sweet nature so he can get her into bed."

Lost soul? Like he was some pathetic loser who had to trick women into sleeping with him. Zach's muscles tensed, his jaw tightening. He edged forward, not surprised when she lifted her chin.

"Move," he demanded quietly.

She must have seen something in his eyes that said if she didn't do as he said, he'd move her himself. She gave him just enough room to open the door, but as he stepped inside, she spoke again.

"Leave Fay alone. Please. Don't use her to make yourself feel…"

He stiffened and turned slowly. "Don't turn coward on me now."

Maddie nodded, her mouth a thin line. "You're right. We're past that." But when she continued, her voice was soft. Regretful. "Don't use her to make yourself feel whole. She deserves better than that."

She deserves better than you.

Breath locked in his chest, he stepped inside, slid the glass door shut, then locked it.

And wished he'd never left his goddamn room.

THE NIGHT HAD turned cold. That was definitely why she was shaking, Fay assured herself as she walked down the sidewalk at Reese's Inn, a motel twenty minutes outside Shady Grove. Not because she was afraid in the least about facing Shane.

It was the bite in the chilled air that seeped past her light sweater. Stung her ears and the tip of her nose. The cold and maybe a bit of leftover adrenaline still pumping through her veins from her conversation with Maddie. Her ensuing dramatic getaway.

Her very strange encounter with Zach Castro.

And for some reason, thinking of Zach did nothing to help calm her erratic pulse or her racing thoughts. So she did what she did best when faced with a situation she didn't want to deal with—she ignored it.

Shoving any and all thoughts of Zach aside, she passed room 107. Her steps slowed as she passed 108…109…110. Shane's room.

She wiped her palms down the front of her jeans and stared at the door. The curtains were drawn, but she could see the flickering light from the TV through them. Heard the muted sounds of it through the door.

He was here—though she didn't see his truck in the parking lot.

She raised her hand to knock. Soon she'd have the answers to all her questions. She'd have the truth.

She lowered her hand. Stepped back and even turned, ready to head back to her minivan. To climb behind the wheel and leave before Shane realized she was here.

Before she did something she couldn't take back.

Oh, God, she really was a coward. And all the *acting as if* wouldn't change it. Unless she actually did something about it.

She knocked, three light taps so soft, there was no way Shane could hear them. But she'd done it. She'd knocked. She hadn't backed down. Not yet.

And because it felt good to do the unexpected, to prove everyone had been wrong about her, she knocked again, loud enough for him to hear.

Now that she'd committed to her course of action, she felt suddenly anxious.

She checked her watch. Almost eight. Her allotted time was dwindling away. She'd promised

Maddie she'd have Bree home by nine and she would—no matter what.

She didn't have much time.

She knocked again, this time using the side of her fist, and a moment later she heard the click of the lock turning. "Hey, babe," Shane said as he opened the door, a self-deprecating smile on his face, his expression welcoming.

"Shane," she breathed, her heart soaring. He was happy to see her. Thank God. Everything really would be all right.

But when she moved to throw herself into his arms, he stepped back, his expression turning puzzled and then hard. "What are you doing here?"

The coldness was back, icing her blood. She opened her mouth, wanting to tell him what happened with the other woman. Wanting to demand he tell her the truth. That he keep all his promises and be the man she needed him to be.

She had to be strong. She had to be the woman everyone else wanted her to be.

"You never came back."

Her words should have been steady. An accusation, one he had to face, had to answer to. Instead she sounded weak.

"Stuff came up," Shane said, searching for something in the parking lot behind her. She turned but saw nothing unusual. "Look," he continued, "this isn't a good time. I'll come over tomorrow."

"But—"

"I said I'll come over tomorrow." His voice was unyielding. He wanted her gone.

All she'd ever wanted was for him to love her. Yet he couldn't get rid of her fast enough.

The worst part? An apology was rising in her throat, one begging him to forgive her. To please, please, just stay with her.

She clamped her lips shut, kept those words inside. Stayed rooted to the spot. She wouldn't beg. Wouldn't run.

She was pushing back.

"A woman came to the bed-and-breakfast," she blurted out, her breath fogging in the cold air. "To see me. About…about you."

He stepped out, his feet bare, his hair mussed as if he'd been sleeping. "What woman?"

Fay shivered. Looked behind him into the room but could only make out the side of a rumpled bed and ugly, tan carpet. "Could we go inside?" Where it was warmer. Where they could sit and figure this out, together.

He pulled the door, keeping it open only a crack. "What woman?"

"I…I don't know. She didn't tell me her name. She was pregnant. She said…she said you were the father."

"And you believed her?"

"No. I mean, I don't know. She…" Fay swallowed. "She said she was your fiancée…"

"You don't trust me," he said flatly.

Her automatic response was to assure him she did. To soothe him, make things right between them no matter what it cost her.

"I guess…I guess maybe I don't," she admitted around the painful knot in her throat. "Can you blame me?"

Surprise flickered in his eyes, followed by confusion. Then they narrowed, the gleam in them bitter. Calculating. "This is perfect," he said, blowing out a heavy breath. He stabbed a hand through his hair. "I'm tired of busting my ass proving I've changed only to have you throw my past mistakes in my face."

"I'm not doing that." Was she? The doubts came back, stronger than ever. She was making a huge mistake. If she loved him, she'd trust him.

Except he hadn't actually denied knowing the woman, her inner voice reminded her. All he'd done was turn this around to make Fay feel as if she was the one doing something wrong.

And she couldn't let him. Not this time.

"I need the truth," she said. "Please. Just…tell me. I need to know."

Leaning against the door frame, he considered her, looking at her in a way she couldn't decipher. Panic set in. Stole her breath. There used to be a time when she knew his every thought, could tell how much he cared for her just by the look in his eye, in the way he smiled at her. She hadn't doubted him or his feelings for her. Hadn't doubted they'd be together forever.

Now all she did was doubt.

"We've come so far, babe," he said, disappointment coloring his tone. "We have a second chance. Do you really want to throw that away?"

"No," she whispered. She'd waited so long for him to come back to her. Had put her life on hold. Could all of that have been for nothing? "Of course not."

One side of his mouth kicked up, reminding her of how much she used to love his grin. How it had the power to make her heart trip. Her pulse race.

But tonight, something was different. Maybe because his smile was more smug than charming. More manipulative than real. Whatever the reason, her heartbeat remained slow and steady.

But her thoughts raced.

"That's what I thought," he said, opening his door. "Now, like I said, this isn't a good time. I'll call you later."

He turned and stepped inside. He didn't want her here. He didn't want her in his room. He didn't want her at all.

"That's so easy for you to do, isn't it?" she murmured.

He frowned at her over his shoulder. "What?"

"It's so easy for you to walk away from me. To turn your back on me."

His shoulders rose and fell with his sigh, and

he slowly, reluctantly faced her, like she was some burden, a noose around his neck he couldn't escape. "You're the one who came here, spouting accusations."

He was still doing it. Still trying to make her feel guilty for wanting the truth.

"You never answered me." Then again, she hadn't asked him a direct question. Wasn't sure she could, not when she was terrified of hearing his answer. But she was even more terrified of leaving here without it.

"Is she telling the truth?" Fay asked quickly, knowing if she didn't blurt the words out, they'd never come. "Are you the father of her baby?"

He scowled. She had to bite her tongue so she wouldn't take her question back.

"No," he snapped. "Do you believe me?"

And that, she realized, was what it all came down to. Whether or not she *chose* to believe him.

She wanted to believe he was honest and trustworthy and faithful. Wanted to go back to how she'd felt this morning—hopeful and happy and brimming with plans for their future. All she had to do was pretend none of this had happened.

"No," she said, unsure if she was speaking to him or herself. "No, I don't believe you."

And she pushed past him, opening the door as she went into his room.

The pregnant brunette wasn't there, but it was obvious she'd been there. That she was staying in this room with Shane, sharing his bed. Clothes were strewn across the cheap, scarred set of drawers—lacy underwear and silky tops. There was a battered copy of *What to Expect When You're Expecting* open on the nightstand and through the open bathroom door she saw makeup and a hair straightener next to the sink.

And as Fay stood there, light-headed and shaking, in the middle of that horrible, cheap room, facing the truth about her husband—her ex-husband—and all her silly, stupid, useless dreams of reconciliation, one thought played over and over in her mind: this was all her fault.

Her fault for pushing when she could have walked away. Her fault for hanging on to something that died so long ago.

Her fault for not being enough for him.

"You can't be here," Shane said, his voice rough. He was angry. At her.

She shook her head, unable to fully understand what was happening. "What?"

He slouched by the open door, hands in his pockets, chin ducked. "You need to leave. I'll call you tomorrow."

"You…you'll call me?" she repeated brokenly.

That was it? Where was his apology? His explanation? He should be tripping over his tongue trying to tell her that this wasn't what it looked like. He should be begging her for forgiveness. Promising to change.

But he wouldn't, she realized with sudden, blinding clarity. He would never change. Would never go back to being that sweet boy she'd fallen in love with, the carefree, charming young man she'd married, the happy father of their children. He didn't love her. Not anymore.

And he never would.

The pain came, swift and intense. The darkness circled her like smog, waiting to soak into her skin, to bring her to her knees. But as it grew closer, thicker, it changed, turned from black to red.

Blood-boiling, vision-hazing red. When it finally reached her, it dug in with sharp claws, riding her back, pushing her to do something to ease its grip. Taunting her with all she'd lost. Tempting her to give in to the building rage burning inside her until she launched herself at Shane, nails scratching, hands pummeling, feet kicking.

Someone was screaming, a hoarse, primal sound that had the hair at the back of her neck standing on end, but she didn't stop. Couldn't. She swung her fists, one after the other, her knuckles connecting with Shane's chin, the side of his head. He swore, low and viciously, then grunted with pain when her knee connected with his inner thigh. He twisted around, clamped his forearm around her waist and squeezed hard enough to stop her breath.

The screaming stopped.

"What the hell is wrong with you?" he snarled, tossing her onto the bed as if she weighed nothing. As if she was nothing. "You really are crazy."

He wiped the back of his hand across his mouth. Spat blood onto the filthy carpet. Fresh scratches marred the left side of his face. His lip was split.

Tears filled her eyes, clogged her throat. She'd done that. She'd hit and scratched and kicked him. She'd hurt him.

And she'd wanted to.

His words rang in her head. *Crazy. Crazy. Crazy.*

She scrambled to the side of the bed, her movements clumsy as she rolled, falling off the mattress onto the floor, landing hard on her knees. Ignoring the pain, she jumped to her feet and ran out the door, the blackness giving chase, the red laughing in delight and her greatest fear echoing in her head.

Crazy...crazy...crazy...

CHAPTER NINE

"WHERE THE HELL have you been?"

Josie tossed her purse onto the unmade bed. When she'd first entered their crappy hotel room, she'd thought Shane was gone, but then the bathroom door had opened and she'd pretended nonchalance by oh so casually turning her back. Showing him how little his anger affected her. That he didn't intimidate her.

That she didn't need him.

"Out," she said with a shrug. Wasn't that what he always said when she asked him where he'd been? *Out*, he'd say with that edge to his tone, letting her know he didn't like to be questioned. Or sometimes he'd give her that lopsided grin, wink and say he'd had things to do. That he'd stopped by the bar after work and had a few drinks.

Then, depending on his mood, he'd either give her the silent treatment, try to charm her out of her anger or make her feel like she was in the wrong.

The last one was the absolute worst.

Not that the other two were much fun. The silent treatment was just so…cold. It always made her feel as if she had to cajole him out of it and she'd end up begging him to talk to her. The charm wasn't so bad, except that it always worked. A few of those grins, a couple teasing remarks and she was forgiving him for anything. Everything.

But when he turned things around, claiming she was overreacting, that she was too immature to handle a committed, adult relationship, that she had trust issues because of her father walking out on her, or that she was jealous because of her own insecurities—well, that really bit the big one.

Because she was always, always left wondering if he wasn't right.

But not today. Today she was right. And he was going to admit it.

"You stole my truck," he said, his voice a low growl.

"I borrowed it," she said with an eye roll as she turned. "I didn't—" Her eyes widened at the marks on his cheek and chin. His split lip. She actually took a step toward him, reaching for him, before she remembered she was pissed at him and stopped. "What happened to your face?"

His eyes narrowed. "You're lucky I didn't call the cops and have them drag your ass back here. Or throw you in jail."

"Uh, in case you haven't noticed, someone broke your face. Maybe you should call them about that. Besides, I didn't steal anything. I borrowed your truck with the keys you left right here—" she patted the nightstand "—after you told me to go ahead and take it if I needed something."

"What did you need that took you six hours to get?"

"Air," she spat out. "Some freaking breathing room, okay? God, you are unbelievable. You're the one who left me, remember? All so you could go out with your stupid friends. What's the matter? Get into a fight? Guess you lost, huh?"

She smirked. Served him right if he got his ass kicked.

"I didn't get into a fight. This—" he jabbed his finger at his mouth "—is thanks to your little visit with my ex-wife."

"What?"

"Fay came here. She attacked me. I told you she was nuts. I told you to stay away from her. To let me handle her."

That skinny, fragile woman Josie had confronted earlier had done that? Guess even mice fought back when pushed too far.

"She needed to know that you and she are never getting back together," Josie said. "And since you didn't seem all that interested in setting the record straight, I took matters into my own hands."

"I'm sick of your crazy jealousy," he said.

Yes, she was crazy. His ex was nuts. Seemed the only one in this equation without blame was him. Funny how that worked.

He stalked over to the mini fridge he'd rented

from the front desk and opened it. And swore as he slammed the door shut so hard it immediately sprang open again. "Did you at least pick up more beer?"

That was the only thing he had to ask her after she'd been gone for six hours?

"Why would I?" she asked. "I don't drink it. Besides, I'm not old enough to buy beer, remember?"

Not that that had stopped her from hitting the bars in college. Easy enough to do in a college town, even if you're underage.

Her being so much younger than him used to be a turn-on for Shane. The fact that he could get some young, hot thing to sleep with him. Leave college and her family for him. Have his kid.

Give up everything for him.

She sat on the bed, hands pressing against the sides of her bulging stomach. Oh, God, she'd given up everything for him. Now she was stuck.

You've made your bed, now you can lie in it, her mother had said in her weary, beaten-down way. As if Josie had gotten pregnant just to make her mother's life more miserable.

Her mom's warning hadn't bothered Josie at the time. While she hadn't been thrilled to discover she was pregnant, she hadn't been ready to slit her wrists over it, either. No, she'd been too busy having fun in the bed she'd made, rolling around with the man she'd thought was going to save her from repeating her mother's life. The man who loved her enough to stay.

But now she was smarter. And being smarter meant no longer being able to shove aside her misgivings and doubts. It meant realizing she'd been an idiot to trust Shane. To fall for him.

It meant her mother had been right.

Josie wasn't sure which one was worse.

Shane grabbed the truck key, and she jumped to her feet. "Where are you going?"

"To get beer."

He was leaving? Now? This wasn't right. He was supposed to have been worried about her and the baby. He was supposed to be out of his mind with jealousy and anger, feeling like shit and wondering what he'd done wrong to push her away. Promising himself—and her—he'd do anything to fix it.

Like she did when he left her alone.

"Fine," she said. "Go ahead. Maybe I'll just call Drew. Have him come over and keep me company while you're gone."

Shane faced her slowly—the first time he'd actually met her eyes since she got back. "Who the hell is Drew?"

"Just a guy I met today," she said, her heart racing with anticipation and trepidation.

Shane's eyes narrowed. His voice grew dangerously soft. "You stepping out on me, Josie?"

Stepping out? God, could he sound any more

like an eighty-year-old man? She widened her eyes, did her best to look innocent. "You're over-reacting," she said, throwing back words he'd said to her many, many, *many* times. "I was just out. Don't get *crazy jealous*."

"Out with some other guy," he reminded her. "For hours."

Actually, she and Drew had spent less than an hour together talking at the diner. After that, she'd driven around aimlessly for a while then ducked into the movie theater downtown to watch Ryan Reynolds's latest romantic comedy. The closest she'd gotten to cheating on Shane was when Ryan had taken his shirt off on-screen. But Shane didn't need to know that.

"Aw, what's the matter?" she asked. "Don't you trust me?"

More of his words used against him. Ha.

He didn't like hearing them, if the tightness of his jaw, the set of his shoulders were anything to go by. For a moment, fear wiggled its way past all the other conflicting emotions inside her, making its way front and center. Shane had never lifted a hand to her. Had never even yelled at her, but now…now he looked mighty pissed off—and capable of anything.

Josie thought of Fay. If she really had attacked him, had he hit her back?

She found herself hoping he hadn't. Sending up a quick prayer that the other woman was okay.

Taking a step back, Josie told herself she could handle anything Shane dished out. That if he hit her, she'd finally have an excuse to leave him. To swallow her stupid pride and go home.

"You want to screw some other guy? Go ahead." With a sneer on his face, Shane looked her up and down, making it clear he found it hard to believe anyone else would want her with her rounded belly and the fullness pregnancy had added to her face. "Hope he likes leftovers."

He walked out, shutting the door behind him. Shaking, Josie sat on the edge of the bed and blinked back tears. She would not cry over that bastard—pregnancy hormones be damned.

This was what she'd wanted. To find out, once and for all, what she meant to him. If she was wasting her time staying with him, fooling herself into believing he would ever change.

She sniffed mightily. Now she knew. When he got back, she'd tell him she was leaving. Whether they were a couple or not, they were still having a child together. He needed to know what her plans were, where she was going.

He needed to give her money for a bus ticket to New Jersey.

Even if she hadn't spent her cash at the diner and then on the movie ticket, she wouldn't have enough to get home.

She barely had enough to buy herself breakfast in the morning.

So, yeah, she'd wait. Because it was the right thing to do, she thought, pushing to her feet and heading to the bathroom. She wasn't hoping when he came back he'd realize how lucky he was to have her in his life. How much he needed her. If he couldn't see that by now, he never would.

She stepped into the dingy bathroom and flipped on the light. She caught her reflection in the tiny mirror above the sink, the dark circles under her eyes, the puffiness of her face. God, she looked like a walking, talking blimp. And it would only get worse. She still had about three months to go before her due date—plenty of time to get fatter.

And she refused to even think about the actual birthing process—seemed like bad engineering to her. After which she'd have stretch marks and flabby skin and saggy boobs. She'd be even more tired, taking care of a crying kid all day, every day.

By herself.

Grabbing the edge of the sink, she lowered her head. Oh, God, what had she done?

Hope he likes leftovers.

A sob escaped her, the sound echoing in the room, taunting and full of self-pity. The tears she'd tried so hard to hold back flowed down her cheeks, big and fat and unending as she struggled to catch her breath. Sinking to the floor, she lay back, her hands on her stomach, her daughter kicking and stretching inside her. As she lay on that disgustingly dirty floor, staring up at the water-marked ceiling, tears sliding down into her ears, Josie realized two very important facts.

One, she wasn't nearly as strong or independent as she liked to believe.

And two, she wasn't able to handle anything Shane dished out. Not even close.

SOMEONE KNOCKED ON his door.

Zach ignored it.

He wasn't expecting anyone—hell, he didn't even know anyone here other than Kane. And as Kane worked nights, Zach couldn't picture his brother dropping by unannounced for an evening chat.

Standing in front of the bathroom sink in a pair of sweatpants, Zach wiped his hand through the steam on the mirror. Rubbed a fluffy towel over his wet hair. The long, hot shower had gone a long way in easing his aches and pains. Unfortunately, it hadn't done anything to stop the thoughts from turning in his head. Thoughts of Fay Lindemuth, the images zipping through his brain, of her sitting under a clear blue sky, her face tipped up to the sun. Of how she'd smelled, so sweet and tempting, in her office. Of her determined expression when she'd driven away.

Driven away to go see her ex.

Zach's scalp stung and he realized he was scrubbing the towel over his hair hard enough to leave a bald spot. He tossed it aside, ran his fingers through his hair several times and called it good.

He had no one to impress.

And he had no reason to be pissed that Fay had gone to see another man. He'd encouraged her to do so, hadn't he? Not that he'd known at the time. All he'd known was that she was trying so hard to stand on her own two feet. He'd given her a nudge. Had let her know it was okay for her to do what *she* wanted, no matter what her bulldog of a friend thought.

There was another series of knocks on his door, louder this time. More insistent.

He shut off the bathroom light and crossed to the bed. Picked up the paperback he'd set on the nightstand. Settled back against the headboard. But when he opened the thriller, he couldn't concentrate on the page before him. He'd seen Fay come back. Had been doing the stretches the physical therapist had taught him when her minivan had pulled up.

She'd sat behind the wheel, much as she'd done earlier. Zach had shut the blinds, blocking his view of her. When he finished stretching, he hadn't been able to resist peeking through the blinds like some damned creep. The minivan had been gone.

Which was good. If it hadn't been, he wouldn't have been able to resist going out there and, once again, insinuating himself into a situation that was none of his business.

She'd saved him from making another mistake, one he couldn't afford. He'd come here to get back on track, to focus on his own future and make some decisions about where that future would be. What he was going to do with the rest of his life now that all his plans had been blown to bits.

And the best way to do that was to stay the hell away from Fay Lindemuth.

She worked here. He slept here. Other than the occasional run-in, there was no reason they ever had to see each other. No reason for them to have a conversation longer than a minute or two. If it came down to it, he'd just avoid her. He'd been trained in evasive maneuvers, had been on dozens of undercover missions where he'd literally been under his enemies' noses and had gone undetected. How hard could it be to avoid one timid hotel manager?

More knocking, a constant, rapid, pounding rhythm that told Zach whoever was disturbing his peace wasn't going away.

Not unless Zach made them.

With a low curse, he got up, walked over to the door and realized he still held his book in his hand. Tossing it onto the chair, he yanked the door open and frowned.

There was no one there.

"You *are* real."

The tone, reverent and excited, had Zach glancing down. It was a kid. A boy in a pair of Iron

Man pajamas and ratty sneakers, his blond hair sticking up in tufts.

"I didn't think you were," the kid babbled on, grinning widely to show two missing front teeth. "I thought Mitch made you up. He's always making up stories about monsters and pirates and killers so I thought that's what you were. A story. But you're not. You're real. And you're staying here. This is so cool. Wait until I tell Harry." The boy's eyes widened, his mouth rounded. Zach was surprised a cartoon lightbulb didn't appear over his head, shining bright as his hair. "You can come to school with me!"

"Kid," he growled, figuring the tone would be enough to scare him off, "go back to your room."

But when he started to close the door, the kid slipped past him.

For being so little, he was pretty fast.

Zach held the door open wide. "Out."

"How come it took you so long to answer the door?" the kid asked, wandering farther into the room. "Is it because you only have one arm?"

Not wanting to be caught in his room with a young boy—a young boy he'd never seen before—Zach stepped out into the hall and looked down the length of it, but no one was around. Where were the kid's parents? "It's because I didn't want to be disturbed."

Standing in front of the bed, the kid scratched his nose. "Then how come you let me in?"

"I didn't *let* you in. You snuck past me."

Which was demoralizing to admit.

The kid shrugged. "You should have pretended to be asleep," the kid said, imparting his great wisdom. "That's what my papa does when he doesn't want to play with us."

"If I was asleep," Zach pointed out with what he considered a bucket load of patience, "all your knocking would have woken me up."

"Yeah. Plus I knew you weren't asleep 'cuz I saw the light under your door." He flopped onto the bed, swung his legs. "Did your arm get blowed off by a bomb?"

"What?" Zach stabbed his hand through his still damp hair. Realized he didn't have a shirt on, which made this entire scenario that much worse. Shit. When he imagined starting fresh in Shady Grove, he'd never imagined spending his first night in jail.

"You need to leave. Now."

The kid gasped and jumped off the bed. "You don't have a foot, either!"

And he raced over, sliding to his knees to check out the bottom of Zach's prosthetic leg.

"Cool," the kid murmured in awe, then reached out to touch it.

That was it. Zach had had enough.

He turned and went down the hallway. If the kid didn't follow, at least he'd be rid of him.

"Is it like a robot leg?" the kid asked, running

up to, then past, him. "Like Luke Skywalker's hand?"

"No." They reached the end of the hall, stepped into the library. Where the hell was everyone? It was just past nine—surely there was a night manager or someone Zach could pawn the kid off on. "Can you find your room from here?"

"Sure. It's upstairs. Want to see it?"

"No. Didn't your parents ever tell you not to talk to strangers?"

He shrugged, his gaze skittering away. "You're not a stranger," he said, defiance in his tone, his little chin set. "You're staying here, which means my mom knows you."

My mom knows you.

Oh, hell, no.

Zach had met three women today, all of them right here, at Bradford House. The teenager wasn't old enough to have a child this age. And while he might like to believe the kid in front of him belonged to Maddie the bulldog, he didn't see much of a resemblance between the olive-skinned, dark-haired Maddie and this pale, blond boy.

But now that he looked closely, he could see a definite resemblance to the very same strawberry blonde he planned on avoiding.

"Where is your mother?" he asked.

Another shrug, but the kid had no sooner lowered his shoulders when Fay stepped into the room, her other son in her arms.

"Elijah...oh," she said, coming up short when she noticed Zach. "Uh...Mr. Castro. Hello."

He nodded. Wished he could cross his arms, but the effect of that particular stance was lost to him forever.

She turned back to the boy. "Where have you been? I was looking all over for you," she said, her tone weary and resigned when she should be ripping the kid a new one for taking off without telling her.

The kid blinked up at her innocently. "I was right here."

She sighed. "It's past your bedtime. Let's get upstairs."

Upstairs. The kid had mentioned that was where his room was. They lived here? Looked like avoiding her might be harder than he thought.

Harder, but not impossible.

"This your son?" he asked.

She seemed taken aback, either at his dark tone or the question when the answer was obvious. "Uh...yes. This is Elijah..." Her words trailed off and she lifted her younger son higher, his arms loose at his sides, head down—out to the world. "He wasn't bothering you, was he?"

"I wasn't bothering him, Mommy," the kid said in his rapid-fire speech. "I just wanted to see him."

Now she frowned at her son. "What?"

"He came knocking on my door," Zach said.

"The only way I could get rid of him was to find out where he'd come from."

"Oh, Elijah," she said. "You didn't."

"He answered the door," Elijah said quickly, shooting Zach a *tattletale* look. "He didn't hafta answer it."

"That doesn't matter," Fay told him. "You know better than to disturb a guest. Please apologize to Mr. Castro."

"But I wasn't disturbin' him! He answered the door."

"Elijah, please..."

The kid rolled his eyes so far back, Zach figured he was looking at his own brain. "Fine." He turned. "Sorry," he muttered, not the least bit sincere. He whirled back to his mom. "There. Now can he come to school with me?"

Fay blushed. Shifted her other son higher once again as she let go with one arm to take Elijah off to the side. "We've already talked about this. Mr. Castro is not a show-and-tell object."

"Mr. Castro is standing right here," Zach pointed out. "And there's nothing wrong with his hearing."

Not exactly true, as he did have some hearing loss in his right ear, but his left one picked up sounds just fine.

"I won't go to school with you," he continued, "and I don't accept your apology."

For the first time since Zach opened the door, Elijah remained perfectly still. "You don't?"

Zach shook his head. "Not until you mean it."

Then again, it was tough to actually mean an apology you were being forced to make.

"He means it," Fay said, nudging Elijah's shoulder. "Don't you, honey?"

But Elijah was watching Zach carefully. "If I say it again and mean it, then will you come to school with me?"

Zach slowly wiped the back of his hand over his mouth, ridding himself of the smile trying to bust loose.

"Elij—"

Zach held up his hand, cutting off Fay's words. He wanted to crouch down, get to eye level with this kid, but he'd probably need help getting back up. "Nope."

The look Elijah sent him was shrewd. "Then I guess I'm really not sorry."

"Of course you are," Fay said almost desperately. "You're sorry because you interrupted Mr. Castro's evening, were nosy and rude."

Elijah rubbed his left eye with a fist. "Nah. I'm not." He yawned. "I'm gonna go to bed."

"I am so sorry," Fay told Zach as Elijah left the room. "I'm not sure what got into him, but I promise he won't bother you again."

"You sure that's a promise you can keep?"

He expected her to assure him she'd keep her son in line. Instead, she sighed. "No. Actually, I can't. Elijah's very…strong-willed. He has a mind of his own."

Seemed to him, when a parent said that about their kid, it meant they either couldn't handle them or couldn't be bothered to try.

"Everyone has a mind of their own," he said.

She snorted softly. Looked away. "Not everyone." Once again the boy in her arms slid down. Once again she hefted him back up. "Anyway, I really am sorry—"

"About what?"

She seemed lost for a moment. "About…everything."

He couldn't stop himself from stepping closer, only to have her scurrying back. He stopped. Remembered he stood there without a shirt, that she could see the end of his amputated arm, his scarred skin. "Everything's a lot for one person to take responsibility for."

"Elijah *is* my responsibility, as is the welfare and comfort of the guests at Bradford House. And I am sorry he disturbed you and made you feel uncomfortable. I will do my best to make sure it doesn't happen again." She struggled with the boy, her hands linked tightly beneath the kid's butt. "Good night."

He was going to let her go. At least, that's what Zach told himself. But when she turned, the light from a nearby lamp caught the side of her face, illuminating a bruise on her jaw—a bruise that hadn't been there when she'd left a few hours ago.

"What happened?" he asked, closing the distance between them, his voice harsh. "Did he hit you?"

"What?" she asked, shrinking back, and he realized he must look like a lunatic, coming at her enraged and shirtless, his hair mussed.

He exhaled through his nose but didn't edge away. He modulated his tone when he spoke again. "Did your ex-husband hit you?"

"How did you know I went to see Shane?"

"Your friend Maddie and I had a little...chat after you left."

"I'm sorry," Fay breathed.

"You're sorry?"

She shifted the kid higher again. "Maddie can be a bit abrasive."

That had to be the understatement of the year. "A bit."

"Did she tell you that Shane hits me? Because he doesn't. Didn't. I mean, he's never hit me. Or the boys. Not even a spanking." Her eyes widened in horror, another blush climbing her cheeks. "He's never spanked the boys," she clarified, then added on a squeak, "or me. I mean...oh, God." She groaned then squeezed her eyes shut tight, her mouth moving silently.

"Are you talking to me?"

"I'm praying that the floor will swallow me

whole and put me out of my misery," she said, eyes still closed. "Did it work?"

He wanted to grin at the hopeful note in her tone, the way she looked like a child making a wish before blowing out her birthday candle, but the sight of that bruise kept any humor from the situation. "Afraid not."

She opened her eyes. "I didn't think so." She smiled at him sadly. "I've never had much luck having my prayers answered."

"What happened tonight?" he asked.

She averted her gaze. "Could we…could we not talk about it? I'm so tired and I need to get him—" she tipped her head toward her sleeping son "—into bed and I just don't want to talk about it. I'm sorry," she added as if she couldn't help herself. Asking him oh so politely to butt out of her business then being sorry for doing so.

He wouldn't push her. Not when he noted the dark circles under her eyes, the weariness in the set of her shoulders. She was clearly exhausted— physically and mentally—so he'd back off.

"You live upstairs?" he asked, sounding pissed, as if her living arrangements were somehow inconveniencing him.

Which they were. Because he couldn't stand by and watch her haul that kid up the stairs. And because now that he knew she lived here, avoiding her would be harder than he'd originally thought.

"Yes. On the third floor."

Damn. Why did it have to be the third floor?

"Don't move," he told her, then turned and headed toward the hallway leading to his room.

"Excuse me?"

He stopped and faced her slowly, saw her frowning at him, her hair frizzing slightly, her body swaying with fatigue. He cursed under his breath. He should leave her alone. She could handle this. She must have carried that kid upstairs to bed dozens if not hundreds of times before.

"I said don't move."

No, he thought, walking down the hallway, he didn't have to help her.

He wanted to.

And that made him an even bigger idiot.

CHAPTER TEN

DON'T MOVE.

Fay shifted. Her arms ached and her lower back was killing her. It was bad enough carrying Mitchell when he was awake, but asleep was worse. He was dead weight, his head lolling, mouth open as he drooled on her shoulder, his body pumping off heat like a furnace, his hairline damp with sweat.

Don't move.

Hadn't that horrible scene at Shane's hotel room been about standing up for herself? About no longer letting people push her around? Yet she was waiting for a man—a stranger—to come back and do…what? Grant her permission to go up to her own apartment? Tell her to put her son to bed?

No. No, no, no. She was not going to backslide. Not now. Not even a little.

If she did, she'd end up where she started—at the bottom of a very large, very steep hill clawing her way back to the top.

If she didn't stay strong, she'd end up at Shane's hotel, their boys in the car, while she begged him to forgive her. To take her back.

When she'd left his room, she'd been frantic,

crying and shaking uncontrollably. But as she drove over the bridge to Shady Grove, calm had settled over her, a numbness she'd embraced, had held on to while she'd gathered the boys and Bree, then taken her niece home. She realized now she'd been in shock and shouldn't have been driving, but she'd gone through the motions, had chatted with Bree, listened to her boys as if everything was fine.

And they'd made it; they were all home, safe and sound. Whether that was due to a higher power watching over them or some hidden, inner strength coming through her she had no idea. But now exhaustion weighed her down and the enormity of what had happened hit her.

Her marriage was over. The future she'd wanted so badly was never going to happen.

She was alone. And she had no idea what to do, how to act or what to feel. Didn't want to feel anything.

She just wanted to go to bed.

Mitch's head began to slide off her shoulder and she hefted him higher. With one last glance at the empty hallway, she turned and walked through the dining room, and made it as far as the kitchen doorway when the sound of uneven footsteps stopped her.

She turned. Zach Castro walked toward her, frowning. Must be his default expression.

At least he'd put a shirt on. The sight of him

bare chested in the library had been...disconcerting. Yes. That was it. She'd been uncomfortable, being so close to a half-naked man who wasn't her husband. Uncomfortable and strangely conflicted, her pulse racing, her mouth dry.

Only because it was unusual to come across someone wearing only a pair of sweatpants in the middle of the bed-and-breakfast. Each room had an adjoining bathroom, so there was no reason for guests to be gallivanting around in their pajamas. Or less than their pajamas.

It hadn't helped matters that he was quite...fit. Or that his pants sat really low on his narrow hips. His shoulders were broad, his biceps and chest well-defined, his stomach rippled with muscles. She'd just been caught off guard by, well, everything. His dusky skin, the tattoo above his heart she hadn't been able to decipher, the way his arm ended, so abruptly, above his elbow.

It was better, much better, now that he'd put on a faded gray T-shirt. But his feet—his foot—was still bare, his hair still mussed as if he'd just gotten out of bed, his gaze flat and unreadable as he reached her.

"I told you I'd be back," he said all low and growly, making it easy enough to gauge his mood. Irritated. Grumpy.

Because of her.

"No, you didn't," she said then cleared her throat. "You said, *don't move*."

He purposely glanced at the spot where he'd left her standing. "You moved."

Nerves fluttered in her stomach. Worry nagged her. Told her not to push him. To accept the blame for upsetting him.

But beneath the nerves there was stillness. A certainty that she didn't need to fear him. A reminder that she was the one who'd had a completely awful, life-altering night. Not him.

And by God, she wouldn't apologize. No matter what.

"Yes, I moved. As I already mentioned, I'm tired and I really need to put Mitchell down and check on Elijah." Lord only knew what trouble her eldest was finding right now. She couldn't even think about it. "Besides," she continued, remembering what he'd told her when they'd been out back, before she'd gone to see Shane, "I'm trying to decide what's right for *me*. Just as a change of pace."

If it bothered him, having his words tossed back at him, he didn't show it. He nodded at Mitchell. "Give me the kid."

Arms tightening around Mitch, she turned, shielding her baby from this hard-eyed, confusing man. "What? Why?"

His mouth, already a grim line, thinned even more.

"Payment for not listening to me," he said, and though it was tough to tell, she could have sworn she detected a thread of sarcasm—and humor—

in his tone. "Spin some straw into gold and you can have him back."

"You know Rumpelstiltskin?"

"Not personally."

"No, I mean, you know the fairy tale."

"Among others." Seeing her surprise, he added, "I wasn't raised by wolves and I didn't live under a rock."

"No. I'm sure you weren't. Didn't." She wanted to add she was also sure he was raised by kind, caring parents, ones who put him first and loved him above all else, like all kids deserved.

But not every kid got what they deserved.

She and Neil hadn't. Not until they'd been placed with Carl and Geraldine Pettit.

She used to think they'd been saved, that her adoptive parents' love and care had made up for the years of neglect and fear and hunger. Now she wondered if the damage had already been done.

"I just...you don't seem like the fairy-tale type," she continued lamely, face heating.

"I don't have a copy of the Brothers Grimm in my duffel bag, but there was a time when it was preferred reading."

"My boys love their stories. Especially Elijah. The darker, the better, it seems."

"You don't like them."

It wasn't a question. "I prefer something... happier."

"They end happily."

"True. But it shouldn't be so difficult to reach happiness."

Zach watched her closely and she wondered what he saw when he looked at her. "Seems to me, the endings that are hardest to earn are the ones most worth having."

She'd never considered that. "But what if they're not?" she asked, thinking of herself and Shane. "Worth it, I mean. The pain, the suffering…what if that's the part that stays with you, that lasts? Not the happiness?"

"Maybe it was the wrong story."

A lump formed in her throat. The wrong story.

She couldn't think about how that pertained to her life right now. Not if she wanted to keep pretending to be strong.

She needed to be alone, in her apartment, hidden away. "I really have to go," she said, and since saying it—several times—hadn't resulted in her actually doing it, she started walking.

Zach brushed past her, blocking her. "Give me the kid. I'll carry him up for you."

"Why?"

His frown deepened, as if that was the dumbest question he'd ever heard. "Because you need help."

It was what her parents and Neil and Maddie always said, too. Now this man before her clearly saw what her family and closest friend knew.

She was needy and weak.

It was humiliating. Worse was how much she wanted to accept his offer when she needed to learn to be independent for herself and her sons.

"You feel sorry for me."

"Why would I feel sorry for you?"

The question, asked so seriously, took her aback. "Because..."

Because her husband left her for another woman, fathered a child with someone else. Because she was so naive, so stupid.

But she couldn't admit any of that, so she just shook her head.

Zach stepped closer, causing those uncomfortable flutters again. That strange sensation of fear and excitement. She swallowed and averted her eyes, looking over his left shoulder.

"One of the hardest things I had to learn after losing my arm and leg," he said gruffly, "was that asking for or receiving help didn't make me weak. It made me human."

Her gaze flew to him. He seemed so sincere, his eyes steady on hers, but she sensed the admission had cost him. And she realized that she hadn't asked for his help. He'd offered it. He could be in his room right now, sleeping or watching TV, but he'd come back out. For her.

She lifted Mitch from her shoulder. His head lolled to the side, but he didn't stir as she transferred him to Zach's left side, where he quickly brought up his arm to support Mitch's butt.

How could Zach hold him, carry him up two flights of stairs with his missing arm and his prosthetic leg?

Maybe this wasn't such a good idea.

"I've got him," Zach whispered, once again able to read her thoughts. He lifted what was left of his right arm to press against her son's back, holding him steady. Safely.

She nodded, and though she wanted to hover, to be there should Mitchell start to fall, she didn't want Zach to think she didn't trust him.

She did. There was no reason for it, she thought, leading him through the kitchen to the back stairway. They didn't know each other—though from what he'd witnessed of her life today, he probably knew more about her than most. But she believed her son was safe with him.

Then again, she wasn't a very good judge of character, so she could be wrong. But he had talked her down after the pregnant teen had confronted her. Had given her the strength and courage to go to Shane. To find out the truth.

It would be nice if he could somehow help her become strong enough to figure out how to live with that truth.

Yes, that would be lovely. He could sweep into her life full time, as he'd done today, giving her pep talks in his quiet, serious way, saving her from the wrath of her friends and family when she dared stand against them. Like some prince in one of those bedtime stories they'd been talking about.

Except he was no prince. He was just a man. With his own battles to fight. His own life to live.

And it was way past time she stopped believing in fairy tales.

NOT ONE OF his better ideas, Zach thought as he reached the second floor.

The kid's head started sliding off Zach's shoulder, and since he couldn't reach it with his arm, he had to lean to the side so it slid back. His leg was stiff and keeping his balance was no easy task, especially carrying what amounted to forty pounds of dead weight. He just prayed the kid stayed asleep.

"He's a sound sleeper," he whispered when Fay stopped at the bottom of another set of stairs, these separated from the rest of the floor by a short hallway.

"Not usually," she said with a sheepish glance over her shoulder.

Well, hell.

"But I think he's out for a few hours at least," she hurried to add as they started up. "He usually doesn't wake up until later in the night. Bad dreams."

Zach glanced at the kid's face, the little guy's eyes moving behind the closed lids, his mouth open, his cheeks red. Bad dreams, huh? *You and me both, pal.*

At the top of the stairs, she turned right, disappearing from view. Thank God she didn't stand there, wringing her hands while she waited to see if he got her son safely to the top.

Sweat formed at the base of his back. On his upper lip. Pain shot up his thigh, but he kept going, slow and steady.

It worked. He reached the top without either of them tumbling down the stairs.

Yet another win for the day.

A big one considering that a few weeks ago he never would have made it up the stairs—let alone been able to carry a kid up them. He was getting stronger. Every day that he got up, put his leg on and walked under his own power was a triumph. Even if some days that triumph ended up hurting like hell.

Fay stood next to an open door, her expression relaxed as if she'd had no doubt he'd get her son up here safely.

She was better at lying than he'd given her credit for.

He stepped into a spacious living room with huge windows on each end, wide-planked oak floors and a cathedral ceiling sporting huge oak beams. Whoever did the renovations on this place had done a good job, especially up here, turning what must have been an attic into a comfortable living space.

Envy hit him, an unusual and mostly unused emotion—until he'd gotten hurt. He'd considered going into construction after the service, had figured he'd work for one of the local home builders in Houston, learn the trade from the ground up and maybe, one day, start his own company.

He shoved the sense of loss aside. No sense thinking about it. Better to focus on the possibilities left to him.

Fay shut the door and brushed past him to pull a colorful blanket off the back of the sofa and cover the older kid—Elijah—who was sound asleep on the couch. On the opposite wall, SpongeBob SquarePants entered his pineapple house on a large-screen TV.

"Thank you for your help," Fay said, holding her arms out for her other son. "I'll take Mitch. Put him to bed."

"No sense handing him off now."

She brought her pinkie nail to her lip only to stare at it as if wondering how it had gotten there. Curling her fingers, she lowered her hand. Tapped it against the side of her thigh. "Yes. That makes sense."

That was him. Sensible.

"His room is this way," she continued, heading past the kitchen toward the hall.

Zach followed, turning into the first room on

the right. The blinds over the window were already drawn, but in the soft glow of two nightlights he made out a set of twin beds. He crossed the hardwood floor, careful not to trip on the edge of a dark rug under the beds as Fay yanked back the covers on the one next to the wall. Zach lowered Mitch onto it then stepped back while Fay tucked the kid in. Smoothing the kid's hair back, she kissed his forehead then straightened and met Zach's eyes.

And Zach had a sudden need to feel her hands on *his* hair. To feel her mouth pressed against *his* skin.

So much for being sensible.

He tamped down the unwanted desire. He was tired. In a state of flux in his life, and he'd spent entirely too much time with her today. Was in danger of getting way too involved in the pretty innkeeper's life.

They went back into the living room, where she shut off the TV. Cleared her throat. "Thank you, again, for your help."

He nodded.

She twisted her hands together in front of her. Separated them to wave at the sleeping kid. "And I'm sorry Elijah bothered you. I can't imagine what he was thinking."

"He'd heard I was a monster. Thought he'd check it out for himself."

She made a sound of distress, her eyes wide, and he wished he'd kept his mouth shut. "I'm—"

"You're sorry. I get it. But what I can't figure out is why."

"Why?"

"Why you think you need to apologize. Unless you told him I was a monster."

"What? No. Of course not."

"Then you have nothing to apologize for."

"Elijah is my son," she insisted. "He did something he shouldn't have. That is my responsibility."

"Your son is your responsibility, but what he does, the choices he makes? Those are all on him. You'd be doing him a favor if you let him reap the rewards and learn the consequences of those choices on his own."

"Thank you for that parenting advice," she said, clearly not grateful but unable to be so rude as to tell him to mind his own business. Must be some sort of fatal flaw, that overriding need to be polite. "I will take it into consideration."

She wouldn't, but it didn't matter to him. As soon as he walked out of her apartment, he could start avoiding her and her kids. Get back to his own life.

"Would you like something to drink?" she asked, already heading toward the kitchen. "I think I have some beer…"

"You don't want me to stay for a drink."

She continued to the fridge, one of those stainless steel jobs with French-style doors. Opened it. "Of course I do." Turning, she held out a bottle. Wiggled it at him when he didn't take it. "It's the least I can do to thank you for carrying Mitch up here and…and your help," she continued quickly, "outside earlier. Before I left." She waved the bottle again, this time swinging it in a wider arc. "Please."

"Is that your way of making us even?"

She blushed, confirming his suspicions. "I just… I'm used to feeling beholden to people for doing things for me, and after what happened tonight…" She shook her head. "I think it's time that changed."

"Starting with me?"

Holding his gaze, she closed the distance between them. Pressed the beer into his hand. "Starting with you."

He set the beer on the table next to a coloring book and what looked to be some hastily done spelling homework. "I don't want a beer."

"How about fifty dollars?"

He laughed, the sound rusty and hoarse to his ears. "I don't want your money."

"That's why I offered you fifty instead of fifty thousand. I knew you'd still say no."

He was curious about why she thought he'd refuse so much money. "That so?"

She nodded solemnly. "After all, what's fifty thousand dollars to a Bartasavich?"

He ground his back teeth together. "That's the second time you've called me a Bartasavich."

"That's because you are a Bartasavich. I met your brother Clinton Jr. last year when he and Ivy were dating. She used to work here," Fay said, as if that explained how she knew that much about him.

Which it did.

C.J. had met Ivy Rutherford over a year ago right here in Shady Grove, resulting in Ivy becoming pregnant. From what Zach had heard, it had taken C.J. months to convince her to give him a shot.

She'd given birth to their son before Thanksgiving and now lived in C.J.'s overpriced penthouse in downtown Houston.

His eldest brother always had been very good at getting what he wanted.

"You're right. Fifty grand is pocket change to a Bartasavich." Zach modulated his tone. "But my name is Castro."

"You can change your name," she said, looking at him in understanding. "But you can't change where you came from."

He knew that. Wasn't that what pissed him off the most?

"Another of Dr. Porter's sayings?" he asked, remembering her quoting what had to be some sort of mental health professional earlier.

Her gaze dropped. "Something I figured out all on my own."

He wanted to know what that meant. Wanted to know more about her, this woman who seemed at times vulnerable and broken only to have flashes of strength and courage. He was curious about her.

And maybe the best way to rid himself of that curiosity, to see if his interest held, was to stick around. To start some sort of relationship with her—a friendship.

But he preferred to be on his own. Friendship required time he didn't have and effort he didn't want to give. Friendship with a woman was worse. There were too many ways to get tangled up. Confused.

No. He and Fay weren't going to be friends. They weren't going to be anything. She'd make up with Maddie or turn to someone else to help her with whatever she was going through. To save her.

And he'd get back to saving himself.

But he couldn't go yet.

"You want to pay me back for helping you?" he asked.

"Yes, please."

He understood the need not to owe someone. Respected her for it. "I don't want a beer. Or money."

"I got that."

He raised his eyebrows at the bite in her tone. The bitterness.

She crossed her arms. "I'm not a complete idiot," she mumbled.

"I don't think you're an idiot at all."

Her gaze met his, pleased and so grateful he wished he had both arms so he could find out who'd made her feel less than and beat the hell out of him.

"If you want to repay me," he continued, "tell me how you got that bruise."

She lifted her hand to her face, her fingers skimming the damaged skin. "I told you Shane didn't hit me."

"That doesn't answer my question."

"But it's the truth."

"Is it?"

His mother used to cover for Michael after he'd hit her. And Michael only ever hit her when she tried to protect Zach. But even though she'd tried to keep Zach safe, she'd still told him to lie to his teachers and their local priest, to say his bruises were from walking into a wall. A fall down the stairs. An accident on the ball field.

She'd been terrified of what would happen to him if Michael found out Zach had told someone.

"It's the truth," Fay said, glancing at a still-sleeping Elijah. "Shane didn't hit me."

"He doesn't deserve your protection."

"It's not like that. I swear."

"But you went to see him," Zach prodded.

"You asked him about that girl who came here this afternoon."

Not looking at him, Fay nodded. "Shane didn't like that. My asking questions. Demanding the truth." Her mouth twisted into a rueful smile. "He's used to me trusting him above anyone else. Believing everything he says. But he didn't get physical with me. Not really. Not until…"

As she trailed off, everything inside Zach went still and cold with rage. He would find the bastard and beat the hell out of him and then he'd get started on avoiding the woman before him.

"Not until what?"

Another blush, this one sweeping color up her throat, blazing on her cheeks. "I hit him." Swallowing, she glanced at her son before meeting Zach's eyes. "*I* hit him. He tried to stop me…tried to grab my arms. That must have been when I got the bruise. I hit him," she repeated in a horrified whisper. "Oh, God, what did I do?"

Zach pulled a chair out from the table. "Sit."

Covering her face with her hands, she slid into the chair—she would have missed, but his reflexes were coming back and he pushed it under her in time. She said something, but with her hands over her mouth, he couldn't make it out, so he wrapped his fingers around both her wrists and tugged her arms down. "What happened?"

Her eyes glistened but she held the tears back. "I… God… I attacked him. I couldn't control myself. I lost it," she admitted as if getting angry was the worst thing that could happen.

"He admitted the baby is his?"

Her laugh was hollow. "He didn't admit anything. I begged him to tell me the truth but he kept evading it, tried to turn it around, making it seem as if I was the one who was out of line for even asking."

Sounded a lot like Michael. He'd often blamed Zach for the abuse. If Zach listened better, didn't make so much noise and was more respectful, Michael wouldn't have to punish him. If he wasn't another man's son, if his presence didn't constantly remind Michael how little he had compared to Clinton Bartasavich Sr., Michael wouldn't have to take his frustration and anger and jealousy out on Zach.

"You had a right to ask," Zach told Fay.

"I did. I absolutely did." She twisted open the beer and took a long sip, surprising him. He would have pegged her for a wine drinker. Or a teetotaler. She took another sip then set the bottle down. "He's been lying to me for years. He's been unfaithful and he's used me. And I still want to call him and apologize. To beg him to take me back." She looked up at Zach, eyes bleak, voice thick with emotion. "Pretty pathetic, huh?"

He wanted to lay his hand on her shoulder. Offer her some sort of support. Some strength.

But what she needed, he couldn't give her. She had to find it within.

He gave an inner eye roll. He sounded like one of the numerous therapists he'd seen.

Or his sister.

He actually wished Daphne was here. She'd know what to do, what to say. But she wasn't. He was. Hell, he'd practically forced Fay to let him carry Mitch up here, had insinuated himself into the situation. He couldn't walk away now just because he was floundering for the right words.

"I'm right-handed," he heard himself say. She glanced at his empty sleeve and he raised his shoulder in a self-deprecating shrug. "I *was* right-handed."

"You've gone through something much worse than what I'm going through," she said, sounding as if she was reciting a speech someone had given her—many times. "I should stop being so selfish and be grateful for what I have. Focus on the good."

Frowning, he tugged on his ear. "This isn't a competition to see who has it worse. Everyone has problems. And getting pissed or disappointed or being sad doesn't make you ungrateful. It makes you human."

He'd gone through all those emotions plenty of times, especially in the past eight months.

"I was right-handed," he repeated, "and now I'm not. But even though I knew my right hand was gone, it took me months before I stopped trying to use it to brush my teeth or pick up a fork." No sense telling her he still did it sometimes. She needed a pep talk. Not reality. "I realized that being right-handed was a habit I'd developed over my lifetime and that if I still wanted to eat and sign my name, if I wanted to dress myself and eventually drive again, I'd have to develop a new habit."

"You taught yourself to be left-handed," she said as if that was the great, wise lesson he was imparting.

Christ, but he sucked at this.

"It's not about learning something new or even relearning things you've had down since you were a kid." Things like combing his hair, shaving or wiping his ass. "It's learning how to accept a situation for what it is and move forward."

She turned the beer bottle in slow circles, her gaze on it. "In other words, you don't want me to call Shane."

"What I want doesn't matter. It's your choice. I'm just saying there are things we all think we can't live without, but you'd be surprised by what you can survive."

Too bad surviving didn't always equal thriving. He knew that better than anyone. Yet here he was giving advice like he actually had his life together.

"I'll let you get back to your evening," he said, needing to get out of there before he started spouting clichés like *it's always darkest before the dawn*. "But for what it's worth, I don't think you should call your ex. You don't owe him anything, least of all an apology. You had every right to confront him and even more right to kick his ass. Don't let him make you think otherwise."

He walked away, past a still-sleeping Elijah, and out the door. He didn't even pause in the hallway, just tackled the stairs with single-minded purpose: to get as far away from Fay Lindemuth as possible. If she did decide to call her ex, he didn't want to be anywhere near her.

Didn't want to be the one to pick up the pieces.

CHAPTER ELEVEN

THE AUDIOBOOK PLAYED through her earbuds as Fay walked on the treadmill, the author-narrator explaining how to overcome all personal obstacles with a little bit of hard work and a whole lot of faith. Which sounded great. Fay wasn't afraid of hard work, though she hadn't had much experience with it. But she was willing to try.

It was the faith part that tripped her up. Because while she believed in a greater power, the author of *The Best Is Yet to Come!* was preaching faith in oneself.

And Fay had no idea how to do that.

Which meant that in her quest for self-improvement and self-empowerment, she was stuck at the beginning.

Okay, that wasn't entirely true. She had made some fairly decent progress the past five days. Progress including, but not limited to, not calling Shane.

And she refused to feel guilty because she'd wanted to. Or berate herself for picking up her phone to do so more times than she could count and, during a weak moment Saturday morning, dialing his number.

The amount of willpower it had taken for her to disconnect before the call had rung through was astronomical. But she'd done it. She also hadn't contacted Maddie.

She wasn't backing down. Not this time. Maddie had put the rules on their friendship. Had given that ultimatum, forcing Fay to choose between trying to get her family back or keeping Maddie and Bree in her life. Now Maddie could be the one to make amends. To apologize.

Fay had done enough apologizing and taking the blame to last a lifetime.

So, maybe she was getting somewhere. Figuratively speaking.

The treadmill's belt moved steadily under her feet. *Literally*, though, she was going nowhere fast. Or slow. The pace seemed quick enough, but then, other than a casual stroll around the block or playing in the yard with her boys, she hadn't exercised since high school gym class.

And as this was the first time she'd used the B&B's fitness room, she would cut herself some slack. Be compassionate with herself.

Another first. And one the author of *The Best Is Yet to Come!* highly recommended.

The narrator droned on. The belt hummed. This exercising thing wasn't so bad, Fay decided. It wasn't so wonderful, either. Mostly it was just…

boring. At least she had the entire fitness room to herself. They only had three guests: a lovely elderly couple from Louisiana visiting the woman's sister, and Zach Castro.

Fay exhaled heavily—more to ease the tension tightening her neck and shoulders than from exertion—and concentrated on the toothy morning news anchor on one of the wall-mounted televisions, the sound muted. A news ticker scrolled across the bottom of the screen and the show switched to the weather forecast, which showed rain, rain and more rain.

This wasn't the first time she'd thought of Zach. As the B&B's manager, it was her job to think of him. Of his comfort. A task she'd been able to do by proxy, asking Gracie Weaver, a high school senior who worked at Bradford House part-time, to make sure Zach had everything he needed.

But no matter how hard she tried to push any and all thoughts of Zach from her mind, they didn't budge. They remained, front and center, begging for her attention.

Attention she didn't want to give. Yes, she appreciated his help, but that was all there was to it. Remembering how he'd looked standing in her kitchen, how he'd sounded—gruff and demanding—as he'd told her she didn't need Shane in her life, made her feel antsy. Unsettled.

Frightened.

So she chose not to think about it. Chose to

forget how his words had warmed her. Had made her feel as if she really could change, become stronger.

He'd made her feel less alone.

But he was a stranger, a guest at the B&B. He wasn't her friend. They had no reason to interact socially, let alone personally.

She *was* alone. If the events of the other day had taught her anything, it was that the only person she could truly rely on was herself. God help her.

It had been a painful, difficult day full of harsh lessons: Damien's lack of support, Maddie's dismissal of their friendship, Shane's disregard for her feelings and how easily he'd tossed aside their family, their future, for someone else.

Hard lessons, but ones she obviously needed to learn. Before those lessons would have beaten her down, kept her down for weeks. Now she was using them as motivation. The people she loved had hurt her—she wouldn't forget that.

The glass door to the fitness room opened and Zach entered, as if she'd conjured him with her stupid, rambling thoughts. He nodded in greeting.

She smiled back, considered offering him a sunny hello, as if she hadn't been a complete and utter hot mess the last time they'd seen each other, but as she was working on being true to her own feelings, she kept her mouth shut.

He didn't seem to mind. Just walked past her to the bench lining the wall. From the corner of her eye she saw him unzip his hooded sweatshirt and take it off. Turning her head, she skimmed her gaze over his back, the material of his black tank top clinging to his broad shoulders. He sat on the long bench and shucked his sweatpants, revealing gym shorts and his prosthetic leg.

He stood, and she averted her gaze. Her breath came a bit faster. Her body warmed. As much as she would have liked to blame her reaction on physical exertion, she needed to be strong enough to admit the truth.

She found him attractive.

In a purely physical way.

A way that was dangerous to her newfound quest for independence. A way that could never, ever be acted on.

He walked toward her and she stared straight ahead, arms swinging idly, chin lifted. Only to have her mouth drop when he got on the treadmill to her left.

"Is that okay?" she asked, then winced at both the question and the volume at which she'd spoken. She took her earbuds out. "I mean…are you allowed to—" she gestured at the treadmill, which he'd kicked up a few notches so that he was walking at a pace considerably faster than hers "—do that?"

The glance he sent her was unreadable. No big shock there. "I don't often ask permission before I do something."

Ouch. Though she was going at a snail's pace, she stumbled. Caught hold of the bars then stepped off the moving belt. "Was that a dig at me?" she asked, proud of herself for getting the question out. For seeking the truth instead of hiding from it.

Maybe there was something to this working-out thing after all. All those endorphins were making her brave.

"No dig," Zach said. "Just stating a fact about myself."

Of course. It was stupid of her to assume he'd been talking about her. He probably didn't think of her at all. Certainly not enough to warrant a comment on how she handled her life.

Except he'd offered her many comments, and opinions, the other day. Ordering her not to cry after the pregnant woman had claimed to be carrying Shane's baby, telling her she needed to make her own decisions instead of worrying about what others thought. Admitting how hard it had been for him to accept help after losing his arm and leg. Making her believe she wasn't as weak as everyone thought.

"I'm just making sure it's safe for you to be exercising. Here. Like—" she nodded at his brisk pace "—that."

She should type up a waiver, releasing the B&B and Neil of any responsibility in case of injury caused while using the exercise facilities.

"It's safe," he said, his left arm bent and swinging, sweat forming along his hairline.

"Maybe you should call your physician. Just to be sure."

She could talk to the doctor. Ask for his or her assurance that Zach wouldn't further aggravate his injuries by pushing his body this way.

"You worried about me, Fay?"

The question, the sound of her name, said so softly, made something quiver in her belly. "I..." She swallowed. "No."

No, she wasn't worried about him, she realized. From what she'd seen, he was one of the most capable people she'd ever met. Certainly one of the most self-aware. He might push himself, but not so much that he'd risk an injury or a setback.

Still walking, his pace quick and even, he watched her while she stood there like a fool, her treadmill running between her feet. How did he do that without falling and breaking his neck? The man only had one leg. Her gaze fell to his prosthetic. Well, one original leg, but he was still way more graceful than she'd ever be, his movements much smoother than they'd been the day they'd met.

The silence, the way he stared at her, as if trying to see inside her head, unnerved her. Her palms grew damp and she wiped them down the front of her yoga pants. "I wasn't worried about you," she blurted out, as usual, caving at the slightest bit of pressure.

No one has died from being uncomfortable.

Maybe not, she thought, but she didn't want to take a chance she'd be the first.

"I don't want you to sue us," she continued.

"What?" he asked and, she had to admit, his scowl was quite intimidating—she blamed the beard.

Good thing she'd recently decided to stop being such a scared ninny.

She twisted her hands together. Too bad being brave was so much work.

"If you get hurt using Bradford House's exercise equipment, you could sue for…I don't know…whatever people who've been injured sue for. Medical bills or living expenses. Lost wages. That, uh…that sort of thing…" She turned her attention to the treadmill's controls, shutting it down while she said, "My brother's made a very good living, and I don't want there to be a chance of him losing everything he's worked so hard for because of…"

"Because of me?"

"Because of *me*. Because I didn't do something I should have." Like thought about liability issues when Neil insisted on putting in the fitness center. Yes, he'd probably already considered it and had plenty of insurance to cover any accidents that might happen—but as the B&B's manager, shouldn't she have taken care of that?

Zach stepped off the belt, turned the machine off then faced her—all done incredibly slowly, every movement controlled. "I won't get hurt, and even if I did, I wouldn't sue you or your brother."

Her shoulders sagged in relief. It had been silly to worry, but worrying endlessly over every little thing was a hard habit to break. "Okay."

She almost apologized for bringing it up but bit her tongue. Even more progress.

His eyes narrowed. "Okay? That's it?"

She nodded. Smiled. "Yes. Thank you."

"You don't want me to sign a waiver?"

"I don't have one. But it's nice that you offered." That he'd asked what she wanted.

"So you're not worried I'll take your brother to the cleaners."

She blushed. Hoped it came off as some sort of exercise-induced flush. "I wasn't really worried about that," she said, climbing down and crossing to get a clean towel and the spray cleaner. "I just… sometimes, when I get a random thought, I focus on it, make it bigger than it actually is. Dr. Porter says it's my way of trying to control my external world. Bring order to it." Spraying the cleaner, she shot him a quick glance. "It's that whole hating-to-be-emotionally-uncomfortable thing again."

Zach crossed to his gym bag. Watching him from the corner of her eye as she wiped down the treadmill, she saw him pull a crumpled piece of paper from his bag then dig around some more. A moment later, he pulled out a pen then smoothed the paper on the bench and began writing.

"What are you doing?" she asked, coming up behind him.

He ignored her. When he was done, he handed her the paper, which was actually a receipt from Keely's Restaurant, a local eatery on Main Street. She scanned what he'd written, but his handwriting was so bad—*I used to be right-handed*—it took her three times to decipher it.

"I release Bradford House and any and all of its owners and employees of all responsibility should I incur any injury while using the fitness center."

And he'd dated it and signed his name.

"Is this actually legal?" she asked.

"Legal enough to make a jury think twice before awarding a multimillion-dollar settlement."

She held it out. "I told you. This isn't necessary."

"Keep it. Then you won't have to worry."

It was one of the nicest things anyone had ever done for her. Oh, there had been plenty of times when she'd been *told* not to worry. And if she disobeyed the order people would sigh and shake their heads, unsure of how to handle her fears. Her parents and Neil had always smoothed the way so there'd be no bumps in the road. While Maddie wanted her to tough it out.

Yes, Zach was fixing her problem, but he wasn't telling her she was silly to worry in the first place. He hadn't made her feel stupid for letting her imagination run wild. He was letting her be her.

She could keep the paper. But she felt foolish, bringing up her fears to him. Worse, she knew in her heart the only reason she'd thought about him getting hurt was because of his disability.

Which didn't seem to be disabling him much at all.

She ripped the receipt in half then in half again. "I don't need it. You won't sue us."

But instead of making him happy, he seemed angry. "Because you figure a Bartasavich has so much money already they won't need to sue?"

"Actually, I hadn't thought of that."

"Then why?"

"I believe you because…" She shrugged. Forced herself to hold his hooded gaze and tell him the truth. "Because I trust you."

More than that, she was learning to trust herself.

SHE WAS KILLING HIM.

Bad enough he'd thought about her the past few days. That she'd slid into his dreams. He'd done an admirable job of keeping those thoughts at bay until today.

He looked forward to working out each day, eagerly anticipated pushing his body to its limits, knowing as he did that he grew stronger. That when he did, he healed more and more. Each morning for the past four days he'd had the entire fitness room to himself, and now here she was, interrupting his workout. Invading his space.

I trust you.

She shouldn't. They barely knew each other.

"My doctor has approved me for physical exercise," he told her, not wanting her to think he'd risk injury. Not after he'd come so far.

She brightened, as if he'd given her a precious gift and not just a few stingy words. "That's good. I mean, I'm sure you were used to working out, right? Before you were hurt?"

"I did what I could, but I actually work out more often now." Pushed himself harder.

"To make up for what you lost," she murmured.

She was right.

She saw him, could read him.

And he didn't like that much at all.

He turned to his bag, pulled out the sling he used when working on his right arm, shoulder and upper back. He hadn't warmed up nearly enough, and would have liked to have gotten at least another fifteen minutes of cardio on the treadmill, but he hadn't been able to concentrate on his steps, couldn't quite find his rhythm with her there.

She was afraid he'd fall.

It nearly unmanned him, having the woman who'd starred in his very heated, very erotic dream last night watching him as if he were a baby taking his first steps.

Christ, but he needed to get laid. A few women had shown interest while he'd worked his shifts at O'Riley's. But he wasn't sure if they were really attracted to him or if he was a novelty. As if having sex with him was a way for them to thank him for his service.

He wished it didn't matter.

Maybe if he accepted what they were offering he'd stop thinking about the woman waiting for him to take his turn, to keep this conversation going. She had dark circles under her blue eyes, her face so pale the freckles on her nose stood out in sharp relief. Her hair, pulled back into a ponytail, needed to be brushed. And washed. She looked tired. And, despite her cautious smile, defeated.

And so sad it made him want to do whatever he could to ease her pain.

"Do you lift?" he asked, the question coming out gruff and not exactly friendly.

She blinked. Blinked again. "Excuse me?"

"Weights," he clarified, scanning her figure with a critical eye. Her long legs were showcased in a pair of snug black yoga pants, but an oversize Columbus Blue Jackets T-shirt covered her from her neck to midthigh. If he had to guess he'd say she didn't have much muscle definition. Not nearly enough strength. "Do you do any strength-training exercises?"

"Oh, no," she said with a breathless laugh. "I don't work out."

He sent a pointed look at her, then at the treadmill she'd been meandering on and then back to her.

She blushed. "I mean, I don't usually work out. I don't have an exercise routine or anything. Today's my first day. Dr. Porter says exercise releases endorphins and that it will give me a constructive, healthy way to cope with some…issues I'm having."

"Issues like your ex-husband?"

"Yes. But mostly it's to help me deal with my… with my illness."

He took an involuntary step toward her. "You're sick?"

"Not physically." As if digging deep within herself, she took a long inhale then pulled her shoulders back and lifted her chin—but couldn't quite meet his eyes. "I suffer from depression and anxiety." She crossed her arms. Uncrossed them. "Dr. Porter says it's nothing to be ashamed of."

The last was said quickly. A burst of words that should have been a challenge to him to disagree. Instead she'd sounded unsure.

He didn't know much about depression except that it was as real as cancer or any other disease.

And absolutely not the fault of the person who suffered with it.

"Dr. Porter's right," Zach said, understanding better now why she so often quoted the guy—or lady. "It's nothing to be ashamed of."

The relief on her face was almost his undoing, and he had the strongest urge to pull her into his arms. But she wasn't his to comfort.

"If you want a release of endorphins," he continued, stepping back, "you'll need to do more than stroll for a few minutes."

"It wasn't a few minutes. It was twenty. And I thought it best to start out slowly and get my body accustomed to exercise."

"That—" he jabbed his thumb at the treadmill she'd been on "—wasn't exercise. You need to push yourself."

"What's with you and so much *pushing*? Were you bullied as a child?"

He thought of the time he'd spent trying to be invisible in his own home, praying he didn't do or say anything that would set off his stepfather. The constant fear, the feelings of resentment and anger that clung to him on a daily basis.

"Yeah. You could say I was bullied."

Sighing, she lowered her head. "This is why I need to keep avoiding you."

He'd expected her to fall all over herself in self-recrimination like she'd done the other day every time she'd worried his feelings had been hurt or she'd said the wrong thing. He hadn't expected a confession.

"You've been avoiding me?"

He'd been avoiding *her.*

Guess he shouldn't have bothered, he thought, irritated.

"Not because of anything you did," she rushed to assure him, going so far as to reach out as if to touch him. He wasn't sure if he was relieved or disappointed when she yanked her hand back before making contact.

"Did you just give me the *it's not you, it's me* line?"

"No. Well, yes. I suppose I did. But it's the truth. After everything that happened the other day, after I embarrassed myself in front of you and said the wrong thing—time and time again— avoiding you seemed the best option."

He'd thought so, too. They had different reasons, but they'd both come to the same conclusion.

Maybe they'd both been way off base.

He scanned the barbells neatly lined up on the rack in front of the floor-to-ceiling mirror. Grabbed a pair of light blue three pounders and held them out to her. "Here." When she didn't move, he twisted them side to side. "Take them."

She tucked her hands behind her back. "Why?"

"I'm going to show you how to properly release those endorphins."

As soon as the words left his mouth, he wished

them back. Shit. That had sounded way too personal, too sexual. And now he had a vision of the two of them in the bed in his room as he showed her all the ways he could make her feel good. Imagined the feel of her hair as it trailed over his skin, how he'd touch that long, lean body of hers. How he'd worship her. Feast on her.

His body stirred. The last thing he needed was a hard-on.

Especially while wearing workout shorts.

Tamping down his arousal, he shoved the weights at her. "Take them."

She did, holding them at her sides. "Thank you, but I've already worked out this morning."

"You have someplace to be?"

"No," she said, drawing the word out.

"Great." He picked up a heavier dumbbell for himself. "We'll start with bicep curls. Three sets of fifteen."

She frowned. "But won't lifting weights make me bulky?"

"It'll make you toned. To gain bulk, you'd have to put a hell of a lot more time in than either of us have."

"Sorry. I'm being stupid," she said.

"You asked a question. That's not stupid."

"No, that's not it. You're offering to help me and my first thought is that Shane doesn't like muscular women. He thinks women should be soft." She sent Zach a rueful smile. "Told you I was being stupid."

Zach's fingers tightened around the weight as disappointment lodged in his stomach. "You're back with him."

Again, the words came without him wanting them to. But these he wouldn't regret. He'd wondered too many times over the past few days whether or not she'd held her ground. Or if she'd gone back to her ex-husband.

"I didn't call him," she said, "if that's what you're thinking."

It had been, but he just watched her. Waited for the truth.

"I wanted to. There were times I wanted to so badly I thought I'd lose my mind. But I didn't call him," she said. "Or lose my mind. At least, not that I'm aware of."

Zach's lips twitched. "Good for you."

She flushed as if pleased by his light praise. "Don't give me too much credit. Part of the reason I didn't call was because after a weak moment, I shut off my phone and gave it to Mitchell to hide."

"Your son hid your phone?"

She nodded. Lifted her hand only to glance down as if surprised she still held the weight. Lowered her arm. "He's good at hiding things. But he's even better at forgetting where he hid them."

"That was very—"

"Pathetic. I know."

"I was going to say smart. You knew your phone was a trigger, so you got rid of it."

"More like desperate. I *could* use someone else's phone or go back to his hotel, but it's a relief not having the option of texting him or simply pressing a button to call him."

"You're making it hard to do. Like I said, smart."

"Shane and I aren't ever getting back together. I know that. I understand it, but I'm not quite sure I accept it yet. But I want to."

She couldn't even see what she was doing, how strong she was being. Couldn't give herself any credit for having the willpower to last this long.

"Then you're halfway there," he told her, hoping she knew he saw her. He understood. "The first step in achieving any goal is to really want it, not just pay lip service to it. That will push you toward taking the necessary steps to make it happen."

"I hope so. Anyway, I'm not giving up, which is a huge deal all on its own. For so long I've held on to the belief that Shane and I would somehow end up together. That he'd change, go back to the man he used to be. That if I was just patient enough, understanding enough, we'd get our happy ending. Now I have to figure out how to make a happy ending without him." Facing the mirror, she began lifting and lowering the weights, determination lining her face, thinning her mouth. "Starting with doing what I want to do. And not worrying about whether he likes it or not."

Zach set his weight down and stepped over to gently touch the back of her hand as it came up. She stopped, looked at him questioningly.

"A little slower," he told her, removing his hand. "More controlled. You want to make sure the muscle is engaged. Better," he said when she started again. "Resist the downward motion." He stepped behind her, pressing lightly on her upper back to fix her posture then on her shoulders so they weren't up at her ears. "Exhale on the contraction as you lift. Inhale on the release. Good," he murmured as she fixed her breathing.

Her lips moved as she silently counted each repetition. When she reached fifteen, she lowered the weights. "I'm not feeling anything. Maybe these aren't heavy enough."

"If you can still say that after your third set," he said, going back to his own weight, "we'll increase you to five pounds."

"Why are you doing this?" she asked.

Because something about her tugged at a place deep inside him. Made him want to know more and more about her. He wanted her to discover her own strength. To realize that happy ending she'd always dreamed about was not only possible, but that she was more than capable of making it happen all on her own.

Mostly he wanted her to stay the hell away from her ex-husband.

As to the reason for that, he wasn't sure. But it might have something to do with him starting to believe his happy ending was possible, too.

He'd be better off avoiding her again, but it was too late for that. He'd stepped over some invisible line, one bringing him closer to her. Putting him into her life. He couldn't go back now.

Didn't want to.

He'd give her the truth. As much of it as he could afford to give.

"Because I know what it's like," he told her, holding her gaze in the mirror, "to be trapped by your own mind. And I've found the best way to deal with feeling helpless is to focus on what I can control and what I can fix."

Understanding and sympathy dawned in her eyes. But she didn't say anything, just went back to carefully lifting and lowering her weights. For the next thirty minutes he worked with her, teaching her proper technique, focusing on upper-body strength. She stayed at three pounds, struggling even with those when they worked on her triceps. By the time they were done, exertion had turned her cheeks a pretty pink and her face glowed. She looked...healthy.

Exhilarated.

"Finish that," he told her of the bottle of water she was drinking, "and drink plenty more the rest of the day. You should also eat some protein after this—eggs or peanut butter are both fine. And if you're sore, don't hesitate to take a couple of pain relievers. Or a long, hot bath with Epsom salts."

"I wish. But if I leave the boys to their own devices for longer than ten minutes, chaos reigns. Elijah has a knack for finding trouble if he's not supervised closely."

"I remember."

The kid had balls, that was for sure. And not nearly enough sense or fear. Then again, the younger kid, Mitch, seemed to have enough fear to cover himself and his older brother.

When she opened her mouth, Zach spoke first. "Don't."

"Don't?"

"Don't apologize again for him coming to my room."

"I wasn't going to."

Which was such a blatant lie he was surprised lightning didn't fry her hair.

"Good."

He sat down on a mat while she tossed her empty bottle into the recycling container and headed toward the door. Bending his knees, he lay back. "Don't forget about the protein and water."

"I won't."

He curled up.

"Zach?"

At the sound of her saying his name, he stilled

in the middle of his crunch, his abs burning. She stood in the doorway in her too-big shirt, strands of loose curls brushing her long neck, enticing and sweet and completely out of his reach.

"Thank you. For everything."

He was the one who was grateful. Grateful she hadn't offered him any platitudes about staying the course on a long, hard road when he'd admitted he understood what it was like to be a prisoner of your thoughts. Grateful she hadn't pointed out how far he'd already come, how his body was healing. How he was almost able to function like any two-legged, two-armed man.

Thankful that during their time together she kept the conversation to a minimum. That she didn't ask any questions, didn't try to dig the specifics out of him like Daphne so often did in an attempt to know every one of his thoughts. His feelings.

"Don't thank me yet," he told her gruffly as he lowered down then did another crunch. "You might feel differently after tomorrow."

She frowned. "What's tomorrow?"

Tomorrow should be the day when he went back to avoiding her. But since that ship had long since sailed, he might as well accept it. *Deal with it.*

New life motto. He'd do well to remember it.

"Tomorrow," he said, "is leg day. Meet me here at 8:00 a.m."

CHAPTER TWELVE

THE DARKNESS WAS BACK.

Fay woke the next morning with it pressing down on her, like a weight on her chest, the pressure unbearable, and she knew, despite how well she'd been doing, despite feeling almost good for so many days, today would be torture.

And to think she'd actually been proud of how well she'd done since leaving Shane's hotel room. Yes, she might have bent a little, but she hadn't broken. She'd been able to function like a real person and not just a robot going through the motions.

No pretending, no *acting as if.* Though it hadn't been easy, she'd faced the pain and disappointment of losing Shane and her dreams of their future together, had let the feelings of sadness come and had dealt with them.

Had survived them.

She'd been confident she'd beaten the darkness for good this time. Had wanted, more than anything, to be strong—for herself and her sons. And maybe even prove she wasn't nearly as fragile as everyone thought.

Wrong. Oh, she'd been so very wrong. And now she was paying the price.

She felt like spun glass, brittle and delicate, as if the slightest movement, the lightest touch and she'd shatter. Her entire body hurt; dull, throbbing pain shot up from her fingers and toes, wrapped around her torso and settled into her throat and head. Lying on her side, staring blindly at the soft glow of the night-light in the hall, she concentrated on taking short, tiny sips of air.

She was alone. Utterly, entirely alone. Despair washed over her, inescapable and expansive. She tried to tell herself it wasn't real, this sense of drowning, of being unable to breathe. Tried to convince herself she was blessed beyond measure with her children and her family and her friends. But it didn't matter how many times she silently repeated every one of Dr. Porter's positive mantras or told herself that the pain would pass—the hopelessness remained.

"Mama?" Mitchell called from the doorway in a loud whisper. "Are you 'wake?" She shut her eyes. Heard his footsteps as he approached the bed. He laid his hand on her cheek, his palm soft and warm, and shook her face none too gently. "Mama?"

She forced her eyes open. Mitch stared intently at her, his brow puckered.

"I'm awake," she managed, her voice rusty and

raw. But she'd answered her baby's question and had not just stared through him.

"Can we have pancakes?" he asked.

Pancakes.

The thought of making them, even from a mix, was daunting. Overwhelming.

She struggled to sit up, pushed her hair out of her face. "We'll see."

Mitch grinned. "Okay!"

Guess she hadn't used the old *we'll see* often enough. He didn't seem to realize that in mother speak it equaled a resounding *no*.

He'd learn soon enough.

She had to get up. Had to get Elijah ready for school, drop Mitchell off at day camp. She could do this. She could.

Act as if...act as if...

And take it one step at a time.

She liked to think it was a spark of strength inside her, trying desperately to flare, that had her getting out of bed. A victory in and of itself. And during the next hour and a half she had a few wins. Along with some scathing defeats.

Yes, she got out of bed, but she only had the energy to pull on baggy sweatpants and a sweat-shirt, sans bra. She brushed her teeth but couldn't find the strength to tackle her hair, settling on a messy, tangled ponytail. The boys ate cereal, not pancakes, and it took all she had to keep smiling, to keep convincing a worried Mitchell that she was okay. She wasn't sad. She wasn't sick.

When she returned to Bradford House after dropping off the boys, all she wanted was to go back to bed. Luckily, when she stepped into the kitchen, it was empty. No close encounters with Damien, no searching looks or pointed questions.

Another victory, even if she wasn't the one who'd made it happen.

Closing the door behind her, Fay crept through the room. Halfway to the staircase, she glanced at the microwave clock.

Eight fifteen.

Meet me here at 8:00 a.m.

She'd totally forgotten Zach's invitation to join him this morning for…what had he called it? Leg day?

Invitation? More like a command.

Well, she wouldn't go. Just thinking about working out made her want to curl into a ball and weep. Plus, she was doing her best not to let herself be bossed around by anyone.

I know what it's like to be trapped by your own mind.

Not even by someone who seemed to understand her so well.

I've found the best way to deal with feeling helpless is to focus on what I can control and what I can fix.

He made it sound so simple, but it wasn't. Not

when she sensed the darkness lying in wait, ready to drag her into the shadows.

It would be so easy to let it. To stop fighting and disappear within herself.

She'd never been good at fixing things. Had always relied on other people to step in, to guide her and, in some cases, take over. To take care of her.

Maybe it was time she started taking care of herself.

Turning around, she concentrated on what she could control—the first step. Then the next, and the next. Through the dining room and hallway, down the stairs she went, step after step, until she stood inside the fitness room, facing Zach on the treadmill.

Without breaking stride he raked his gaze over her, taking in her baggy clothes and ballet flats—not exactly gym-friendly footwear. She lifted her hand to smooth her hair, but really, the snarled mess was well past that point, so she lowered her arm to her side.

She braced herself for what came next. A comment about her appearance, either given with concern over her mental health and overall well-being or said in a resigned tone, letting her know how frustrated he was that she'd let her illness win again. He'd advise her on how she should be living her life, telling her happiness was a choice and she needed to decide to stop being sad. Then he'd remind her that everyone had problems and obstacles to deal with, but they didn't let those things stop them from living healthy, productive, joy-filled lives.

All things she'd heard before from family and friends, said with love and concern. Things she'd be thrilled to never hear again.

Holding the side bar, Zach stepped off the belt. Fay tensed, the ache in her body going deeper, growing stronger. This was a mistake. He didn't really want her here.

"You're late."

That was it? Two words said without any condemnation or judgment?

He wasn't waiting for her to fall apart. There was no pity in his gaze. Just patience. Understanding.

I know what it's like to be trapped by your own mind.

Her relief was swift and intense, knocking her back a full step. "I…"

I'm sorry. I'm so sorry for being late. For making you wait. Please don't be mad at me. Please don't walk away from me.

She swallowed the apology, along with her explanation that she wasn't feeling well and that she'd had to take the boys to school and day camp. "Yes. I'm late."

Something flashed in his dark eyes, something that might have been respect. Pride. But it was gone so fast she couldn't quite decipher it.

Couldn't quite bask in it.

"You need to warm up," he said, nodding at the treadmill next to him.

"I'd really rather not," she murmured.

Frowning, he shut off his machine. Climbed down to stand before her. "Then why are you here?"

Because she was trying so hard to be strong. Because she wanted to get better.

Because she didn't want to be alone.

"I don't know," she admitted, feeling like an idiot. What was it about this man that had her constantly making a fool of herself in front of him? "I felt better. Yesterday," she explained. "After I worked out."

She hadn't done much, but the effort it had taken to lift and lower those puny weights had given her something to focus on, something else to think about other than Shane. And at the end, when she'd been a bit sweaty, her breathing harder than normal, her arms and shoulders pleasantly sore, she'd felt triumphant, as if she'd passed a major test.

"That's good."

She nodded. "It is good. It helped."

"But you don't think it'll help today?"

"That's part of it. If it doesn't, I'm not sure I can handle the disappointment. All the therapy, the meds and the tips and tricks to deal with my depression and anxiety, they're all just pieces of a puzzle," she said, hands fluttering uselessly. "All part of my treatment. Sometimes they don't work at all, or there are a few missing pieces, or the finished picture is completely different from what everyone expected. But at other times they fit together perfectly and I feel almost normal—"

"Normal is subjective."

He said it with such conviction, as if it were the absolute truth.

She prayed he was right. She'd never been described as normal. She'd been too quiet as a child. Too clingy. Too sensitive and serious as a teenager, always lost in her own thoughts.

"I guess my normal would be pretty close to how I felt yesterday after I left here. So, yes, I'm afraid it won't work today, but I'm..." She stopped. Inhaled deeply but couldn't meet his eyes as she told him what truly frightened her. "I'm also afraid it will."

Lowering her head, she shut her eyes, hating her own cowardice.

She sensed him shift. Felt him draw nearer, but she didn't dare look at him.

"You're afraid that if it works," he said close to her ear, his voice whisper soft, his musky scent surrounding her, "you'll start to believe it's a miracle cure. You'll start to think that this one specific thing is the key to getting your life back. But deep down you know that's impossible. There are no miracles. And one day you'll try to use this key but the door won't open and you'll be trapped. Locked once again in your own mind, wrapped up in darkness. Unable to see a way out."

Her eyes flew open and she stared at him, heart racing, mouth dry. Yes, that was it exactly. How did he know? How could he see her so clearly when it seemed as if no one else could?

Why did it scare her so much?

"You must think I'm pathetic," she whispered. "Scared of my own shadow."

"You're not pathetic," he said simply. "We all have our fears."

"Even you?"

"Even me." He slid her a sideways glance. "You don't believe me."

She quickly tried to school her features, as he'd obviously read disbelief on her face. Well, she'd never been very good at hiding her emotions. No use expecting that to have suddenly changed.

"No."

Her face heated and she chewed on her pinkie nail. Why had she said that? Now he would be angry with her. Accuse her of thinking less of him. Or he might ask her to leave. Or maybe he'd give her the silent treatment, turn his back on her and walk away.

But he didn't look angry. More…thoughtful. Considering.

Considering her.

Wrapping his fingers around her wrist, he gently tugged her hand down, his grip loose, his skin warm. Her pulse jumped and she wondered if he felt it.

Wished she was brave enough to turn her hand around, to link her fingers with his.

"I don't lie," he said, his words quiet and soothing, as if he knew her stomach was jumping, her head spinning.

She swallowed and pulled free of his hold. Took a step back. Being so close to him was too confusing. Too frightening.

"I didn't mean to imply you were being untruthful. I'm just…surprised…that you're afraid of anything. You're so…" She waved her hand over him. "Together. From what I've seen, you have more than your fair share of self-control."

"You pissed that I have self-control?" he asked, one side of his mouth kicking up. The small smile made him look younger. Less severe, more handsome.

It made her wonder what he'd look like if he smiled at her for real.

Oh, good Lord, Maddie had been right. She really was losing her mind.

"I'm run ragged by my scattered thoughts. I let my feelings rule my world and often blurt out whatever comes to mind. There are days when I can't even get out of bed. So, no, I'm not angry you have self-control. I'm envious. And while I don't think you were lying about having fears, I do think you may have been stretching the truth in an effort to make me feel better. Which is very kind of you."

His smile widened into a full-on grin. Her mind blanked for a good five seconds. Well, she thought, when the power to do so returned, she'd wondered what his real smile would be like. Now she knew—devastating.

"I'm not a liar," he repeated, "and I'm not particularly kind."

"You've been nothing but kind. At least to me."

He'd been honest, had helped her see she needed to stand up for herself. He hadn't made her feel less than for needing a push.

He had kindness in him. More than he even realized. But she'd seen it. Had experienced it. And she'd never forget it.

"Eight months ago," he said, as calmly as if they were discussing today's breakfast menu, "I was afraid I was going to die. Seven months ago I was afraid I'd never walk again. Six months ago I was afraid I'd never be able to live on my own." He shrugged as if it was no big deal that he'd had to fight for his life. "Like I said, we all have our fears."

Shame filled her for thinking he'd been spouting platitudes at her. For being so wrapped up in her own problems she'd assumed he was just being nice, trying to make her feel better.

She'd thought only of herself and not about what he'd gone through. What he was still going through.

"And now?" she asked.

"Now I'm afraid that no matter how hard I work, how far I've come—"

"There will always be a piece of you that's different," she finished for him softly. "That there will always be something inside you that remains broken."

It was her fear, as well.

He shook his head. "I know there will always be a part of me that's different. Hard to pretend otherwise," he added, waving his empty sleeve. "And I'm not sure I can ever fully accept that. And that scares the hell out of me."

I know what it's like to be trapped by your own mind.

"But," he continued, "I can accept it right now. For the next—" he checked his watch "—hour or so, I can do what needs to be done to keep myself healthy. To get stronger. And for those sixty minutes I can pretend that everything is okay."

"Act as if."

Though she'd said the words under her breath, he heard. "Right. I can act as if. And so can you."

His belief in her was perplexing. She didn't believe in herself—how could he? But it was also flattering. And enticing enough to make her climb onto the treadmill and begin to walk. A moment later, Zach returned to the treadmill next to her.

Having him beside her helped her ignore her fear and pain—if only for a little while. Made it possible to shove aside expectations, to stop worrying about what would happen an hour, a day or a week from now. Having him beside her made it possible to be in the moment.

To be in *this* moment. With him.

JOSIE KNOCKED ON the back door to Bradford House, three hard raps that hopefully told Fay Lindemuth she meant business. Straightening, she hugged herself, the cold and damp seeping into her skin. The rainy spring day did nothing to improve her mood.

Which had been pretty damn crappy to begin with.

Guess that happened when you spend yet another night alone in a cheap hotel with no money and no options.

No options other than tracking down the lousy, lying, cheating bastard who'd gotten her pregnant then decided he'd rather be with his skinny, pale ex-wife.

Josie knocked again, hard enough to bruise her knuckles. When the door opened, she bit back her scathing comment meant to put Fay in her place.

Squeezing her eyes shut, she inhaled carefully. Maybe lack of sleep combined with gnawing, relentless hunger had made her delusional. She opened her eyes. Nope. He was still there, an apron tied at his waist, huge, muscular, tattooed arms crossed, bald head gleaming. "You look just like The Rock." She narrowed her eyes and craned her neck so she could see his face—he had to be at least six-five. "You aren't—are you?"

Because meeting a famous movie star would go a long way toward making this day a lot less sucky.

"No," The Rock impersonator said. "And I think he prefers to go by Dwayne Johnson now."

"I guess you get mistaken for him a lot, huh? Must be a pain."

"It's not too bad. It's actually how I met my husband."

"Your husband is a fan of The Rock's... I mean... of Dwayne Johnson?"

"Not really. But he seemed to be a fan of the tiny, tight wrestling shorts I wore when I dressed up as The Rock for a Halloween party."

She scanned him from bald head to booted toe. "I bet."

He raised an eyebrow—just like the real Rock would do—and relaxed enough to uncross his arms. "Guests usually use the front entrance."

Right. Back to her purpose in being there. "I'm not a guest. I need to speak with Fay Lindemuth. Immediately," she added, just so he wouldn't get the crazy idea that she could be put in some corner to wait.

His gaze turned downright frosty. "What do you want with Fay?"

"With her? Nothing, really. I just want to know where my fiancé is."

"That son of a bitch. Shane did this to you?" he asked, jabbing an accusatory finger at her bulging belly.

"Well, technically, we were both there when it happened," she said drily.

His lips flattened and he stood aside, all serious and very *Downton Abbey* butlerish with his perfect posture and lifted nose. "You'd better come on in." She stepped inside the small foyer and he shut the door. "This way."

She followed him into a bright, airy kitchen that looked like something out of one of those home and garden television shows that her mom loved to watch, all gleaming wood and high-priced tile floor and fancy countertops. A timer dinged, and the butler or cook or whatever he was pulled out a tray of muffins. He set them on the six-burner stove.

"You can wait here," he said, tossing his pot holders on the large center island as he passed it. "I'll find Fay."

He left Josie alone in that fancy kitchen with those wonderful-smelling muffins. Her stomach growled. Her mouth watered.

She glanced at the doorway then hurried over to the muffins. Chocolate chip.

She moaned. They just had to be chocolate chip. She could resist any other flavor, she assured herself—blueberry or cranberry, anything but chocolate chip.

Yeah, she was lying to herself. So what? At this point, lies were all she had.

After another glance at the door, she plucked a muffin from the tin.

It was blazing hot, but that didn't stop her from breaking off a large chunk and popping it into her mouth. "Shit."

It was hot. Burn-the-top-of-your-tongue-and-the-roof-of-your-mouth-so-you-can't-taste-anything-for-two-days hot.

She was too far gone to care.

"That's a bad word."

Whirling around, she almost dropped the muffin, but hunger and desperation had granted her ninja-like reflexes and she saved it. She held on to it, despite the heat soaking into her palm, and stared at the little kid standing next to the fridge. She wished she could shove the rest of the muffin in her mouth. "What?"

"*Shit* is a bad word," he told her as Fay walked in with another boy, this one a few inches shorter and a bit rounder, holding her hand. "Right, Mom?"

But Fay was too busy staring at her in what

could only be described as stunned horror to answer her son.

Her son. Josie squeezed the muffin into crumbs.
Fay's sons, hers and Shane's, the boys he rarely
talked about, the ones he had practically nothing
to do with. Every time Josie asked about them—
how old they were, when she could meet them—
he evaded the questions. Almost as if he didn't
know the answers.

Or just didn't care.

Why the hell had she thought it'd be different
with her and their kid?

"Wha-what are you doing?" Fay asked.

Josie glanced at the muffin. Great. First she
swore in front of Shane's kid, now she'd been
caught stealing. She might fudge the truth a bit,
might be on the abrasive and aggressive side, but
she wasn't a thief.

If she started down that long slide, she might
not be able to stop at one muffin. God, go a few
hours—okay, more like a day and a half—without
food and suddenly it's like she was in *The Hunger
Games*, willing to do anything for a quick bite. She
set the rest of the muffin on the counter. Brushed
the crumbs from her fingers.

"I'll pay for it," she said, sounding more de-
fensive than she'd planned, but then, not much
had gone according to her plans lately. She pulled
her shoulders back, reminded herself to be strong.
That she was there for a reason. A good one.

She was the one in the right here.

"Where is he?" she asked as the older kid—Evan? Ethan?—poked her stomach.

"Elijah," Fay said, springing forward to grab his arm and yanking him back as if saving the boy from the snapping jaws of a freaking alligator, "don't touch her!"

Josie's face heated. "I don't have cooties."

"Why can't I touch her?" Elijah asked.

Fay tugged him back several more steps before letting go. She blinked while she thought over his question. "Because…because it's impolite," she finally said. "And you might hurt her."

He turned back to Josie, looking up at her with his big blue eyes. "Did it hurt?"

"No. But you still shouldn't do it. It's weird to touch someone you've never met, especially their stomach."

He nodded as if that explanation was better than the one his mom had given him. "Are you gonna have a baby?"

"Well, I didn't swallow a basketball."

His eyes wide, he bounced on his toes a few times. "Can you *do* that?"

She rolled her eyes. "Of course not."

He frowned, looking so much like Shane, Josie could have cried. "Then why did you say you could?"

"I didn't say I could." And she was arguing with a kid who probably still believed in Santa

Claus. "Look, never mind. Yes, I'm going to have a baby. A girl."

Your sister.

She glanced at Fay, wanting to see her reaction to the news that she was having Shane's daughter, giving him a girl while Fay had only sons. She wanted the other woman to be jealous. To feel as insecure and scared as Josie did.

She wanted to hurt her.

The realization hit her hard, had her knees buckling, her vision going gray. She reached out for the counter but started to slide to the floor, anyway.

Only to have Fay rush across the room in an effort of superhuman speed and catch her before she hit the ground.

"Here," Fay said, sounding breathless, "let's get you to a chair."

"I can do it," Josie muttered, shifting out of Fay's reach. She lifted herself onto a stool at the counter, embarrassed to have almost fainted in front of this woman. Ashamed at wanting to hurt her just because Shane had stomped on Josie's feelings.

"Are you sure you're okay?" Fay asked, and when Josie glanced her way, both Fay and the younger boy were wearing identical worried expressions.

"I'm fine. I missed breakfast, that's all."

Not a lie. Just not the entire truth.

"Ivy had a baby," Elijah said. He knelt at Josie's feet and peered up, as if checking out the undercarriage of a car. "How'd it get in there, anyway?"

Josie snorted. "Yeah. Not going to answer that one."

"There you are," Not The Rock said as he entered the room. He scowled at Josie then glanced at Fay, who was filling a glass with ice from the dispenser in the refrigerator. "This young lady wanted to talk with you."

"I don't want to talk to *her.*" Josie wished she had the energy to get to her feet, but her head still felt like it was stuffed with cotton. "I want to talk to Shane. I promise, what I need to say to him will take less than five minutes, then I'll get out of your hair."

And out of Shane's life.

"Shane's here?" the huge bald guy asked, eyes narrowed on Fay.

"You know my dad?" Elijah asked Josie.

"No," Fay said.

"Yes," Josie said at the same time.

Baldie crossed his massive arms. "Fay…"

"Shane's not here," she said.

Cotton-filled head or not, Josie got to her feet. Swayed slightly but waved off the guy's outstretched hand. "He's here. He has to be." Her voice was unsteady, her hands shaking. "He has to be."

Fay and the guy exchanged a look. "Damien, could you take the boys out to check the mail?"

He hesitated and she laid her free hand on his forearm. "Please."

Josie looked away. It was obvious these two were more than coworkers—they were friends. Fay had this man, her sons and probably others— parents and siblings and girlfriends—she could turn to, could talk to. People who jumped to her defense or rushed to her aid.

While Josie had no one.

The boys raced out with Damien lagging behind, shooting curious, worried glances over his shoulder. Ignoring it, Fay set the water in front of Josie. When Josie stared at it, Fay slid it closer. "Take a drink. You could be dehydrated."

Josie sipped the water. Cleared her throat. "Thanks."

"Shane left you," Fay said, making what should have been a question sound like a statement.

"Yes. Almost a week ago."

"You haven't heard from him since?"

Josie considered lying, but really, what was the point? If anyone knew what she was going through, it was this woman. "No. He won't answer my calls or my texts."

There was no pity in Fay's eyes, only understanding. Sympathy.

Josie hated it.

Lips pursed thoughtfully, Fay exhaled heavily. "What are you going to do?"

Josie snorted out a humorless laugh. "If I knew

that, I wouldn't be here. I don't want him back, I just need to talk to him. If he wants you, fine— I'm not waiting around this stupid town for him to come to his senses." But maybe that wasn't true. Maybe she did want him back. If only so she wouldn't be alone. She took another sip of water, stared at her glass as she asked, "He's really not here?"

"I haven't seen or spoken to him since last Wednesday."

Wednesday. The day Josie had first confronted Fay. The day she'd taken Shane's truck and met Drew. The day she'd gone back to the hotel and found Shane with those marks on his face, bruises and cuts Fay had given him.

"He left that night," Josie said. "We got into a fight and he took off. Said he was getting beer. I figured he'd drive around for a while, maybe go to a bar with his stupid friends. When he didn't come back, I thought he was trying to hurt me for pissing him off." She met Fay's eyes. "That's what he does. If you upset him, he finds a way to get back at you. To make sure you pay."

Fay looked stricken, as if hearing a new and extremely disturbing fact. "Yes," she said, her voice strained. "I know."

"When one night turned into two, I thought he had come here, that he was with you and your sons."

"And you've been waiting for him at the hotel ever since."

Put that way, it made her sound pathetic. Like some loser who couldn't take care of herself or her baby.

"I didn't have anywhere else to go," Josie said, a snap of defiance in her tone.

"What about your home? Your parents?"

"That's not an option."

"Why not?"

"Because when I called my mom yesterday she told me I'd made my choice by sleeping with Shane and now I had to deal with the consequences of my actions."

Josie never should have called, but she'd been desperate. "I'm nearly seven months pregnant and have nothing for a baby—no crib or clothes or those onesie things—but I guess it doesn't matter, since the hotel manager told me the room had only been paid up until today." Her eyes stung, but she'd shed enough tears already. Self-indulgent tears over Shane. Pleading ones while on the phone with her mother. "I'm screwed. I can't go home and I can't stay at the hotel. I have no job, I'm homeless and I'm completely on my own." The baby moved, and Josie laid her hand on her stomach. "We're on our own."

Shane was gone. He wasn't going to love her forever. It was time she accepted that and moved on with her life.

But before she did, there was one thing she had to do.

"I'm sorry," she said, the words rushing out of her on a soft exhalation. "I'm sorry for coming here and messing up your afternoon. And I'm sorry for the other day, too. For the things I said and how I acted. I won't bother you again."

She turned and headed toward the door, her stomach rumbling, her body heavy with fatigue.

"Are you hungry?" Fay called.

The question was so unexpected, Josie answered truthfully as she faced the other woman. "Starving."

"Why don't I make you a sandwich? You can eat and we can talk."

"You want to talk? With me?"

"Yes." Fay crossed to the counter and picked out another muffin, handed it, along with a banana, to Josie. "You can nibble on these while I put your sandwich together. What's your name, anyway? I don't think we ever got to that."

"My name's Josie." She paused for a moment, trying to make sense of what was happening. "Why are you doing this? You should hate me."

"Maybe I should, but I don't." Fay's smile was quick and on the sad side. "Then again, I've never been very good at feeling the things I'm supposed to. Why start now? As for why I'm doing this… I guess because I can. Because I want to, but more importantly, because I choose to. The question is, what do you want?"

Confusion, suspicion and gratitude all tumbled

around inside Josie, fought for dominance. She didn't trust Fay. Didn't want to trust her. But what if she did? What if she took a chance and let herself believe in something good?

To believe someone was good.

She was hungry enough, tired enough and brokenhearted enough to try.

"I'd like to talk," Josie said. "And I'd really, really like to eat."

Fay smiled. Nodded. "I'm glad."

The weird thing? Josie believed she meant it.

CHAPTER THIRTEEN

HE'D INTERRUPTED SNACK TIME.

Shit.

Both of Fay's sons were in Bradford House's kitchen. Zach couldn't handle Elijah with his rapid-fire questions and endless energy. The kid was so busy racing around the island waving a banana as if wielding a sword that he hadn't even noticed Zach yet.

But the younger one had. Mitch sat on a stool at the large island, chocolate from a muffin smeared on his face, eyes wide and panicked, his body half turned on the high stool, poised to jump off and run should Zach make any sudden moves.

Where was their mother?

"Hey!" Elijah cried, stopping so suddenly when he spotted Zach he almost toppled over. "What are you doing here?"

There went his slight hope of being ignored.

"Making my dinner." Zach and Mitch kept a wary eye on each other as Zach crossed the room and set his grocery bags on the counter next to the refrigerator. Mitch's lower lip trembled. His eyes glistened.

Zach narrowed his gaze. "Don't even think about it."

Mitch ducked his head fast enough to give himself whiplash. But he didn't cry, just kept his chin tucked to his chest, his eyes squeezed shut.

Good enough.

Zach unloaded a package of chicken breasts and a container of rice.

"You're not allowed to do that," Elijah said running up to him, banana still waving. "No one can touch anything in here 'cept Damien or my mom. Or Gracie," he added, "'cuz she works here. Luke used to work here, too, but he quit 'cuz he got a job in Pittsburgh. But you don't work here so you can't touch anything."

"You said that already."

"'Cuz you're touching stuff," Elijah said, with a silent *duh* at the end. He hopped, all wound up and agitated, as Zach opened one of the lower cabinets. "And you're not allowed."

Zach closed the door, opened another and took out a saucepan. Set it on the stove. "Your mom and Damien both said I could use the kitchen."

Elijah stilled. "Are you sure?"

The kid was a little young to be so suspicious. But then again, living with Michael had taught Zach how to mistrust adults at a young age, too. He hoped like hell this kid hadn't had that mistrust beaten into him.

"I'm sure."

"Oh. Okay."

And he took off, slashing and stabbing with the banana. Whatever invisible foe he was fighting must be a bloody mess by now.

Zach tucked the container of rice between his side and his right arm, twisted the lid off with his left hand. He and Fay had come to an agreement that morning during their workout. She'd wanted to repay him for his time, and while he'd never take her money, he'd realized over the past six days that eating two meals at O'Riley's or another restaurant downtown each day wasn't doing his wallet or his fitness goals any good. By preparing his own meals he could focus on giving his body the nutrients it needed to get stronger and save money, too.

As long as Zach stayed out of the kitchen between the hours of 5:00 a.m. and 3:00 p.m., cleaned up after himself, and didn't use any of the bed-and-breakfast's food, Damien didn't have a problem with it, so Zach had stopped at a grocery store after work.

He hadn't planned on anyone else being in here.

He poured rice into the pan then turned to the sink to add water. From the corner of his eye he noticed Mitch now stood at the end of the island closest to Zach, watching him. Elijah had pushed one of the heavy chairs from the table to the counter.

"Where's your mother?" he asked the kid.

"In her office." Elijah stood on his toes—not

the brightest idea considering how close he was to the edge of the chair and his proximity to the stove. "She's helping Josie get situated."

Situated? Must be a direct quote.

"Why don't you and your brother go find her?" Zach asked, setting the pan on the stove.

Elijah shook his head, hair flapping all around. "We're supposed to wait for her here." He climbed onto the counter and sat, feet swinging against the lower cabinets. "What are you doing? Can I help?"

"No. And get down."

"Why?"

"Because I'm going to turn on the stove."

"I can do it!" Elijah said, reaching across the front burner for the knob.

Swearing, Zach grabbed the kid around the waist and set him on the floor.

"That's a really, really bad word," Elijah whispered in awe. "When Uncle Neil said it at Bree's soccer game, Grandma Gerry hit him on his head."

"Then I guess you'd better not ever say it." At least not in front of his grandmother.

But Zach could tell by the look on the kid's face he was going to shout it out the first chance he got.

Zach moved the rice to one of the back burners and turned the flame on.

"Get down," Zach said when Elijah once again climbed onto the chair. "And move away from the stove."

"Why?"

"Because it's hot."

"I won't get burned."

"Get. Down."

Elijah didn't move.

The kid had balls. Or else he was spoiled and too used to getting his own way.

"You didn't count to three!" Elijah yelled when Zach scooped him up again. "You're supposed to count to three!"

The kid wiggled, but Zach held firm, carrying him past a wide-eyed Mitch standing with his back against the refrigerator. Setting Elijah on a chair at the large table, Zach crouched so they were eye to eye. "I don't count to three," he said, "and I don't give second chances. When I tell you to do something, you do it."

Lower lip sticking out, Elijah crossed his skinny arms. "Why should I?"

Because I'm bigger. And even with one arm, I'm still stronger.

That was how Michael would have responded. And with sharp rebukes, stinging slaps and bruises.

But Zach didn't need to use force to show he was in control.

"Because I'm the adult and you're the kid, which means you will listen to me whether you like it or not."

"I *don't* like it."

Zach shrugged. "It doesn't matter. If you want to stay in this kitchen with me, you'll do as I say.

If you don't, I'll haul your butt back to this corner where you will sit, in silence, until your mother comes to get you."

"You're not the boss of me," the kid grumbled, red faced. "You can't make me sit here."

"Try me."

The stare down lasted thirty long seconds until Elijah dropped his gaze. Swung his legs—back and forth—narrowly missing Zach's knee. "I just wanted to help."

Zach sighed. How many times had he stood on a chair at the counter next to his mother or Abuelita while they cooked? "You can help," he heard himself say then winced. *Aw, hell.*

"I can?" Elijah hopped down, forcing Zach to rear back so he didn't get clipped in the chin. "Want me to stir the rice?"

"You can help," Zach repeated, holding on to the chair as he straightened, "but you're not allowed near the stove. Understand?"

"Yeah."

Zach thought about correcting him, having him say *yes, sir* as he'd been taught, but at this point, he'd just take this small victory and leave the rest be. "Wash your hands. You're on salad duty."

"Okay!" He galloped over to the large sink, as if ripping lettuce into pieces was the most exciting thing he'd done all day.

Zach went back to the stove. "What are you

doing?" he asked Mitch, who stood on the chair his brother had dragged over.

"I want to help, too."

"You're scared of me," Zach reminded him.

"I'm not." But he didn't sound too sure about that. "Not anymore."

"Lucky me."

Mitch nodded, Zach's sarcasm going right over his blond head.

Zach looked to the doorway again. How long could it take to get one guest situated? "Wash your hands. You can help your brother make a salad."

Mitch smiled—like an angel to his brother's devilish grin—and scrambled off his seat. Zach pushed the chair farther down the counter and preheated the oven.

"I'm ready!" Elijah announced, bouncing over like a kangaroo amped up on speed. He hopped onto the chair, banging it against the counter. "Can I cut something? I'm a real good cutter."

"Sure. Let me get you the biggest, sharpest knife here."

"Really?" Elijah asked breathlessly, eyes glazed in pure anticipation.

"No. Not really. You're not old enough to use a knife."

"Uh-uh, Mommy lets me use a knife all the time."

"Are you arguing with me?" Zach asked quietly.

"No!" Elijah rushed out. "It's okay. I don't need a knife."

"Way to make it seem like your idea." Zach took produce out of one of the grocery bags—lettuce, tomatoes, a cucumber and some carrots. "We'll need a bowl for the salad."

"I'll get it!"

Elijah bent his knees so that his butt rested on his heels momentarily then sprang up and jumped off the chair, landing a good three feet away.

Mitch tugged on Zach's jeans. "I washed my hands."

Zach noted the wet spot on his jeans, the water and soap suds dripping down the kid's arm. "You do know you're putting together a salad, right? You're not performing surgery."

Mitch nodded and climbed onto the chair.

"Hey!" Elijah yelled, carrying a stainless steel bowl as he raced over. "Get down! That's my spot!"

Elijah climbed up and tried to shove Mitch off, but Mitch held on to the counter ledge, his little face set, eyebrows lowered. "No. I'm standing here."

Zach would have thought Mitch would give in to his brother. Guess the little guy was tired of being pushed around. Literally.

Zach knew how he felt. Too bad any time he'd tried to stand up to Michael the resulting beating was that much worse.

Elijah gave a battle cry that had the hair on the back of Zach's neck standing on end and then launched himself at Mitch, wrapping his arm around his brother's throat in a choke hold. Mitch, obviously the recipient of this particular move before, jammed his elbow in Elijah's stomach.

Zach tugged on his ear while Elijah tried to strangle his brother and a red-faced Mitch kicked and elbowed like he was fighting off a dozen attackers.

"Take it outside," Zach called over their grunts and muttered taunts—*poop face*, *stupid head* and, Zach's personal favorite and one he might borrow should the need arise, *toe crud licker*. "Or knock it off!"

Mitch stopped immediately, his arms going limp at his sides. Elijah took the opportunity to try to twist Mitch off the chair by his neck, but Zach snatched Elijah's wrist, pulled him off his brother and set him on the ground.

A recurring theme with this one.

"Get another chair," Zach told him, once again crouching to the kid's level.

Lower lip sticking out, shirt a wrinkled mess, Elijah's chest heaved, his hands fisted. "That's my chair!"

"Not anymore it isn't."

"How come I have to get another chair? I had that one first!" He stomped his foot, jutted out his chin, reminding Zach of Fay's determination to stand on her own two feet. To push back.

"You have to get another chair because, one, I said so," Zach told him, lifting a finger for each reason. "Two, you tried to get in a cheap shot with your brother after he'd stopped fighting. Three, you're a little too used to getting your own way, and four—" his pinkie joined the three already up "—you're the big brother and that's what big brothers do. They take care of their little brothers."

"That's not fair!"

"Life's not fair, kid. Deal with it. It'll help you build some character."

Zach straightened and turned his back on Elijah. A moment later, with even more muttering about how mean Zach was and how Mitch was a baby who always got his way, Elijah walked away.

"Good job trying to get out of that headlock," Zach told Mitch, "but next time, knee or punch him in the nuts."

Mitch winced and covered his own crotch with his hands. "Mommy says that's not nice."

"You want to be nice? Let him strangle you. You want to win, you do whatever it takes to get him off you. Even if that means fighting dirty."

Eyes wide and thoughtful, Mitch frowned. "I don't want to be strangled."

"No one does, kid. No one does."

Sliding the package of chicken closer, Zach heard the sound of a chair being pushed across the tile floor. A moment later, Elijah shoved the chair against the counter with a thud and climbed onto it.

Mitch eyed his brother warily then looked up at Zach. "My mom always stands between us when we help her in the kitchen."

"Yeah?"

He nodded solemnly. "It's so we don't fight."

"You won't fight."

"We won't?"

"If you even think about fighting, I'm tossing both of your asses out of here."

Pressing his hands against the counter, Elijah hopped up and down. "That's a—"

"Bad word," Zach said, rinsing the lettuce. "I know." He tossed the lettuce to Elijah, who caught it in both hands. "You can tear that up and put it into the bowl."

While Elijah did that, Zach set a tomato on the counter and chose a serrated knife. "After I cut this," he told Mitch, "you can put the pieces in with the lettuce."

But when he pressed the knife against the tomato, the edge slipped and the tomato rolled across the counter.

"You can't hold it 'cuz you only have one hand," Mitch told him.

Great. A play-by-play while he cooked. Zach slid the tomato back into place. "Right."

"I could hold it," the kid told him, all earnest and helpful. "So you can cut it."

"I've got it. But thanks," he added, seeing the disappointment on the kid's face.

He pierced the tomato with the tip of the knife then cut. Repeated it twice more until he had four thick slices.

"Does it hurt?" Mitch asked.

Zach laid the slices flat on the counter, began chopping them. "The tomato?"

Mitch shook his head. "Your arm." He brushed his fingertips against the hem of Zach's sleeve. "Does it hurt?"

"No."

"But it hurt when it got chopped off. Right?"

Not exactly what had happened, but close enough. "Yeah. It hurt then."

"I'm sorry you got your arm chopped off," Mitch said, leaning slightly against Zach's side, his body warm, eyes sincere. "But I'm glad it doesn't hurt now."

Zach's throat tightened. An odd ache spread in his chest. He'd had plenty of people offer him their condolences since he'd been injured, had been looked at with sympathy and pity, but he'd never been affected like this.

Damn it. He had liked it better when the kid was scared of him.

JUST WHEN FAY thought her day couldn't get any more bizarre, she found the boys in the kitchen with Zach, backs to her as they worked side by side at the counter. Her sons weren't arguing, pushing or trying to stab each other's eye out with a fork, a knife or—if no other option was available—a spatula.

Obviously she'd walked into an alternate dimension. Maybe she could stay here forever.

Leaning against the doorjamb, she watched her small blond boys and the darkly handsome, broad-shouldered Zach, their heads close together. Zach said something, a low rumble that scraped pleasantly against her skin, the words unclear. Mitchell smiled up at him in his innocent, hopeful way while Elijah giggled, the joyful sound filling the space.

Seeing her sons so happy, so content should have thrilled her. Filled her with gratitude. Instead she chewed on her pinkie nail, feeling empty and bereft, as if she'd lost a vital piece of herself. As if the scene before her was somehow tainted. Wrong.

All because Zach was the one teasing laughs and smiles from her sons.

All because Shane wasn't.

Shane should be. He should pick them up from school and day camp and take them to the park several times a week like Fay's mom did. He should teach them how to fish and play card games with them, like Fay's father did. Cheer them on at their soccer games or take them into Pittsburgh for a Pirates or Pens game like Neil and Maddie did. He should help her tuck them in at night, read them story after story, get them water when they were trying to delay their bedtime, soothe them when they had a bad dream, hug them and kiss them and assure them he loved them.

He should *show* them how much he loved them by being there for them, by being in their lives each and every day, even if the only way that was possible was with a quick phone call or text.

But he didn't love them. Not the way they needed to be loved. Not the way Fay wanted him to. He hadn't even seen them last week, had come to her in the middle of the night, slipped out of her bed early in the morning.

He'd never be the father they deserved.

The hits just kept coming, each one harder and more painful than the last. For so long she'd believed holding on to Shane was the right thing to do because she loved him.

But she'd loved him too much.

Hadn't loved herself and the boys enough.

Accepting that Shane wasn't the man she thought he was, admitting she was as much to blame as him for choosing to believe his lies, for settling for so much less than what she gave, were the first steps in finally getting over him.

Time to focus on the future. To focus on what was best for her children.

As if sensing her, Zach lifted his head then slowly turned to watch her from over his shoulder, his expression unreadable, his gaze searching.

She straightened and crossed her arms as if that

alone could protect her from his intense gaze. He saw too much. Saw her way too clearly.

The darkness she'd been struggling with all day pushed against her with a vengeance, punishing her for daring to fight it.

Laughing at her for foolishly believing she was strong enough to win the battle.

"Boys," she said, her sharp tone slicing through the air. Elijah whirled around in surprise; Mitch's mouth trembled. She never raised her voice at her sons.

It reminded her too much of her early childhood, before Carl and Gerry took them in. A volatile life filled with fear, uncertainty and hunger.

A life she didn't want to touch her sons. Ever.

But she'd never felt this sense of urgency before. She wanted to grab the boys, sweep them out of the room and upstairs, away from Zach Castro and his handsome face, stoic patience and controlled demeanor. From his kindness and solid, steady presence and his quiet insistence that she was strong enough to do anything. To be anyone.

If she wasn't careful, she might start actually believing him.

She forced a smile. Tried again, this time modulating her tone. "Boys, you shouldn't be bothering Mr. Castro."

He might get angry at them. Lord knew they could overwhelm even the most patient soul— Elijah with his nonstop movement and defiant attitude and Mitchell with his neediness and end-less questions.

And Zach was a guest. One who'd already done more than enough for her. She didn't want to take advantage of him. And she really, really didn't want to feel indebted to him.

She already owed too many people, and she'd rather she and Zach be on more even ground.

"We're not bothering him," Elijah said, turn-ing back to his task, unconcerned. "We're helping him make dinner."

"He said we could," Mitch added, eyes worried as he glanced at Zach. "Right?"

Zach nodded. "Get your new guest settled?"

"Yes. No. I mean…" She shook her head. "Josie's not exactly a guest."

Mitch tugged on Zach's empty sleeve. What had happened to her son's fear of him? For goodness' sake, she was only gone fifteen minutes. Had the entire world gone mad?

"Josie has a baby in her tummy," Mitch told Zach. "Ivy had a baby in her tummy but now he's out but he can't care for us until he grows some more. He's boring. And he smells funny."

"He came out through her vagina," Elijah said, hopping onto Mitch's chair with him—the better to join the conversation and give his little brother a light shove in the back. "But we still don't know how he got in there."

"I know," Mitch said, raising his hand like he was in class at his preschool. "She swallowed it."

Zach's eyebrows rose. "Yeah?"

"Yep," Mitch said, all enthusiasm and earnestness. "But it's super small, like a seed, when they swallow it."

"Nuh-uh," Elijah said, his condescending sneer reminding her of Shane. "That's not how it happens. The daddy puts the baby in the mommy."

Mitch faced him. "The daddy feeds the mommy the seed."

"No, he gives her a shot," Elijah said. "Ryan's brother told him the daddy pokes the mommy."

Oh, dear Lord...

Face flaming, Fay's eyes met Zach's. If he was uncomfortable with the topic of conversation, he didn't show it. Just held her gaze easily, a smile playing on his lips.

"The daddy's a doctor?" Mitch asked.

Elijah shrugged. "Probably a nurse." He looked at Zach. "Is that how it happens?"

"Close, in some ways," he said, his deep voice serious, but when he glanced at Fay there was a definite glint of amusement in his dark eyes. "But way off in others."

"Boys," Fay said weakly, stepping forward before they decided to draw a diagram or contemplate more on what *poking* meant, "it's time to go upstairs."

"We're not done," Elijah said, jumping onto his

own chair. Then back to his brother's. Then back to his again. "I have to finish stirring the salad dressing."

"I'm snapping beans," Mitch said, holding up a green bean. "Look."

And he snapped it in half.

"Good job. But I'm sure Mr. Castro has had quite enough of your help for one day."

Elijah continued jumping from chair to chair. "No, he hasn't."

"He only has one hand," Mitch told her as if the man in question wasn't standing next to him. "So he needs us to help him 'cuz it's hard for him to do stuff like cut tomatoes and snap beans."

"Can't argue with that," Zach said, and she wasn't sure if he was talking to himself—accepting his limitations—or her.

She wanted to insist her boys march themselves up to their apartment and spend the few hours until bedtime in some quiet activity so she could wrap her head around the events of the day. But she didn't like forcing her children to do something they didn't want to do and the chances of them actually listening to her were slim to none.

And the last thing she needed was to prove her ineffectiveness as a mother in front of Zach Castro.

"Fine." Yes, she was giving in to them, but honestly, she didn't have the strength to force the issue right now. "You can finish helping Mr. Castro. I'll just…" She looked around the spotless kitchen.

Felt useless and unnecessary. She pulled out a chair from the table and perched on the edge of it. "I guess I'll just sit here and wait."

Well, that had come out quite pitiful. Not that the boys noticed. Or cared. Elijah stirred something in a small bowl and Mitchell snapped another bean.

"Everything okay?" Zach asked.

"Everything's fine," she said, giving him a grin that was more toothy than chipper but was the best she could summon at the moment. "I just don't want the boys to be a nuisance—"

"They're not."

"That's kind of you to say, but I'm sure you have better things to do than supervise my children—"

"Not really."

"Still," she continued, proud of her firm tone, of her persistence in the face of Zach's dark, assessing gaze. "I never would have told them to wait for me here if I'd known you were going to be making your dinner."

He stilled. Nodded as if realizing some hidden meaning in her argument. "I see."

"You see what?"

"The real reason you don't want the boys around me." He shrugged, but the movement was stiff. Angry. He began to move toward her, away from the boys. "You don't trust me."

CHAPTER FOURTEEN

"ACTUALLY," FAY TOLD ZACH, "this has nothing to do with you."

And what a relief it was to say that, to mean it. To know that her feelings, the thoughts in her head, were focused on her choices, actions and emotions and nothing else. No one else.

"I need to stop turning to other people for help so often," she continued, "especially with my sons. I rely on my parents or Maddie—or I *used* to rely on her—to watch them, to step in and handle things when I get overwhelmed. But I need to handle things on my own."

It was the only way to protect herself. To finally become and remain strong.

It was the only way to stay out of the darkness.

"But just when I think I'm getting the hang of doing for myself," she continued, "of handling something on my own, I find my sons standing next to each other, with a virtual stranger, and they're not even trying to tear each other's heads off."

Zach's eyebrows rose. "And that's a bad thing?"

She shrugged, feeling small and irritable. "No,

it's wonderful. It's just…they never behave this well for me," she admitted on a whisper. "At least, not very often." She sighed. "Maddie says it's because children are like dogs, they can sense when a person means what they say and who is really in charge. She says I'm too lenient with them, that I let them walk all over me and I'm too nice. Dr. Porter says I'm afraid of conflict, even with my children, because I fear people leaving me, not liking me and being upset with me."

"And what do you think?"

She blinked. That wasn't something most people asked her. They usually told her what to think, how to act. Her own fault, she knew, for letting it happen so often, for doing as she was told without argument. "I think they both have valid points," she admitted. "But they're wrong. I'm not afraid of losing my sons' love or worried about having them upset with me. Or at least, not much." She stared at her hands in her lap, couldn't meet his eyes. "Maybe I am too nice. I don't want them upset or sad or disappointed, but it's only because I hate for them to feel the way I feel sometimes, even for a minute. And because…because I owe them. So much. I have to make up for what I did."

"Your depression isn't your fault," Zach said quietly, his body between her and her sons, his voice soft so they couldn't hear from across the kitchen. He watched her intently, and when she didn't look back at him, he brushed his fingertips over the back of her hand. "It's not your fault."

"I know my illness isn't my fault, but that doesn't make me feel any less responsible on the days I'm unable to get out of bed to play with my sons. But what I need to make up for is what happened two years ago. I...I took some pills," she said, voice raw, throat tight. "I didn't mean to. At least, I don't think I meant to, but the truth is, I don't even remember. I was completely submerged in the darkness and the only way out that I could see was to take those pills and just...disappear. I couldn't take the pain anymore."

Now he held her hand and she clutched his in return. "You're a survivor."

She shook her head. "I'm weak."

He shifted closer, his knee pressing against her thigh. "No. You're strong. Suicide isn't a choice. It's part of something bigger. People don't commit suicide—they die from it like any other illness. But you beat it. You survived. And you're still surviving. You're taking care of yourself and your kids, you're working, you're getting stronger each and every day. You don't owe your kids anything other than your love, time and attention."

"I hope you're right."

"I am."

If only she could be that confident. Well, she was working on that. Making small strides. But she did wish she could leap ahead and be happy and healthy now. Right now.

"I just… I don't want to ask for help all my life," she told him.

Zach glanced at the boys—both snapping beans into teeny, tiny pieces—then pulled out a chair and sat facing her. "Everyone needs help now and again."

"Maddie doesn't," she said, shooting for a breezy, dry tone but sounding more petulant than anything else. "Neither do my parents or Neil."

It was an unpleasant realization she'd come to a few nights ago as she'd lain awake in bed, staring at her ceiling. Her parents, her brother and her best friend didn't need her. "I have to be more like them," she continued, rubbing her thumbnail along the edge of the table. "I want to be."

"You think not accepting or asking for help will cure you of your depression?"

"Not at all. I'm not even sure my depression can be cured. But it can be managed. I can manage it by making changes in my life."

"Like being more independent."

Her shoulders sagged with relief. With gratitude. He'd listened. More than that, he understood. "For a start."

"Changes like taking control of your life. Being the one who offers help instead of asks for it?"

"That, too."

"Is that why you took in your ex-husband's pregnant fiancée?"

Fay's jaw went slack. "Ex-excuse me?"

"Your new guest," he said as Mitch giggled in the background at Elijah's impersonation of a mutant ninja turtle battling evil with two green beans. "It's the girl who came here last week, right?"

"I don't remember telling you that."

"When the boys told me that your new guest was pregnant, I figured it out."

Of course he did. Didn't she already know he was intuitive? That he saw too much?

It was extremely annoying.

"I didn't plan on letting her stay here," Fay said, and wished she didn't sound so apologetic. She'd done nothing wrong; there was no reason to worry he would be disappointed in her or think less of her. "It just sort of happened."

He remained silent for a moment then nodded slowly as if her nonexplanation made perfect sense. "What about your ex?"

She touched the ring she still wore, hidden under her shirt. Forced her hand away. "Shane walked out on her last week. She hasn't heard from him since."

"So you gave her a room."

"And a job."

Fay waited for him to tell her she'd made a huge mistake. That she was naive, too trusting. That

Josie would take advantage of her. That's what Neil would say. What her parents would be thinking.

At least with her and Maddie not being on speaking terms she could avoid hearing it from her, as well.

But Zach didn't say any of those things. She almost wished he had.

"Paying for your husband's sins?" he asked quietly.

She jerked, her fingers once again wanting to touch the ring, feel the symbol of her marriage, of her hope for the future.

She wished she could deny it. Admitting she felt guilty over Shane's choices meant she wasn't as ready to let go of those hopes, of that future, as she'd claimed. As she needed to be.

And maybe she wasn't. But she would be. Until then, she'd just have to act as if she was already over him.

"Josie has nowhere to go," Fay said, as close to an honest answer as she could give. "No one to turn to. She's young and scared and alone. And I understand what she's going through."

Zach nodded. "Because he left you, too."

"No. Because we both trusted him. We loved him. Now we're left to wonder how we could have been so completely fooled. So stupid to believe his lies. And while I can't speak for Josie, I'm also left wondering if I didn't get exactly what I deserved."

Zach's expression hardened. "That's bullshit."

"That's a bad word!" Elijah, of the bionic hearing—when it came to cursing—shouted gleefully.

Zach ignored him.

Fay flushed with shame and embarrassment. Ducked her head. No, she thought, staring at her feet, her breathing ragged, her fingers curled into her palms, she wasn't ashamed or embarrassed. She was insulted. And so angry she could barely see straight.

Swallowing, she forced her head up. "It's how I feel."

"You're not to blame for the choices he made."

"You're right. I'm responsible for the choices *I* made. I chose to believe Shane. To believe he was still the same man he used to be. My entire life was about him, what he wanted. What he needed. How to get him back." She stood, her knees unsteady but her voice surprisingly firm. "Now I'm feeling gullible and stupid. Both of which," she continued when Zach opened his mouth as if to argue, "I not only have a right to feel, but maybe I need to feel in order to finally break this cycle. And the last thing I need in my life at the moment is one more person telling me what I should think, and what I feel is wrong.

"Boys," she called, brushing past him toward her sons, "get down. We're leaving."

"But you said we could stay!" Elijah reminded her.

"I've changed my mind. Come on." She clapped

her hands as if the sound alone carried some magical power capable of convincing her sons to obey her. "Tell Mr. Castro thank you for letting you help and let's go."

Mitchell scrambled down and ran over to her, pressed his body against her leg. "Thank you," he told Zach, as solemn as a judge thanking a jury for their time.

"You're welcome," Zach responded in kind.

"*We* were helping *him*," Elijah said. "He should thank us."

"He *let* you help him…" And she was not going to allow herself to get sidetracked by a seven-year-old's strange logic. She straightened her shoulders. "Thank Mr. Castro and get down."

Elijah jumped from his chair to Mitchell's and back again. "No. I don't want to."

There was the rub. And the reason he didn't listen to her. Because she hated to make her children do something they didn't want to. Couldn't handle them being upset.

No one has died from being uncomfortable.

She slid Zach a glance, almost expecting him to give her an arrogant look, as if he'd heard his own words playing in her head. But his expression was neutral. Expectant. Waiting to see what she'd do next. How she handled this.

A test for her to fail? She had no idea.

"I understand you don't want to." It was important to her that the boys knew she heard them, took their feelings into consideration. "But you have homework and we have our own dinner to make."

Unconvinced, Elijah kept right on jumping. "No."

Forcing Fay to fall back on the tried and true. "I'm going to count to three." She didn't bother adding what would happen when she reached three—mainly because she had no idea. "One…" He leaped back and forth. Back and forth. "Two…" He changed to a hop, squatting low then swinging his arms as he bounced. "Three…"

More hopping.

Her face flamed. This wasn't going her way at all. She was completely inept at dealing with her own child, and, best of all, Zach got to witness the whole scene.

And after she'd stood up for herself so well only moments earlier.

"Elijah," she began, stepping forward, only to stop.

She had no idea what to do next. She could yank him down and drag him upstairs, but that might scar him for life. She could plead with him, but that had stopped working on him years ago. She could offer to let him stay up past his bedtime or to buy him a new video game, but that seemed counterintuitive to him learning to obey her because she was his mother and for no other reason.

Then Zach took matters into his own hands and took away the second chair.

"Hey," Elijah cried, red faced and sweaty, "I'm jumping on that!"

"You're done jumping," Zach said, as if he didn't care one way or the other that Elijah was close to tears, his shoulders rigid and up to his ears—sure signs he was about to throw an epic tantrum. "You're going to get down and thank me for letting you help with my dinner, then you're going to go upstairs and do your homework and whatever else your mother tells you to do. And you're going to do it all without complaining or arguing."

"I don't need your help," Fay told him, which was a lie; even her own sons looked at her as if waiting for her nose to grow.

Maybe she could use a bit of assistance, but she didn't like that he'd taken over without asking what she wanted.

Didn't like that he hadn't given her any choice.

Suddenly Elijah jumped down, said, "Thank you," to Zach and headed up the stairs.

Yes, clearly she was an independent, self-sufficient woman who needed no one.

Well, she wouldn't thank Zach for his help or apologize for being so sharp with him—no matter how badly she wanted to do both. Chin lifted, she took Mitch's hand and headed toward the staircase.

And told herself she wasn't disappointed when he let her walk away.

AFTER TWO DAYS of cold, rainy weather, Friday had dawned crisp and clear, the temperatures climbing into the high sixties.

Warm enough, Zach had thought, to enjoy a beer on the patio off his room.

That illusion had been shattered as soon as the sun started sinking. His breath frosted in the air, the cold stung his ears and the tip of his nose.

Still, he remained outside. Once he put on a jacket over his sweatshirt, the cool breeze became tolerable. And he had a great view of the sun setting behind the rolling hills to his right. Could hear the hoot of an owl. The rustle of the wind through the trees.

It was peaceful. Bradford House quiet behind him, the other guests either in their rooms or out for the evening.

Headlights cut through the twilight, bounced off the windows at the back of the B&B. A moment later, Fay pulled into her parking spot. She and the boys had been getting into the van when he'd stepped onto the patio not twenty minutes ago. They hadn't noticed him.

Not that she would have acknowledged him. For the past two days she'd done her best to pretend he no longer existed. If he entered a room where she was, she left, as if suddenly remembering she had somewhere else to be. If he walked by her, she averted her gaze and kept right on going, as if she didn't see him. She also no longer showed up to work out with him in the mornings.

She wasn't avoiding him, like she'd admitted to doing at the beginning of the week—she was completely ignoring him.

He couldn't say he cared for it much.

Guess he had more of his father's arrogance in him than he'd realized.

So far he'd made it easy for her to pretend he didn't exist by not starting any conversations or trying to engage her in any way, not even a simple greeting.

He hadn't pushed her.

Mainly because he hadn't expected her to hold out this long.

That she had—and that he was on the receiving end of her anger—irritated him to no end.

And made him proud as hell.

"Nice night," he called, setting his beer aside as she walked past him, arms swinging.

Her steps slowed but she didn't start, didn't whirl around, proving what he'd suspected—she'd known he was there all along.

She stopped and faced him. The setting sun behind her cast her face in shadows but haloed her head, made her hair look darker, more red than blond. The colors encircled her, the oranges and reds shimmering along her arms and legs as if they'd originated within her.

It reminded him of when he'd first seen her

last week sitting in the sunshine, a sweet smile on her face. There was nothing sweet about how she looked now with the wind lifting the ends of her hair, nothing soft about the set of her shoulders, the tilt of her chin.

She looked strong. Powerful.

And so beautiful it hurt him just to breathe.

Her shoulders rose and fell on a long sigh. "Yes. It is a very nice evening."

A response, if not exactly an invitation to prolong the conversation. He'd take it.

And push for more.

"You forgot something," he said as he stood.

She glanced at her purse strap on her shoulder then opened her palm where he assumed she carried her keys. Startled when she looked up to find him walking toward her. "No, I didn't."

"The boys?" He'd expected them to burst out of the minivan the moment she'd turned off the ignition, Elijah racing around, talking a mile a minute, and a grinning Mitchell chasing after him.

He'd found himself looking forward to it.

Surprisingly, he'd had a good time with them the other night, listening to their chatter, answering their questions. He wasn't used to being around kids, but he'd gotten a kick out of Elijah's imagination and energy. Had found Mitch's sweet smiles and eager-to-please personality endearing.

"They're with my parents." She hesitated as if

unsure whether or not to tell him more. "The Blue Jackets are playing the Pens in Pittsburgh," she said as if that explained it all.

Which, he supposed, it did. The Pens, he knew from working at O'Riley's, were Pittsburgh's professional hockey team. Her brother, Neil, played for the Blue Jackets. "You don't like hockey?"

"I love it."

He noted her robotic tone, as if she'd been programmed to respond exactly that way to that specific question. "You sure about that?"

"I like hockey. I've just seen enough of it to last a lifetime. Endless practices when Neil was little, driving hundreds of miles to games, weekends spent sitting in cold rinks when he had a tournament. For years, my entire life revolved around hockey. Revolved around my brother playing hockey," she corrected. "So I'm taking tonight off. Because I want to. Although," she continued, "part of that decision might be because Maddie will be there."

"Guess I'm not the only person you don't want to see."

"I… You…" She pressed her lips together. Gave a sigh and met his eyes. "No. You're not the only one."

Her admission didn't make him feel any better. Or, he realized with a start, any less alone.

Which was nuts. He didn't mind being by himself. But he wanted to be with her.

He wanted to spend more time with her, to keep her talking. And she was already edging toward the door. Away from him.

"Are you hungry?" he asked, stilling her escape.

She blinked. "Excuse me?"

"I ordered pizza," he said, checking his watch. "It should be here any minute."

She stared at him blankly. "You ordered pizza?"

"I ordered pizza. And salad and wings." The back of his neck warmed and he grabbed it. Squeezed hard. He didn't need to recite the menu. He just needed to ask a straightforward question— no matter how afraid he was of not getting the answer he wanted.

"Will you have dinner with me, Fay?"

It came out gruffly. Impatient and bordering on irritated. Not quite the romantic invitation he was sure a woman like Fay dreamed of.

Her eyes widened, her face paled.

Then again, that wasn't the response he was used to.

"You want to have dinner with me?"

Did she have to sound so freaking appalled? Like he'd asked her if she wanted to go out and find some stray cats they could string up by their tails.

He shoved his hand into his jacket pocket. Curled it into a fist. "Yes."

She took a step back. Then another. Christ, she might as well kick his ego in the balls.

"I don't think that's a good idea," she finally said, glancing at the house over her shoulder as if gauging her escape.

"Why not?"

More blinking. At this rate, she'd have a seizure or something. "Because you're a guest at Bradford House and I'm the manager."

"You have rules about eating meals with guests?"

She frowned. "Well, no, but…but I'm working tonight."

"And you don't eat when you're working?"

"Yes. No. I mean, I can eat—"

"Just not with a guest." When she didn't respond, he moved in closer. "Or just not with me?"

"Both."

"You're still pissed at me."

She tipped her head to the side. "Are you asking me if I am? Or telling me?"

He opened his mouth to ask why that mattered when it hit him—that was the problem. Three nights ago in the kitchen, he'd told her what to think, how she should feel. As if he was somehow inside her head. Knew her heart.

Just like everyone else in her life did.

He was an ass.

"I'm asking. Are you still pissed at me?"

"I'm trying to be."

Fighting a smile at her grudging tone, he nodded. "You're doing a good job."

"I don't like being angry," she said, like a guilty secret.

The breeze picked up, carried her light, sweet scent to him. "Because it's uncomfortable?"

I'm not comfortable being emotionally uncomfortable.

"Because it's dangerous."

Dangerous? "I don't understand."

"I don't like to lose control of my emotions. I have to keep them in check so I don't make another mistake."

"What was your first mistake?" When she hesitated he continued, "Taking those pills?"

She nodded. "My second was attacking Shane the way I did," she finally said, shivering though the wind had died down. "At his motel room? I shouldn't have gotten so upset. I need to be more careful."

"After everything your ex did, you deserved to get a few licks in. My opinion," he added, not wanting her to think he was saying how she felt was wrong. Just that it was different from his own view.

"He wasn't always like that," she blurted out, then bit her lower lip, her brows drawing together. "At least, I don't think he was. But maybe my memories are skewed. No one else seems to remember Shane being sweet or doting or fun.

Maybe I made it all up. Saw what I wanted to see. Pretended he was who I needed him to be. But for so long, all I did was remember how he used to be, how *I* remembered him being. All I could focus on was getting that man back." Her smile was small and sad. "It was hard, seeing the truth, realizing that everyone around me had been right about him. That I'd been so wrong. Harder yet to accept the part I played in my own misery. So when I finally took some responsibility for my own choices and actions—after years of being told that was exactly what I needed to do—and then you told me it wasn't my fault, that I was wrong, I…"

He raised his eyebrows. "Wanted to rip my throat out?"

"I lashed out at you," she said slowly. Softly. "Because I thought you were different. That you saw something in me that no one else had. Some inner strength or willpower. But when you look at me, you only see what everyone else does. Weakness."

Son of a bitch. He'd really messed up.

And now he had to make it right.

But to do that, he'd have to open up. Would have to share a piece of himself and his past that he'd never shared with anyone. It was either that or let her walk away. For good.

There was no choice. Not for him.

"When I was a kid," he began, only to stop.

Shift. His chest was tight, his palm sweaty. "When I was a kid," he repeated, quick and sharp, as if getting the words out faster would make this easier, "my stepfather used to hit me." Zach snorted. "Actually, he used to beat the hell out of me."

She made a sound of distress. Reached for him. "Zach, I—"

Shaking his head, he stepped back and her hand fell to her side. "Look, I'm not going to get into the gory details. Suffice it to say, he was a drunk, and a mean one at that, but even sober he found ways to make my life miserable. He resented me because I was another man's son. Hated me because he was jealous of my father's wealth and power and that the child support Senior sent each month paid for the house he lived in. The food he ate. And since he couldn't take his frustrations out on Senior, he took them out on the next best thing."

"You," Fay said, her face white.

"I walked around my house like a ghost, trying to be invisible, hoping he didn't see me. That he'd somehow forget I was even there. But it didn't matter how quiet I was, how respectful or obedient. I'd always end up doing something to set him off."

"He made you think it was your fault," she whispered.

Zach nodded. Held her gaze. "It wasn't. I realize that now. Someday, I hope you realize that what your ex did to you, how he treated you, wasn't your fault. But I shouldn't have demanded it of you the other night. I let my past, what happened with my stepfather, color my judgment. I said some things I had no right saying. And I'm sorry. I'm sorry for upsetting you. For making you feel in any way less than."

"Less than what?"

"Less than the capable, strong, amazing woman you are."

At his quiet, sincere words, color flooded her cheeks. "Oh," she said weakly, staring at him as if stunned. She swallowed. "Oh."

He couldn't help it—he had to touch her. He slid his fingers over the back of her wrist. She twitched but didn't pull away, so he pushed for more, wrapping his fingers around her hand and tugging her a step closer. "Do you forgive me, Fay?"

She stared down at their hands for a moment. "Yes," she breathed. "I forgive you."

He wanted to pull her to him, wrap his arm around her and hold her. Feel those soft curves pressed against him. Inhale the scent of her skin. Taste her mouth. But when she lifted her head, he didn't see an answering desire in her eyes. He saw confusion. Fear.

Guilt.

"Thank you." He squeezed her hand gently then let go. "Have a good night."

He turned and headed back to the porch. He'd

take his beer inside, wait for his dinner to show up and spend the rest of his evening alone. Thinking about Fay. Wanting Fay.

Yeah. Sounded about right—it was the way he'd spent the past few nights.

Goddamn her.

He swiped up his beer and headed toward the French doors.

"Wait," Fay called, and it was as if he no longer controlled his own body. It stopped, despite his brain wanting it to keep right on walking, to step inside his room and shut the door firmly behind him.

Instead he stood there, his back to her, his jaw aching from grinding his teeth.

In the reflection in the glass, he watched her approach only to hesitate at the edge of the patio. She lifted her hand to her chest, her fingers lingering there for a moment before she lowered her arm.

"I've changed my mind. I think I am hungry after all."

CHAPTER FIFTEEN

SHE WAS NERVOUS.

Which was ridiculous, Fay assured herself. There was nothing to be nervous about. Zach had invited her to join him for pizza and she'd accepted, that was all.

But she'd accepted after she'd already turned him down, had been avoiding him for the past two days and admitted how much he'd hurt her the other night.

Yes, well, perhaps there was good reason to be nervous.

But this was Zach. Zach who thought she was capable and strong and amazing—words no other person had ever used to describe her. But he'd looked her in the eye and had spoken with complete sincerity. Wanting her to believe him. Willing her to.

Plus, he'd apologized for what happened the other night. *He'd* apologized to *her*.

That was a rarity in and of itself. She was used to being the one offering up contrition, hurrying to show her remorse, begging for forgiveness, promising to change.

Do you forgive me, Fay? he'd asked, and the low timbre of his voice had tugged at something deep in her belly. There'd been no way she could refuse.

But maybe her turnaround about dinner was too little, too late. He was still standing in front of the doors to his room, his back rigid, his left arm bent in front of him.

She went hot then cold all over. Crossed her arms and cleared her throat. "Unless you've changed your mind."

Finally, he faced her, and she saw he held a bottle of beer in his hand. The same hand that had held her hand only moments before. Her palm still tingled. She could still feel the warmth of his skin.

He walked toward her and it took all she had to stand her ground. There was something almost predatory about him now, as if he was stalking her—hunter to prey. Something heated and raw in his eyes, in the way he held himself. Something…sexual.

The thought both thrilled and terrified her, though she wasn't sure which emotion came out ahead. Not that it mattered. She couldn't possibly be seeing what she thought she was seeing. It was only her very active imagination taking over once again. Her own wayward thoughts coloring her view of things because of her reaction to his touch, which had been surprising in its intensity. Her entire body had warmed, her blood seeming to thicken and slow as it moved through her veins in a way that could only be described as one thing.

Desire.

Terror edged out excitement. How could this be happening? She couldn't be attracted to another man. She was still getting over Shane. Still reeling from the events of last week that had upended her life, made her question everything she'd thought she wanted.

No. No, these…sensations she experienced when she was close to Zach, the surging pulse and quickened heart rate, were defense mechanisms. Ways for her to handle the loss of her husband, of the future she'd dreamed of for years. Like a rebound relationship, one meant to boost her confidence, to stroke her ego. To help her move on.

But she wasn't ready to move on. She needed time to process her loss. To grieve it properly. To heal.

And anyway, she couldn't believe that someone like Zach Castro—confident and sexy and strong—would be interested in her in any way other than friendship, at best.

A project, at worst.

"You changed your mind about the pizza?" Zach asked when he stood before her, a scowl on his handsome face, his knuckles white around the beer bottle.

"Yes." The pizza and nothing else.

"Are you feeling sorry for me, Fay?"

At the moment she was busy feeling sorry for herself. She didn't want him to see her as someone who needed his help. Who needed him to fix her messed-up life.

She wanted him to see her as his equal.

But then she realized what he was asking. Why he was asking it. "I feel sorry for the little boy you were," she said, knowing her words were inadequate for what she felt. For the depth of emotion, of sadness over him being abused. But she wouldn't let him see how much it tore her up. She'd stay strong. For him.

She smiled. "This isn't a pity date." A fierce blush heated her face so quickly, so intensely, her eyes watered. "Not that this is a date," she rushed out, horrified by what had just come out of her mouth, then realized she was making it worse. "Not that I wouldn't go on a date with you... I mean... I don't want to go on a date with you..." She squeezed her eyes shut. "I think I just blacked out for a moment. Please tell me I've been passed out on the ground this entire time."

"Sorry," he said, not sounding sorry at all. Actually, he sounded almost chipper. "But if you were unconscious, you were talking the whole time."

She opened her eyes, forced herself to meet his gaze, because that's what a strong, confident, independent woman would do.

So far being strong, confident and independent was extremely overrated.

"You must think I'm an idiot," she said.

"You have no idea what I think of you."

But she did, she realized with a jolt of pleasure. He thought she was capable and strong and amazing.

A slow, satisfied grin spread over her face as a car pulled into the parking lot, a Panoli's Pizza sign on the side.

"So, are you going to share your pizza with me or not?" she asked, having no idea where she'd found the courage to ask such a question.

She preferred only asking questions she knew the answers to. It was safer that way.

The car stopped and the driver—a local boy Fay recognized from church—got out then opened the back door for the food. "You sure this isn't a pity date?" Zach asked.

"Not a date," she said, touching her ring under her shirt, hoping he understood that this couldn't be any kind of date. It was too soon.

"Not a date," he repeated. "Not a pity pizza party. What would you call it?"

She had no idea. Technically, their eating together could be construed as a date. It hit all the high points: two single adults about to share a meal where they would converse about their lives. Get to know each other.

Yes, put that way, it definitely sounded like a date.

"I'd call it two friends having pizza and beer on a Friday night," she said.

"Is that what we are?" he asked quietly, probably so the approaching pizza delivery guy didn't hear him. "Friends?"

She felt like there was more to his question. Something hidden and dangerous that, if found, if probed too deeply, would blow up in her face. Tear her life apart.

"I'm not sure. But I wouldn't mind if we were." She glanced at the pizza guy, who nodded in greeting, his hands full with a bag of takeout containers on top of a large pizza box. She stepped closer to Zach and lowered her voice. "Not to pressure you or anything, but I could really use a friend." She smiled. "And I really love Panoli's Pizza."

Holding her breath she waited—seemed she was always waiting for someone else to decide what would happen next. But she'd taken a chance. Had stepped out of her comfort zone and offered Zach her friendship.

She really, really hoped he accepted it. That he accepted her.

"Far be it from me to keep a friend from her favorite pizza," Zach said as the pizza guy reached them.

She smiled, relieved and grateful and maybe more excited than pizza with a friend warranted.

"Hey," the kid said. He checked the slip taped to the bag. "I have a large tossed salad, house dressing, order of bread sticks, dozen hot wings and a large loaded pizza for Castro."

"That's me," Zach said.

Fay took the food from the kid while Zach pulled out his wallet. "I'll run up to my apartment and get us some drinks then meet you in the kitchen," she told him before heading toward the house, feeling like a pizza thief, scurrying away with his order. But if she stayed, he'd argue with her about who should carry the food inside. While she was sure he'd be fine balancing it all with one hand, she had two, so why should he struggle when she was able to help him?

Shifting the food to one arm, she opened the back door and stepped into the kitchen. "I'm back," she told Gracie Weaver, who had covered for Fay while she dropped the boys off at her parents' house and was now at the table reading a paperback. "Thanks for staying late. Any problems?"

"Nope. I gave the couple from DC a couple of suggestions for dinner, told them about Thad Sircy's band playing at the Barn Door. They said they might check it out."

Fay set the food on the table. "Great. Did the bridesmaids arrive?"

They were expecting a party of four from Buffalo who were celebrating a bachelorette party and bridal shower over the weekend.

"Not yet." Gracie closed her book and stood and stretched gracefully. A pixie with big, expressive gray eyes, curly light brown hair that reached her waist and a penchant for wearing thrift store finds, the talkative eighteen-year-old was a favorite among Bradford House's staff and guests.

And now that Fay was no longer on speaking terms with Maddie, and Ivy had moved to Houston, Gracie was also the closest thing to a girlfriend Fay had.

What that said about her current social situation, she had no idea. But she was extremely glad to have Gracie in her life. And that Gracie had decided to attend the University of Pittsburgh in the fall and continue working at Bradford House.

"I didn't know you were getting Panoli's," Gracie said, and, before Fay could stop her, she'd set aside the bag and opened the pizza box. She wrinkled her nose. "This thing is like a cancer pie. And I mean that literally. Processed meats are death bombs just waiting to go off in your body."

"I'll keep that in mind," Fay promised as she crossed the room. "But I didn't order the pizza. One of our guests did."

And the only reason she didn't tell Gracie that it was Zach's food—and that Fay would be sharing it with him—was because she wanted to get up to her apartment and drop her purse and keys off. Not because she was afraid Gracie might get the wrong idea about their dinner.

Not because she didn't want anyone to know about it.

After discussing tomorrow's work schedule, Fay and Gracie said their goodbyes and Fay went up to her apartment. She purposely did not check her reflection in the hallway mirror, just as she didn't change out of her baggy sweatshirt or worry about her hair. This wasn't a date, she reminded herself as she opened her refrigerator for the drinks. It was pizza. With a new friend. A very handsome, extremely interesting, completely male new friend.

Maybe her current social situation wasn't so bad after all.

"YOU DIDN'T HAVE to wait for me," Fay said as she entered the kitchen carrying a six-pack of beer in one hand, a bottle of wine in the other.

Zach stood and took the wine from her. He'd been sitting at the table for almost ten minutes. Long enough to wonder if she'd changed her mind.

He hadn't liked how disappointed he'd been at the thought. "To tell you the truth, I'm half afraid to eat anything."

Setting the beer on the table, Fay smiled. "Ah. You spoke with Gracie."

"Little hippie girl with long curly hair?" he asked. Fay nodded. "I wouldn't say I spoke with her. She did all the talking." And he meant *all*. The kid barely paused long enough between words to take a breath. "I've now been thoroughly informed on the dangers of processed meats and animal fats."

He hadn't had the heart to tell the kid he didn't eat like this every day. That this was one of his twice-weekly splurge meals and that this was the first time he'd had wings or sausage-laden pizza in over two months.

Fay got plates and bowls from a cupboard, set them on the counter to grab two forks and a roll of paper towels, then carried it all to the table. He opened the wine for her—a fairly easy task even with one hand—and poured her a glass. Since he'd already had a beer, he stuck with water. He divided the salad between the bowls and they started eating.

"You got a haircut," she said a moment later, setting her fork down as if this was some huge discovery.

He ran his hand over the back of his neck. "Yeah. Kane said I was scaring his customers."

"Your brother told you to cut your hair?"

"It helps that in this instance he wasn't speaking as my brother, but as my boss." While he could tell his brother to kiss ass, saying that to one's boss wasn't the best idea.

"And your beard is trimmed."

Zach forced himself not to rub his fingers over it. He shrugged. "I figured I might as well. Since they offered it at the barbershop." He noticed her frowning, playing with her salad and not eating. "Something wrong?"

"I didn't notice. Outside. I didn't notice you got a haircut."

"That hardly makes you a horrible person," he said. "One time my sister, Daphne, cut six inches off her hair and I didn't notice it for over a week."

Fay stabbed a piece of lettuce. "I met your sister, did I tell you that?" He shook his head. "When she was here for Kane and Charlotte's wedding over Christmas. She's very pretty and seemed extremely nice."

Finished with his salad, he wiped his mouth with a paper towel. "She's both, plus she's smart. Smartest one in our family." He pointed at Fay with his fork. "But if you tell her I said that, I'll deny it. Her ego is already big enough."

"You love her."

"She's a pain in my ass, but I'm crazy about her," he said. Setting chicken wings and a slice of pizza on his plate, he looked up to find Fay smiling hugely at him. He couldn't help but grin back. "What?"

"It's nice. That you and she have that bond."

"What about you? You and your brother seem pretty tight."

"We are, but the balance of power in our relationship has always been skewed." She took a bite of salad and chewed thoughtfully for a moment.

"Neil's always been my protector and I've always been his responsibility. I guess it never bothered me until recently. And while I appreciate all he's done for me, the financial support and this job, I think it's time I stopped relying on him so much. I just wish I knew where to start."

She looked so nervous, as if she'd committed some great sin wanting to stand on her own two feet. As if her brother would be upset with her. "Tell him what you told me. I'm sure he'll be proud of you for wanting to be more independent."

"He will be. He only wants what's best for me. I hate to bring it up now, though. Neil and I haven't spoken much since Maddie and I broke up."

"Broke up?"

"It was more than a fight. Maddie and I have been friends—were friends—for twenty years and now we're not. Breakup seems like an apt description to me."

He couldn't argue with that. "How does your breakup affect your brother?"

"He's Maddie's boyfriend, so he's in the middle. Which is why I think he's only called me once and texted me twice since it happened."

"Your brother and your best friend are a couple?"

She sipped her wine. Nodded. "They were high school sweethearts and have a fourteen-year-old daughter together, but they split up when Neil went pro." She chose a piece of pizza. "Three years ago they got together again."

"Sounds almost as convoluted as Daphne's relationship with Oakes," he said drily.

"Ivy told me about that. It must be…strange… Your sister being in a relationship with one of your brothers."

"Strange is one way to put it."

"Does it bother you?"

"No," he admitted. "Don't get me wrong. I'm not crazy about them being together, but like I said, Daphne's smart. She knows what she wants and she goes after it. I trust her decisions. And Oakes is a good guy. Even if he is a Bartasavich."

Chewing, she frowned. Swallowed. "But you're a Bartasavich."

"So Daphne keeps pointing out to me."

"You don't like your family?" she asked.

That was tougher to answer than he'd expected. "Hard not to like Oakes." Though Zach gave it his best shot. "And Kane's been good to me, giving me a job at O'Riley's."

His brother never treated him like an invalid. Gave him the same workload he gave his other employees and expected Zach to perform his duties just like everyone else.

"But, no," he continued, "I don't like C.J. He's too much like our old man. Arrogant, bossy and condescending."

"Oh." She broke off a piece of crust. Nibbled on

it. "I can see that. But Ivy's with him, so he must have some redeeming qualities."

Zach snorted. "Yeah. His bank account."

He expected her to get pissed, to tell him that her friend wasn't some gold digger, but instead she laughed, the sound light and musical and so freaking rare, he sat there stunned, unable to look away.

Wanting, more than anything, to hear the sound again.

"Have you met Ivy?" Fay asked, still smiling, her face glowing. "Believe me, if she'd wanted a man just for the size of his bank account she could have pretty much anyone she wanted. No. She loves C.J. Which tells me there's a good reason why she chose him. Why she's stayed with him."

He'd only met Ivy a few times since he'd returned to the States after his injuries. She was, hands down, one of the sexiest, most confident women Zach had ever met. "You may have a point," he conceded.

"Thank you." Fay's grin broadened and she flushed. "Maybe you don't think much of your brothers because you didn't spend a lot of time with them growing up."

"Time enough," he said, debating a third slice. "Weekends and holidays at Senior's house. Until I was old enough to refuse to go."

"You spent weekends at your father's house?"

"And holidays. We all did."

The holidays had been the worst. He'd wanted

to be home with his mother and Daphne, with his grandparents and extended family, but had to endure Thanksgivings and Christmases with Senior. It hadn't been so bad when Senior had still been married to Rosalynn, Oakes's mother. She'd done her best to make the holidays warm and cheerful, had tried to include Zach in the festivities even though it must have been hard for her to have the product of one of her husband's affairs opening presents under the tree with her own son.

"I don't understand," Fay said. "How could he let it happen?"

"What do you mean?"

She leaned forward, looking fierce and angry, her hand fisted on the table. "How could your father let you stay with your mother if he knew your stepfather was beating you?"

"Simple. He didn't know."

Shaking her head, she sat back. "How could he not?"

"He wasn't around much. And," Zach admitted, "I never told him. I never told anyone."

"Because you didn't want them to take you away from your mom and sister," Fay said, eyes knowing and sad.

"I couldn't let that happen. If I lived full time with Senior, he'd stop sending my mom child support. But mostly I was afraid if I wasn't there, Michael would take his anger out on her and Daphne."

Fay reached over, laid her hand on his wrist.

His pulse jumped under her fingers. "I'm so sorry, Zach. Your father should have noticed."

Her understanding blew through him. All those years he'd done his best to hide his bruises. Had made excuses or lied to the few people who questioned his black eye or split lip. But his father never asked.

He'd never noticed.

"He should have," Zach agreed, going with instinct and turning his hand so they were palm to palm. He linked his fingers with hers, stared at the sight of their joined hands, her fingers long and slender, her skin pale and warm. "But he was too focused on himself, on his own needs to pay attention to any of his sons. C.J. always walked the straight and narrow, and Oakes had his mom and stepfather and two younger brothers, but Kane... he got involved in drugs and didn't get clean until a few years after his daughter, Estelle, was born. And I just walked away. Senior was selfish. He seduced my mom when she was barely nineteen. She worked for him, she trusted him—hell, maybe even loved him—and he took advantage of her. And now, because he's sick and can't walk or talk or feed himself, I'm supposed to forgive and forget. It doesn't work that way."

His father hadn't earned Zach's forgiveness, and he'd never once asked for it. Had never admitted his mistakes or apologized for them.

"No," she said softly. "I suppose it doesn't." Her

fingers curled tighter around his. "Did he ever find out about what your stepfather did?"

Zach shook his head. "After a while it didn't matter. Mom kicked Michael out and we moved on. When I was old enough, I took my mom's maiden name so I wouldn't have to be a Bartasavich."

"But it's not that easy, is it?" she asked quietly. "You can change your name, but it doesn't change where you came from. *Who* you came from." She rubbed her thumb over the back of his hand. Back and forth. "Neil and I were adopted by the Pettits— I was almost nine, Neil was going on eleven. Before that our last name was Douglas."

"What happened to your parents?"

"Our biological parents were neglectful."

"You were taken from them?"

"Not until after our mother died. She killed herself. Neil and I found her one day after school."

He squeezed her hand, knowing what she was thinking. "You aren't your mother."

"I'm not, but there are way too many similarities."

"And one big difference. You survived."

"I survived," Fay agreed. Shook her head. "After Mom died, our father left us." She slipped her hand from his and he immediately missed the contact. She stood and picked up her salad bowl as if unable to sit still, unable to look at him when she spoke. "Before that, no one knew how bad it was. They didn't know there were days the only time we ate was at school, or how our father would disappear for long stretches and our mother wouldn't be able to get out of bed." Reaching for his bowl, she glanced at him. "Like you, we were careful not to let anyone know."

Before she could straighten, he took hold of her wrist. "Did they hurt you?"

"No." She tugged lightly and he freed her. "They weren't physically abusive. At least, not to us. But their relationship was volatile. Unhealthy. Neil took care of me. He made sure I took baths and walked me to school and did his best to get something in my belly each day, even if it meant stealing a candy bar from the grocery store."

Neil's always been my protector.

"You were lucky you had each other," Zach said gruffly, imagining her as a little girl, tiny and scared and hungry.

"I'm the lucky one. But when we were put into the foster-care system, they split us up. I was placed with the Pettits while Neil bounced around from foster home to foster home. I was so unhappy and scared without him. Carl and Gerry— my parents—did all they could to get him placed with them, but it took almost a year before he finally came to live with us. They started adoption procedures shortly after that."

"A happy ending," he murmured, standing and crossing to where she stood by the sink.

"A hard-earned one," she said, following his

line of thinking back to when they'd discussed happy endings the night he'd first arrived. "Luckily, it was also the right story. From there on out, Neil and I grew up with two loving, giving parents, and all I pray is that their influence, their guidance, is stronger than any memory or genetic influence our biological parents left us."

"I think that's up to you."

She ducked her head. Sighed. "That's what I'm afraid of."

He didn't like that. Didn't like her doubting herself. "You still don't know, do you?"

"Know what?"

"How strong you are. How capable."

Her eyes were wide, her throat working. "You give me too much credit."

"And you don't give yourself nearly enough." He closed the distance between them, careful not to touch her again—because touching her led to him wanting to continue to touch her. To hold her hand. To brush her hair back. Kiss her. "I don't see weakness when I look at you," he said, remembering what she'd said outside.

"You...you don't?"

"I don't." His fingers twitched with the need to pull her closer, so he stepped back. Shoved his hand into his pocket. "When I look at you I see..." Light and warmth. Peace.

His future.

The thought shook him. But he couldn't pretend it felt anything less than right. Than real.

"When I look at you," he repeated, his voice rough, "I see strength and courage and endless possibilities."

CHAPTER SIXTEEN

THE LAST PERSON Fay expected to see walking up to Bradford House on Mother's Day was Maddie. But no matter how hard she squinted, no matter how many times she blinked, the image of her ex-best friend stalking up the sidewalk in a cobalt blue sundress and pair of low heels, her dark, loose hair flying behind her, remained.

So much for a peaceful Mother's Day.

Fay, sitting on one of the comfy chairs on the wraparound porch, marked her place in the romance book she was reading and set it aside. She sipped her iced tea as Maddie stomped up the stairs, glad her hands were steady because her heart was racing.

"Hello, Maddie," Fay said, all outward calm and composure. Pride swelled at how well she could fake it. *Act as if...act as if...* "Happy Mother's Day."

Maddie wiped the polite greeting away with the swipe of her hand. "What do you think you're doing?"

"Just enjoying this beautiful day."

That was true. It was a gorgeous Sunday complete with blue skies, a brilliant sun and mild temps. And Fay had been enjoying it immensely. Until a few moments ago.

Maddie slammed her hands on her hips. "I mean, why aren't you at your parents' house?"

"Because you're there." As it was obvious Maddie actually was not there, Fay frowned. "Because I *thought* you were going to be there."

Maddie blanched. Swallowed. "Ouch."

Fay refused to feel guilty. Much. Maddie was the one who'd put the limits on their friendship. Who'd given Fay the ultimatum.

She was the one who'd walked away.

And she had no right to come here after over two weeks of no contact, not even a text, and act as if she was the one who'd been wronged. The one who'd been hurt.

"You'd really avoid your own mother—on Mother's Day—just so you don't have to be around me?" Maddie asked.

"I didn't want to, but I thought it would be..." Easier. "Best."

"Gerry is crushed."

Talk about ouch. Fay dropped her gaze, hating that she was hurting her mother in any way. "She understands."

Fay and the boys had gone to Mass earlier with her parents and she'd explained why she wouldn't be attending their weekly brunch. But she'd let them take the boys, just for a few hours, to help make up for her absence.

No, Gerry hadn't been thrilled, but Fay had stood firm, and with her father backing her up, she'd managed to hold her ground.

And now Maddie was here trying to push her around.

Maddie paced, her skirt swirling at her knees when she turned. "Are you trying to punish me? Because the only people you're hurting are yourself and Gerry."

"This isn't about punishment," Fay said as she stood.

Maddie stopped in front of her. Sneered. "No? Then what is it about?"

"It's about no longer doing things just to make other people happy."

Maddie's mouth worked soundlessly for several seconds. "What is going on with you?" she finally managed. "First you let Shane's pregnant girl-friend—"

"Shane's pregnant *ex*-girlfriend."

"Move in here and you give her a job." A fact Fay wasn't surprised Maddie knew, since Fay had felt it only right to tell Neil what was going on at his business. "Then you decide to have Elijah skip a grade—"

"What?" Fay asked, eyes narrowing. "How do you know that?"

Maddie had the decency to look abashed. "Harper may have mentioned it in passing."

"Isn't there some sort of law about teacher-student-parent privilege?"

"I think that's doctors. And lawyers." Maddie frowned. Wrinkled her nose. "And priests."

"Well, teachers should be included in it." Fay had gone to Harper Kavanagh—a second-grade teacher at Shady Grove Elementary School—to discuss the possibility of Elijah skipping first grade and going into second starting this fall.

She should have known Harper, recently engaged to Maddie's older brother Eddie, would say something to Maddie.

"Don't blame Harper," Maddie said. "The only reason she said anything was because she thought I already knew." She sighed. "Do you really think moving ahead a grade is the way to go?"

Fay bristled but fought her rising irritation. She was sure Maddie didn't mean to be insulting—or to speak to Fay in that condescending tone. "I do. More importantly, both his current teacher and Harper agree he should be moved up."

On the advice of Dr. Porter, Fay had held Elijah back from entering kindergarten when he'd turned five. The psychiatrist had felt that Elijah wasn't emotionally mature enough to handle school. But the past few months he'd been acting out in class, complaining that school was boring. His current teacher had recommended, based on his progress this past year and his age, that he join the other kids his own age when school started again.

But ultimately, the choice was left up to Fay. And she'd chosen to trust her gut and agree with the switch.

And she didn't need anyone questioning her decision. Not even if that person had good intentions.

"If that's all," Fay said, gathering up her book and tea, hating that Maddie was chasing her away from what had been a peaceful few moments, "I need to get back inside."

"Wait," Maddie called, stopping her before she could open the door. "I miss you."

Fay turned. Raised her eyebrows at Maddie's begrudging tone. "Really?"

Maddie rolled her eyes. Crossed her arms only to drop them again. Sighed. "Yes. Really. I must have picked up my phone to call you a hundred times."

"But you didn't," Fay said softly. "You didn't, because you didn't think you'd have to."

Holding Fay's gaze, Maddie nodded. "You're right. I thought you'd call me. I was wrong."

"Obviously."

"No. I was wrong for giving you that ultimatum. I knew it that night, but I couldn't stop myself. I was so frustrated. So..." She shook her head, her eyes glistening with unshed tears. "I was so scared for you. For what could happen if Shane hurt you again."

Fay's head snapped back as if she'd been slapped.

Well, she guessed she deserved that. Hadn't she given her loved ones reason to be afraid? "Shane is out of my life," Fay told her. "Not because of anything you or anyone else wanted. It was my decision. It had to be my choice."

"I know."

But Fay wasn't sure she did. Clutching the book to her chest, her glass growing slick with condensation in her other hand, she pulled her shoulders back. "I've always been there for you. I never, not once, turned my back on you. I stood by your side when you got pregnant, I stayed there after you had Bree. I never judged you. Never questioned your decisions. Never threatened to pull my love and support if you didn't do what I wanted you to do."

Maddie was crying now, tears silently streaming down her face. "I know. I…" She wiped her face. Sniffed. "I was wrong. And I'm sorry. I'm sorry for getting so angry with you. I'm sorry I walked out and didn't call. That I withheld Bree from you. But mostly, I'm sorry for letting you think, for even a moment, that I don't appreciate you or cherish our friendship. Because I do. You're the best friend I've ever had. Not just because you're always there for me, but because you're kind and funny and smart. You've got the biggest heart of anyone I know, and it kills me that I hurt you."

Fay's own tears went unchecked. "I'm sorry, too."

"You don't have anything to be sorry for."

But she did. And it was time to accept responsibility for her part in how she and Maddie had gotten to this place. "When something went wrong in my life, I looked to you or Neil or my parents to fix it. I expected you to. I was complacent. Repeating the same mistakes over and over again, expecting a different result and then getting upset when that didn't happen. I leaned on you all, too much. But now…now it's time I stand on my own two feet. And maybe, once I get really good at it, you all will be able to lean on me once in a while."

Maddie sent her a tremulous smile. "Well, you're kicking ass so far with it."

Fay grinned. "Yeah?"

"Definitely."

They both moved at the same time, their hug a rocking one that had Fay's tea sloshing down Maddie's back. She yelped and sprang back. Laughed then wiped her eyes again. "Now, will you please come back to your parents' place with me? I'll give you my slice of coconut cake."

"Only because you don't like coconut cake."

"True. But I'd make the same offer even if it was Gerry's dark chocolate-espresso torte."

"Wow, you really are sorry. Let me just put these inside and tell Damien I'm leaving."

Fay slipped inside, put her book and glass in

the kitchen, and explained to Damien, who was covering for her so she could have Mother's Day off, what was going on. A few minutes later she stepped back onto the porch to find Maddie sitting on the steps, her face tipped up to the sun.

"Ready," Fay said, shutting the door behind her.

Standing, Maddie linked her arm with Fay's and they walked side by side toward Maddie's pickup parked at the curb. "Bree is going to be thrilled. She's so worried the boys didn't do anything for you for Mother's Day, so she might be helping them plan something."

"That's sweet, but the boys both made presents at school. Mitchell made me this bracelet," she said, lifting her hand to show Maddie the ribbon bracelet with felt flowers strung on it. "And Elijah made a painting of flowers in a pot—the base his handprint, the stems his fingers and his thumbprints the petals. Plus, they brought me breakfast in bed."

Which had been the nicest surprise of all.

"Soggy cereal and burned toast?"

"No." Fay fidgeted, turned her bracelet this way, then that. "Actually, it was huevos rancheros."

Maddie whistled. "Fancy. I didn't know Damien dabbled in Mexican cuisine."

Fay cleared her throat. "He doesn't."

"The boys made huevos rancheros by themselves? Doesn't that involve frying eggs?"

"They had help, just not from Damien."

Fay would have been happy to continue walking—in silence—following that statement, but Maddie stopped. And as their arms were still linked, Fay had no choice but to stop, too. "If Damien didn't help them, who did? Please don't say Shane," she murmured, her eyes closed. "Please, please, don't say Shane."

"Of course not Shane." She still hadn't heard from him, and neither had Josie. As far as Fay was concerned, Shane was out of their lives forever. It was getting easier and easier to accept. "Zach helped them."

Maddie frowned. "Who?"

"Zach Castro. Kane Bartasavich's brother?" she added when Maddie continued to look confused. "You met him the night we argued—"

"The veteran?" Maddie asked.

"He was in the service, yes." She waved her hand in front of Maddie's face. "Are you okay? You've stopped blinking."

Maddie shook her head and they started walking again. "Fine. Just…surprised. I hadn't realized you two were such good buddies."

"We're friends, yes." Ever since they'd shared pizza just over a week ago, they'd spent more and more time together. In the fitness room in the mornings working out. In the kitchen in the evenings while he cooked dinner. He'd even gone out back with the boys several times to kick the soccer ball around.

"And he brought you breakfast in bed?"

"Of course not." Though the idea of him in her room, all broad and dark and serious, was strangely...enticing. Not to mention frightening. "He told me the boys asked him to help make me a special breakfast, so I pretended to be asleep while they let him into the apartment and cooked. The boys brought in the food and their cards and gifts and by the time I was done eating, Zach was gone."

Maddie's eyes narrowed. "Leaving you to do the dishes?"

"The kitchen was spotless."

"Oh, boy. He's got it bad."

"Got what bad?" Fay asked as she rounded the front of the truck to the passenger-side door.

Maddie stared at her over the hood as if she'd sprouted a second head. "He's interested in you."

"Don't be ridiculous. We're friends."

"Hmm...so you said. But no guy goes to so much trouble for a woman he wants to be 'friends'—" she made air quotes "—with. Trust me. Zach Castro is looking for more."

Fay felt suddenly warm. From standing in the sun, likely. Though this heat seemed to come from within her body. "You're reading into things. Zach isn't... He doesn't think of me that way."

"Why wouldn't he?" Maddie asked, sounding truly baffled.

"Because I'm not the type of woman a man like Zach would be attracted to."

"You're beautiful, smart and kind. Those seem like pretty good reasons to me. But far be it from me to try to convince you of something you don't want to believe."

"No?"

"Nope. I've learned my lesson about being bossy. Besides," she continued as she opened the driver's-side door, "I have a feeling sooner or later, Zach will do the convincing for me."

"I'M HEADING OUT," Zach told Kane at the end of his shift.

Kane, behind the bar pulling a beer, looked up. "I want to talk to you."

"So talk."

"The back booth. I'll meet you there."

Zach narrowed his gaze on his brother. "You're taking this boss thing a little too seriously. Next thing I know you'll want me to call you sir and bring you coffee."

"I can get my own coffee, but I like the *sir* part. Let's practice now."

Zach shrugged. "Okay. How about, kiss my ass? Sir."

"Not bad," Kane said, handing a customer the beer. "But the tone was way off. It needs more reverence. And a hint of groveling wouldn't hurt, either."

"I'll keep that in mind," Zach said drily.

He grabbed a bottle of water from behind the bar and crossed to the last booth. Sat down.

He had no idea what Kane wanted to talk about, but he wished his brother would get over here and spill it, whatever it was. He doubted it was about his job performance. He was always on time, worked hard and tackled any assignment given to him to the best of his ability. Hell, he'd even started working behind the bar. He wasn't the fastest bartender, but so far everyone had given him a break.

No, he wasn't nervous about the conversation. He just didn't want to be here. He was anxious to get home.

Home. Christ. It was a room with a connected bath, not a home. But it felt like one. Felt more like one than any other place he could remember. And he wanted to get there before Elijah and Mitchell went to bed, maybe kick the ball around. He wanted to see Fay. Talk to her.

Yeah. He was an idiot. Wrapped up in some woman who was still hung up on her ex while banishing Zach to the dreaded friend zone.

He'd gone willingly. It was better than nothing and gave him the opportunity to spend more time with her and the boys.

Gave him time to try to convince her to see him as something more than a friend.

Kane slid into the booth opposite Zach and tossed some papers on the table between them.

Not papers, Zach realized. College brochures. "What's this?" he asked. "I thought Estelle was going to UH."

Kane's eighteen-year-old daughter lived with her mother in Houston, and though she'd made noises about attending college on the East Coast, she'd decided to stick close to home and attend the University of Houston in the fall.

"She is. These aren't for her," Kane said, nudging the pile toward Zach. "They're for you."

Zach snorted. "I'm no frat boy."

"No fraternity would have you. I'm not saying you should live on campus and pretend to be a twenty-year-old."

"What are you saying?"

Kane leaned forward, the intensity and intelligence in his gaze reminding Zach of their father. Guess certain traits you couldn't escape no matter how hard you tried. "I'm saying you can't hide forever."

What the hell? "I'm not hiding."

"You're not living, either. You've been here for three weeks and you've yet to make any significant strides toward…hell…toward anything." He tapped the pile of brochures. "It's time to make some decisions about what you want to do with the rest of your life."

"You sound just like the old man."

If he'd wanted to piss Kane off, it didn't work. He just nodded. "Sometimes even a complete ass can be right. Look, I've been where you're at—"

"No," Zach said quietly, holding Kane's gaze. "You haven't."

"Okay. Not exactly where you're at. I had all my parts when I got out of the service, but I still had to decide what to do with the rest of my life."

"It's easier for you," Zach said. "You had more options than I do."

Kane's expression hardened. "Bullshit. You and I both know you can do anything you set your mind to."

Though the compliment warmed him, Zach sneered. "Because I'm a Bartasavich?"

"Because you're too stubborn to quit and too stupid to know when you're beaten." Kane stood. "You came here for a reason. It's time to figure out what that is and to make some plans for your future. At least think it over." Then he shocked the hell out of Zach by laying his hand on Zach's shoulder. "If you need someone to talk to…"

Zach's throat was tight, and he had to clear it before speaking. "Yeah. Thanks."

Kane, seemingly as unsure about this new brotherly bond as Zach, patted his shoulder awkwardly then went back behind the bar.

Zach's mind spun. He hadn't thought about his future and the possibilities since before he got hurt. Though one of his reasons for coming to

Shady Grove had been to figure out what came next for him, he'd avoided thinking about it because that meant facing what he'd lost. Accepting it. It meant letting go of his old plans, of the life he'd always thought he'd have.

He thought of Fay and the boys. Of how his life had been these past three weeks. Thought of how his future could be.

Kane was right. It was time to make some decisions. Time for new plans.

Time for him to embrace his future.

Josie walked next to Drew toward his car. They'd just had lunch with Mr. and Dr. Constable, the very nice couple who wanted to adopt her baby.

"Tell me I'm doing the right thing," she said as Drew slid into the driver's seat next to her.

He immediately turned toward her. He always did that—listened to her. Cared about what she had to say. Though it had been less than a month since they'd met, they'd become good friends, though she often wondered if there was a possibility of them being more.

"You're having second thoughts?" he asked, turning the car on to blast the air-conditioning.

"No. Yes. I don't know." She was always hot and uncomfortable, couldn't sleep through the night, had to pee all the time and hadn't seen her feet in weeks. She was due to have her baby girl in eight short weeks.

And then she was going to give her daughter away.

"I'm just…scared, I guess. What if the Constables aren't as nice as they seem?"

"Well, they seem pretty great to me."

True. They were perfect. Married for fifteen years, he was some hotshot attorney and she was a pediatrician. They would be wonderful parents.

"They are great. It's just…what if she hates me? For giving her up?" Josie asked quietly, rubbing her stomach as the baby kicked.

"She won't hate you. The Constables are going to tell her that you only wanted what was best for her. And she's going to know who you are," he said, reminding her of the agreement the lawyer handling the adoption had written up. The Constables would send her pictures and updates and tell the baby all about her. She could even visit if she wanted, but Josie wasn't sure she'd ever be up for that.

Leaving her baby once was going to be hard enough. Doing it again and again might be more than she could handle.

"She's going to know you love her," Drew said, touching Josie's arm. He was always doing that, touching her arm or her shoulder, her lower back as they walked. It made her feel connected to him. Safe.

Made her realize how stupid she'd been for so

many years, being with guys who treated her like a possession. Who'd treated her badly.

Guys like Shane.

She hadn't heard from Shane since he left her at the hotel. But the attorney had tracked him down—he was working on a road crew in Maryland—and had gotten him to sign the papers giving up his rights to their baby. He hadn't even tried to get her to change her mind.

He was probably thrilled to be let off the hook. No third kid wanting his time and attention and money.

Part of her had hoped he'd come back. That he'd realize what he'd lost and beg her for another chance. Beg her to keep their baby so they could be a family.

Thankfully a bigger part realized she was better off without him.

She was over him. *Mostly.* It was hard to completely stop thinking about a guy when you carried his baby. But at least she no longer wanted him back.

Progress. Slow but steady. For the past two and a half weeks she'd been living at Bradford House, working for Fay and even becoming friends with her.

Plus she had Drew in her life. They hung out several times a week and every weekend, finding time after school—he was actually a year younger than her and would be graduating high school in a few weeks—and work. But she couldn't help thinking about what Shane had said about a guy not wanting another man's leftovers. It worried her.

"I'm just getting nervous," she told Drew as they sat in the parking lot, the bright sun beating down on the car. "It's all moving so fast."

"That's understandable. But for what it's worth, yeah, I think you're doing the right thing. It's unselfish."

She'd never thought of herself as unselfish. Had always put her wants first. But Drew was right. Keeping her baby would be selfish. Though she already loved her baby more than anything, she couldn't take care of her. Not in the way she thought her baby deserved.

She wanted the best for her daughter. A home with two parents who could give her all the advantages in life that Josie had always envied. Her baby girl would have love and support.

What more could she ask for?

"Thank you," she said to Drew, taking his hand in hers.

He smiled, and her heart flipped as he squeezed her hand. Held on. "What for?"

"For…everything. For being there for me. For going with me to the attorney and meeting the Constables and taking me to my doctor's appointment last week. Thank you for being my friend. You were right—that day we met, I needed one."

Something in his eyes flashed, and his smile dimmed. What had she said wrong? "No problem. I'm glad I could help."

He tried to tug his hand free, but she held on tight. "What's the matter?"

"Nothing."

"Drew...come on. Tell me. You already know more about me than anyone else."

Sometimes it scared her, how close they'd gotten in such a short time. When she was with Drew, she felt like the old her. Not the girl she'd been in high school or those few months in college, but the one she'd been so long ago it seemed like an entirely different life. When she'd been a kid and had still believed she could accomplish anything if only she tried hard enough.

And she knew him, too. Knew he'd been sick as a child, diagnosed with leukemia at the age of eight. That he'd moved to Shady Grove with his mom from California two years ago and now his mom was engaged to a firefighter.

She even knew his sins. How he'd used Gracie, the sweet girl who also worked at Bradford House. Had told her he loved her only to dump her after sleeping with her. How a few months later he'd slept with his best friend's girlfriend only to discover what a bitch she truly was. How guilty he still felt about hurting Gracie. Betraying his friend.

"I don't want to be your friend," Drew said, then winced. Swore. "I didn't mean it like that. I just…" He exhaled heavily. "I like you, Josie. I like you a lot."

"You do?"

"I know you're not in a position to start…anything…right now. I understand. All I'm asking is that you give me a chance to be more than just a friend. Give us a chance to see if we can be something more."

"I don't know." Getting involved with another guy was scary, but so was being alone. She didn't want to rush into anything, didn't want to be with Drew just so she *wasn't* alone. But she couldn't pretend she didn't care about him. "I like you, too. I mean… I've thought about us being together."

He grinned. "Yeah?"

She nodded. "It's just…I'm scared. I don't want to make another mistake."

He leaned forward, giving her plenty of time to evade, but she didn't want to. He pressed his mouth to hers, his kiss warm and so sweet that tears stung her eyes.

"I don't think we're a mistake, Josie. We don't have to make any promises or put a label on it. We can go slow. I'm in no hurry. And you're worth waiting for."

"You're the first guy to think so," she whispered. "You're the first guy who's really seen me. The first guy to like *me*."

The other guys she'd been with had wanted sex, and if she hadn't given it to them, they had walked. They hadn't cared about her. But Drew cared. He thought she was worth waiting for. He thought she was special.

She kissed him, tried to show him with that one kiss everything that was in her heart. "I can't make you any promises," she told him when she leaned back, "but I think I'd like to try. I'd like to try with you."

Her baby kicked, and Josie thought the baby agreed with her. The future was waiting for them, and it was time Josie stepped into that future and became the person she was always meant to be.

CHAPTER SEVENTEEN

SHE'D NEVER HAD a male friend before.

Oh, she had friends, Fay thought as she turned off the light in the boys' room. But most of them had been female. After she met Shane, got married and had the boys, a few of those friendships had drifted away. She understood, she'd been at a different point in her life than most of her girlfriends, and she hadn't been much for going out even when she'd been single.

She'd always just wanted to meet that someone special who'd love her forever.

So, yes, she thought, picking up a plastic T. rex from the hallway floor, she'd had friends, still had them now that she and Maddie had made up, but never a male friend.

She stepped into the living room and saw Zach looking out the window at the sun setting behind the hills.

Guess things had changed more than she'd realized. Life was funny that way.

She looked at him while his back was to her. His shoulders were broad, his legs wide apart. Ever since sharing that pizza, they'd gone from working out together in a haphazard way to planning to meet in the fitness room early in the morning before she started her day with the boys and he left for work at his brother's bar. They'd progressed to doing things friends do—they hung out. Cooked and ate meals together. Sat on the patio or played with the boys in the yard.

It was nice.

And lately, super confusing.

She liked him. But even that thought brought a hint of panic. Of nerves.

They were friends. Just friends.

Yet Maddie had scoffed at that. Had insisted that a man like Zach wasn't looking for friendship from Fay. That he was attracted to her. Interested in her.

Fay's grip tightened until the dinosaur's pointy claw dug into her palm. Ridiculous. Why would he be interested in her? She was passably pretty, yes, but she was sure there were plenty of women he'd met at O'Riley's who were prettier.

Who were at a better place in their lives.

She might no longer be broken, but she was still a work in progress.

Still, Maddie's words had flowed through Fay's brain all week. Yes, she found Zach attractive. She wasn't dead. He was a handsome, interesting man, but she was in no place to look for anything beyond friendship.

But she had to admit to being curious. There

were times when he looked at her when she could have sworn she saw something in his eyes, a flare of something that made her excited and nervous at the same time.

She thought about him. Dreamed of him, dreams she had no place dreaming, of him kissing her, holding her, touching her.

Guess she wasn't as mended as she thought.

He sensed her behind him, turned, and her heart did a strange flip-flop. Her throat dried.

"Good idea with that kickball game," she told him, putting T. rex in the box next to the couch. "They were wiped out and both fell asleep immediately."

"I don't blame them," he said, crossing to sit on the couch. He stretched out his right leg, rubbed his thigh.

"Does your leg hurt?"

"It's okay."

His limp was barely noticeable now, and he went up and down stairs with much greater ease. He was talking about buying a truck, a modified one if need be, so he could gain even more independence.

She got them each a beer. Handed one of the bottles to him then tapped the top of hers to it in a toast. "To a lovely Saturday."

They'd spent almost the entire day together, had done a quick upper-body workout that morning, then he'd watched the boys while she checked in new guests and helped Josie with the housekeeping. After lunch, they'd taken the boys to the park and out for ice cream and ended their day with a cookout and kickball.

She couldn't remember a nicer day.

He took a drink. Rubbed his thumb up and down the bottle's neck. "I'm thinking of going to school. To college."

She grinned. "Oh, Zach, that's wonderful. Where do you want to go? What do you want to study?"

He lifted a shoulder as if it was no big deal, but it was. "I'm going to apply at Pitt. If I get in, I want to enroll in their sports medicine and nutrition program. I thought…I thought I could be a personal trainer. Focus on helping people with disabilities or illness."

Tears stung her eyes, but she willed them back. This was no time for them—even happy ones. "As your first unofficial client, I can say that is a fabulous idea."

He slid her a sidelong glance. "Yeah?"

She nodded. "Definitely." But then something occurred to her. "Will you keep your job at O'Riley's?"

"I'm not sure. I guess that depends on the workload. I haven't studied in twelve years, and even then I was a mediocre student—I didn't take it that seriously. I might need all that time just to make sure I pass my classes."

"I'm sure you'll do great," she assured him. She tucked her legs under her. Sipped her beer. "But even if you don't continue working, you'll still stay in Shady Grove? Commute to Pittsburgh?"

"Maybe. Or maybe I'll get an apartment in the city. Something close to campus."

"Right. Of course. That's…that's smart."

And made perfect sense. Why would he continue to live in Shady Grove and drive forty minutes each way if he didn't have to? With his family's money, he clearly didn't need a job to make ends meet.

It was stupid of her to feel disappointed. The man couldn't live here forever. At least, not at Bradford House. That he'd been here so long was unusual, to say the least, and as she'd told him when he first arrived, his room was booked by other guests for next weekend, anyway.

And while Pittsburgh might be too far for a daily commute, it was certainly close enough for them to still see each other. To continue their friendship.

So why did she feel so lost? As if something precious was slipping through her hands?

Oh, God, she thought, scared and shaken. She felt like she was losing him.

Which was crazy. He wasn't hers to lose. They weren't involved. She needed time. Months or maybe even years to figure out who she was on her own. She was in no hurry to put her heart on the line.

Wasn't sure she'd ever be ready or willing to do so again.

"I'll miss you," she blurted out, because the silence was pressing in on her. Because she had to say something, and *I'll miss you* was better than what she really wanted to say.

Please stay. Don't go. Don't leave me.

"I mean," she continued hurriedly, "we'll miss you. Me and the boys and Josie and Gracie and Damien and…everyone."

Yes, that about covered it.

She shut her eyes on an inner groan. Ordered herself not to say any more. What had already come out of her mouth was bad enough.

Zach nodded, and she had no idea what it meant. There were still times, like now, when she had no clue what he was thinking. And, being a taciturn man, he didn't offer extra words unless necessary.

But she was slowly getting stronger. Bolder. Or at least, brave enough to ask for what she wanted.

"Will you miss us?" she asked, then held her breath.

He looked at her, something heated in his gaze. "I'll miss you," he said, his voice rough, the sound causing gooseflesh to cover her arms. "You and the boys and everyone."

She felt as if she was on the edge of a precipice, afraid to make the wrong move, scared she'd tumble down into an abyss. Terrified, as always, of the unknown.

But there was one thing she did know for sure. Zach was leaving Bradford House. He wouldn't be around much longer. Oh, they could pretend they'd keep in touch, and they might actually follow through—for a little while. But soon enough he'd move on with his life. He'd become busy with classes and studies. He'd meet new people. Make new friends.

He'd meet new women. Women who didn't have kids or emotional baggage. Women he hadn't seen at their lowest points. Women who were strong and healthy. Who knew what they wanted and went after it.

She wished, so desperately, that she could be one of them.

"Zach?"

"Hmm?"

She swallowed. Met his eyes. "Do you want to kiss me?"

ZACH ABOUT CHOKED on his beer. He coughed, wiped his mouth with the back of his hand. Had she edged nearer to him, somehow? It seemed so, as her thigh was pressed against his, her face close. Too close.

"What?"

She blushed, and he had to bite back a groan. She was killing him. Had been killing him for

weeks. He'd been thinking of her, had been attracted to her since the first moment he saw her
kneeling in the yard, the sun on her face. And now
she was sitting here, so near, looking so pretty
with her hair down and curly, her hands clutching her bottle of beer like it was a lifeline, asking
him if he wanted to kiss her?

Goddamn it.

"Do you want to kiss me?" she repeated, and
he was surprised. He hadn't thought she'd be
brave enough to repeat the question—but then
again, she'd been gutsy enough to ask it in the
first place. "It's okay if you do." Her eyes widened. "Or if you don't," she added quickly. "I was
just wondering and thought I'd ask since you're
leaving soon…"

She trailed off, looking miserable—embarrassed
and shy but also determined, as if proud of herself for putting the question out there. For taking
this step.

A step he hadn't been brave enough to take first.

"It's just," she continued when he remained silent, "Maddie seems to think you're…"

He narrowed his eyes. Even though she and
Maddie were back to being bosom buddies, he
still wasn't crazy about the bombshell and how
she'd treated Fay. "Maddie seems to think what?"

Fay's blush deepened, flowed into her neck.
He had the strongest desire to press his lips there,

where her skin was heated, to kiss her until she forgot all about her unease.

"She thinks you're attracted to me," Fay finished quietly. She gave a quick shake of her head. "I told her she was crazy. I told her we were just friends. I'm sorry if I've made you uncomfortable."

But he wasn't uncomfortable. He was surprised and amped up, but not uncomfortable. And he was really tired of being in the friend zone. He'd put himself there, had set himself up for this, but only because she'd needed time to get over her ex. And Zach hadn't wanted to push her, hadn't wanted to take advantage of her.

But she was right. He was leaving. In less than a week he needed to be out of his room. They wouldn't see each other every day.

So when she started to stand, he put his hand on her arm, stopping her. "I've wanted to kiss you since the moment I first laid eyes on you."

She blinked, her mouth open. Her hand trembled once. Twice. Beer sloshed out and onto her shorts. She didn't seem to notice. "You… No…" She shook her head. "No, you didn't."

"I did," he told her quietly. He took the bottle from her before she dumped it all over herself. She was so pretty, with her fiery hair and those bright eyes, her long, bare legs. "And I've wanted to kiss you every day since."

"Oh." She licked her lips. "Well, that's…" Her

hands fluttered, and she settled them in her lap. "Wow."

He couldn't help it. He smiled. "Yeah. Wow. But do you want to kiss me?"

He didn't move. Could barely breathe as she mulled that one over, worrying her lower lip with her teeth.

"Yes," she whispered. "I want to kiss you."

Triumph surged through him, but he tamped it down. Felt like a schoolkid on the couch at his mom's house fumbling around with his first girl-friend. Fay was on his right side, so he had to turn to touch her. He laid his hand on her shoulder, his fingertips brushing the side of her neck.

Then he slowly slid his hand around to cup her neck and drew her close. Closer, until their mouths were inches apart, their breath mingling. He waited, holding on to that anticipation, until she finally drew her hands up, settled them on his shoulders.

And he kissed her. Brushed his lips over hers once. Then again. When he leaned back, her eyes fluttered open. She looked serious, as if the weight of the world was on her shoulders, and his ego deflated.

Looked like he was out of practice.

But then she cupped his face, smoothed her fingers down his cheeks and chin. And she smiled at him, shy and sweet and lovely.

His control snapped.

He pulled her to him and kissed her again, this time a long, slow, deep kiss that seeped into his bones, settled into his veins. Her taste, her scent, surrounded him; the feel of her hair, of her skin, was all he could think about.

Tugging her closer, he settled back against the sofa so that she lay half on top of him. He kept the kiss controlled, but his blood burned. He kept kissing her until she melted against him, her body soft and sweet smelling, her hands caressing his shoulders. Her fingers playing with his hair.

She was so warm, so responsive, her tongue hesitantly touching his. He couldn't stop. He slid his hand down her back, settled it just above the curve of her ass. He cursed the bomb that had taken his other arm, wished he could wrap both of them around her, hold her tight.

She moved her hands down to both of his upper arms, squeezed his biceps, her mouth moving more confidently over his, and he slid his hand around to her waist and then up her side. Kept it still, his fingers against her rib cage, his thumb under her breast. He didn't want to rush her or take more than she was ready to give. But it felt as if he'd wanted her forever, and it had been so long for him, he couldn't stop himself from shifting his hand higher. Brushing the pad of his thumb over her straining nipple.

She moaned into his mouth, arched into his touch, and he did it again. And again.

He wanted, more than his next breath, to strip her bare of her tank top, glide his hand up her smooth thigh, press his face to her breasts, touch her at her core. Take her.

Make her his.

The thought sobered him. Breaking the kiss, he sat up, settling her back in her own space. She looked dazed and thoroughly kissed, her skin pink from his beard. He brushed her hair over her shoulder and his forefinger caught the gold chain around her neck, pulling it free of her shirt.

He curled his finger around the chain, lifting the ring on it away from her chest. "What's this?"

Though he'd spoken quietly, she flinched. Tried to tug the necklace from him, but he held firm. He grasped the ring between his forefinger and thumb. Stared at the simple silver band.

And knew what it was. What it meant.

But he needed to hear her say it.

"Tell me," he said, pushing the words out past the tightness in his throat.

She dropped her gaze, her throat working. When she spoke, her voice was barely a whisper. "It's my wedding ring."

Her quiet confession rang in his ears, built into a roar, an angry scream. She'd looked at him, soft and sweet, and told him she wanted to kiss him. She'd put her hands on him. Damn it, he could still taste her, could feel the imprint of her touch, her fingers against his cheek, her hands in his hair, her body against his.

All while wearing the ring another man had given her, hidden under her clothes like a secret. Close to her heart.

Zach's fingers ached, and he realized he was squeezing the ring as if he was strong enough to crush it. To destroy it and whatever hope it symbolized to her.

"Were you thinking about him?" he asked, staring at the ring, wondering how something so small could mean so much. Could have so much freaking power.

"What?"

He met her eyes, hardened his heart against the tears glistening there. "Were you thinking about him when you were kissing me?"

Her mouth trembled. "No."

He wanted to believe her, wanted to trust her. But he held the truth between his fingers.

He slowly, carefully lowered the ring so that it once again hung between her breasts, then stood and headed toward the door.

She scrambled to her feet. "It's not… The ring… It doesn't mean anything."

He went absolutely still. Even his heart seemed to stop beating. Before he knew his intention, he turned and stalked back to her, not stopping even when she flinched, her shoulders rounding, her chin lowered.

"Oh, no. You don't get to stand there like some beaten kitten," he said, incredulous. Infuriated. He edged closer, his voice a low growl. "You chose to hold on to the man who used you. Who betrayed your trust, took your love for granted and left you and those boys. He hurt you time and again, but you were the one who put that ring around your neck, wearing it like some goddamn medal of honor. You. So don't give me any bullshit about it not meaning anything. You can lie to yourself, but don't you ever, *ever* lie to me."

"I won't... I'm not," she insisted, her voice thick with unshed tears.

Unable to look at her any longer, wanting space and needing to get the hell away from her before he cracked and accepted her pitiful excuses, took whatever scraps she had to give him, he stalked to the door.

Made it into the hallway before she reached him.

"Zach, I...I'm so sorry," she said, standing in the doorway, her hair wild, her eyes sad, that damn ring like a beacon against her shirt. "Don't go. Please. We can discuss this."

"There's nothing to discuss. I'm not interested in your excuses or apologies. But there is one thing you can do for me."

"Anything," she promised quickly, reaching for him. He stepped back and she blinked. Wrapped her arms around her waist. "I'll do anything to make this up to you."

He kept his voice flat. "You're confusing me for your husband. I don't want you to make it up to me. I don't need you groveling and small to make myself feel like I'm worth something."

Even if her not seeing that worth ripped him up inside.

"My room here is booked until next Friday." He wasn't going to let her run him off early. He still had some pride—battered and bruised though it was at the moment. "And what I want is for you to leave me the hell alone."

CHAPTER EIGHTEEN

FAY HAD NEVER been so nervous in her life.

And that was saying something, she thought as she walked up the long, wide hallway toward Zach's room, her legs heavy, her feet dragging. She'd spent most of her life being scared, worried and nervous.

Somehow she'd hit a new high. Or low, depending on how you looked at it.

Either way her palms were damp, her stomach turning, and honestly, if she walked any slower, she'd be going in reverse. Worse, much, much worse than the nerves wreaking havoc on her senses, the darkness she'd evaded for so many days had returned, pouncing on her the night Zach had kissed her. The night he'd left her. Surrounding her when she'd been tossing and turning in her bed.

She'd almost succumbed to it. When Mitchell had come into her room bright and early Sunday morning wanting his breakfast, she'd stared at him blankly. Then rolled over, tuning him out.

Thank God she'd realized what she was doing almost immediately. Scraping together every bit of strength she had, she got out of bed. Fed her sons. Dressed them and herself and went to Mass with her family. Even had coffee with Maddie after.

She didn't let the darkness win. Would continue to fight as long as it took. Because she was worth fighting for.

She stopped at the end of the hall. Stared at the closed door. Zach was worth fighting for, too.

But it wouldn't be easy, getting him to listen. Getting him to forgive her. It had been five days since he'd left her. He'd been so angry. So disappointed.

So hurt.

She hadn't seen him since. Had given him the space he'd requested.

What I want is for you to leave me the hell alone.

More like the space he'd demanded.

As usual, she'd ignored her own wants to honor someone else's. But he was leaving tomorrow and she couldn't let him go without…well…she wasn't sure.

She just couldn't let him go. Not yet.

She knocked on his door, two hard raps, then stood back, hands clasped at her waist.

He opened the door, dark and glowering at her, his hair mussed, his mouth a flat line. "Are you kicking me out early?"

It took her two tries, her mouth flapping wordlessly, before she could speak. "No. No, of course not. The room is yours until noon tomorrow."

He nodded. And started to close the door.

Frustrated at his stubbornness, irritated by his rudeness, she went with instinct. And pushed past him, slipping into his room before he could shut her out.

His eyes narrowed to slits. "I see where Elijah gets it," he muttered.

She frowned. "Excuse me?"

"Never mind. I take it you have something to say?"

She did. Absolutely. She was just having a hard time finding her words now that she was face-to-face with him. "You're leaving tomorrow."

"That's been established."

"Right. It's just…the boys are worried they won't get a chance to say goodbye." True. Just not the entire truth.

"I'll be sure to see them before they go to school."

He'd been so good to them. Though he no longer wanted anything to do with her, he'd still spent time with the boys this past week. "They'll appreciate that. They're going to miss you." Having come this far, she pushed forward. "I'm going to miss you, too."

His jaw tightened as if he wanted to say something but wouldn't allow himself.

She wished she had his self-control.

"I'm sorry," she said, the words scraping her throat raw. "About the other night."

He finally met her eyes. "You have nothing to be sorry about."

"I do. I never meant to hurt you."

"You're allowed your feelings." He dropped his gaze for a moment then lifted it once again. "You're still hung up on your ex. I knew it. I just chose to ignore it."

"I'm not hung up on Sha—" But she couldn't say his name. Not when it felt as if he was here, standing between her and Zach. "I'm not hung on him. I swear." She stepped toward Zach, heartbroken when he backed up. "I'm not sure I can explain it, but I'd like to try. If you'll let me."

"It doesn't matter now."

"It does to me. You deserve an honest explanation and I deserve a second chance."

She thought he'd refuse her, but he nodded. Sat on the edge of the bed and gestured for her to go ahead.

"You were right. I wore my wedding ring because it was a symbol of what Shane and I had. What I thought we'd have again. At least, that's why I used to wear it. I should have taken it off years ago, if not that night I left him in that hotel room. I should have tossed it in the river, but it had become a part of me. It reminded me what we had, but also of what I'd hoped to have again. Getting rid of it meant the end of that dream."

"And you're not ready to let go of that dream."

Feeling edgy and restless, she lifted her hands.

Let them float back to her sides. "I'd chased after it for so long that giving up meant I had to admit everyone else was right. I had to accept what a fool I'd been all these years. How stupid I was for believing in a fantasy."

Zach sighed. "You don't have to say that. You don't owe me anything. Not even an explanation."

"This isn't just for you. This is for me, too. I've spent my whole life worrying about what other people think of me, of them telling me I was wrong, and I just... I couldn't handle the thought of that happening again."

She'd been prideful and foolish.

"I took the ring off right after you left that night," she continued. She'd set it aside for the boys, in case one of them wanted it when they got older. "I took it off because I don't need it anymore. And I...I wanted you to know that. I've let go of that dream."

Zach stood and her heart leaped, but he didn't reach for her. "Now I know. But it doesn't change anything."

How could he say that? It changed everything.

"I don't think of him," she blurted out, her heart racing. "I didn't think of him when you kissed me. Not for one second. In that moment, it was as if something inside me burst free. I couldn't have thought of anyone but you even if I'd wanted to. I know you believe that I still love Shane, but I don't. I don't even think of him," she repeated on a whisper, "because there's no room for him in my head anymore. There's only you. Only been you for weeks."

Her words seemed to blow through him, and his head snapped back. She thought he was going to send her away, but instead he yanked her to him and kissed her. She thought she'd be prepared for his kiss this time, but it still rocked her to the core. She kissed him back, loving the feel of his mouth on hers, his hand on her waist, holding her close.

She wanted to show him what he'd come to mean to her, that what she said was true—she thought only of him. Dreamed of him. She kissed him hard, unsure and nervous but still eager to be with him. He pulled her close, his arousal pressing against her belly. She felt an answering tug deep in her core, and her mouth turned hungry. Demanding. Her hands skimming over him— arms, shoulders and chest.

He tore his mouth away, pressed his forehead against hers, breathing hard. "The boys—"

"They're spending the night with my parents." It was a chance she'd taken. One she'd hoped would pay off.

He raised his head, a question clear in his eyes, his breathing already coming faster.

She cupped his face, his beard thick and scratchy beneath her palm. "Please don't send me away."

He covered her hand with his. Searched her eyes. "Are you sure?"

Her heart swelled. She loved that he asked. That he cared about what she wanted. But what she wanted tonight, right now, more than anything, was him.

Bringing their joined hands to her mouth, she turned his and pressed a soft kiss to his palm. And told him the absolute truth. "I've never been more sure about anything in my life."

ZACH DIDN'T KNOW what he'd done to deserve this woman coming to him, but he wasn't about to waste it.

I deserve a second chance.

She did. They both did.

He kissed her again, trying to take things slow, but she was so soft, so responsive, her body pressed against his, her hands smoothing over his shoulders, down his arms—

He pulled back, but she shook her head. "Let me," she whispered, her fingers trailing over his right shoulder, down his bicep before drifting away.

He thought she'd be put off by his amputated arm, maybe even disgusted by it. That she'd change her mind and leave him, but she didn't go anywhere. She stunned him by dragging her long fingers down his chest, lower and lower until she reached the hem of his T-shirt. Sliding her palms under the material, laying them flat against his stomach, she dragged her hands up, bringing the shirt with them. When it bunched at his chest, she tugged and he raised his arms, allowing her to pull it up over his head.

He stood, hand fisted at his side while she studied his tattoo, her nails lightly tracing the eagle, globe and anchor, the insignia of the Marine Corps. "Semper Fidelis?" she asked, reading the small script.

"Always faithful."

She smiled. And rocked him back on his heels when she pressed a warm, wet, openmouthed kiss there. Straightening, her fingertips grazed his chest, his stomach, before sliding up the sides of his waist, around the front of his shoulders then down his arms—both arms.

He flinched.

She stilled, her hand on the bottom of his amputated arm, her touch light. "Does it hurt?"

He shook his head, unable to speak. She caressed his neck, traced his collarbones, trailed down his stomach. His breath caught. His willpower waned. He quickly stepped back.

"I want to undress you," he admitted, lifting his hand, "but it might take me a while."

She smiled, serene and confident, like a goddess—powerful. Power he'd helped give her, he realized, by wanting her so badly. By letting her just be her.

She lifted her arms over her head, the hem of her shirt rising to show a glimpse of pale skin. "I'm not in a hurry. Are you?"

He was afraid he was. That he would rush this. Would ruin this. But he forced himself to take it slow as he worked first one side of her shirt up, then the other. Past her ribs, then over her silky white bra until he was able to pull the top over her head and toss it aside. His breath whooshed out. She was all pale, creamy skin, the globes of her breasts rising and falling quickly with her breath, her waist narrow, her belly slightly rounded.

"You're beautiful," he told her, unable to believe his good fortune.

She blushed, color washing over her chest and climbing her neck. "I'm not—"

"You are." She was lovely and sweet and so much stronger than she knew. He slipped his finger down the valley between her breasts. Swept it up and down. Transfixed by the sight of his dark finger against her white skin. "You have no idea how much I want you."

"I've never been with anyone…else," she said breathlessly. "This way."

Zach was glad she hadn't said his name, hadn't brought him here. But if possible, her confession made him want her more. She was so brave, asking for another chance. So honest, giving him the truth, letting him see her. Know her. The least he could do was give it back to her.

"I haven't been with anyone since the explosion," he admitted. "I don't want to disappoint you."

"You won't. You couldn't."

He was afraid he would. That he wouldn't be able to love her the way she deserved. The way he so desperately wanted to.

He kissed her, taking his time, showing her with his mouth and tongue how much he wanted her. How much he planned on cherishing her.

He was careful to keep things controlled. To keep his desire for her contained. But she kissed him back, her mouth open and giving under his, her hands smoothing over his bare skin. He tried to focus on her taste, but her bare torso against his drove him wild, the press of her breasts against him making him groan.

But it wasn't enough.

Reaching behind her, he undid her bra. She broke the kiss to look at him in surprise.

He grinned. "Luckily, I perfected one-handed bra removal back in high school."

She laughed, the sound like a balm to his nerves, and he kissed her again, sitting on the edge of the bed with her on his lap. He used every bit of skill he had, kissing her, touching her until she was breathing hard, her hips wiggling against him.

He lay back, bringing her with him so she straddled his hips. Lifting his head, he took the rosy tip of one breast in his mouth, licking and sucking until she gasped and writhed against his arousal. He switched to the other breast, his fingers molding and cupping the one he'd just relinquished.

Pressing her hands against his chest, she arched into his touch, her face upturned, eyes closed.

She leaned back far enough to kick off her shoes and slide out of her shorts while he struggled to get out of his jeans, feeling like a fumbling virgin. He had his prosthetic on, felt her watching him as he took it off and set it aside. She didn't hesitate at the sight of his scarred leg, crawling over him until she straddled him once more.

He put on the condom he'd pulled from his pocket then guided her over him. Onto him. She was hot and wet and so beautiful, it made his chest ache.

She was his home.

Unable to stop himself, he lifted his hips, going deeper, and she moaned, her eyes on his, her hands on his chest. Then she began to move, slowly, hesitantly at first and then with more confidence. Sweat broke out along his upper lip and temples. She was so tight, so passionate and giving, he couldn't hold back. He pumped into her again and again, taking what he wanted, what he needed until he came with a hoarse cry.

She collapsed on him, still breathing hard, her body warm and, thanks to his lack of finesse, unfulfilled.

He brushed her hair from her face. "I'm sorry," he managed, breathing hard, his heart racing, the aftershocks of his orgasm still rocking his body.

"Don't be sorry," she said, smiling down at him. "It was really nice."

He winced. *Nice.* She might as well have cut off his balls and told him he didn't need them anymore.

"No," she said, correctly interpreting his expression. "I meant it was great. Really. I've never...you know...during the, uh...actual act..."

He narrowed his eyes. "You've never come during sex?"

Her face was pink and it was a pretty sight, her above him, their bodies still connected, her skin warm against his, her cheeks flushed. "No. Well...I haven't, technically, had a...an orgasm." She cleared her throat. "Uh...ever."

"You've never pleasured yourself?" he asked, shifting onto his elbow.

She blinked and he could tell she'd rather be talking about anything else, but they were naked and had just done possibly the most intimate act two people could engage in, so he wasn't going to let her be embarrassed. "It's just not...something that's ever been that important to me."

"No?" he asked, his voice soft. "Well, it's important to me."

And he flipped them over so that she was beneath him.

FAY'S HEAD WAS still spinning from the way Zach had—with one arm—reversed their positions when he kissed her. His mouth moving over hers again and again, his beard scratchy but in a pleasant way. Long, slow kisses that drugged her mind, slowed her senses, his tongue sweeping into her mouth.

She was so confused. They'd already made love and it had been nice. Very nice. If a bit quick. But it had been a long time for him, she reminded herself. And it was flattering that he hadn't been able to last longer. That he'd wanted her that much.

Maybe that was why he was kissing her now. Though he'd reached climax, perhaps he wanted to do it again. Or maybe—

"Stop," he murmured.

She jerked guiltily. Let her hands drop from where she'd been stroking his hair. "Sorry."

"Not the touching. Stop thinking."

He kissed his way down her neck, his lips leaving a trail of fire over her skin, his whiskers abrading softly, his hand smoothing up her side then cupping her right breast. He dragged his thumb across the straining peak. Then scraped it with his nail, plucking and rolling it gently between his fingers as he settled his mouth on her opposite breast and sucked.

A moan rippled up from her throat. "Wha-what are you doing?"

"If you have to ask," he said, his lips moving

against the wet, sensitized peak, "I'm not doing it right."

It felt right. It felt…decadent. And almost frustrating. Her body reaching for something, heading toward it but unable to get there. Her hips lifting of their own accord, a silent plea, one she couldn't fathom. Couldn't put into words.

"I'm going to teach you how to please yourself," he told her, his mouth trailing between her breasts and down to her stomach. He kissed each hip. Dipped his tongue into her belly button. "Then, when you think of me, when you think of us like this, you can touch yourself." He groaned, pressed his forehead to her stomach, his breath brushing the curls at her apex. "I can picture it. I can see you, skin flushed pink, breasts bouncing as you pleasure yourself."

Her mouth dried. As if his words had made it a reality, she saw it, too. She whimpered. "You're there," she gasped.

He stilled, his body tense, his expression fierce. "Where?"

She shook her head, but his gaze was so intense, so seeking, there was no way she could hold back. No way she could refuse him anything. "Teaching me." She stroked her hands over her breasts, lost in the shared fantasy. In the encouragement and heat in his eyes. "Telling me wha-what to do," she whispered, feeling wicked and powerful as she pinched her own nipple. Slid her other hand down her stomach. Lower. "Watching me."

"Fay," he breathed, his gaze heated and hungry—for her. For how she made him feel. He stopped her hand, trapping it there below her belly button. "I'm going to teach you," he promised, pulling her hand away, holding it by her hip. He slid down and nudged her thighs apart with his shoulders. "But not now. Now I'm going to touch you. Taste you. I'm going to be the first man, the only man, to make you come."

The possessiveness in his voice thrilled her. Scared her.

She should protest, should end this madness, but she was too far gone. When he kissed her inner thighs—one then the other—she forgot everything but the feel of him, the scrape of his beard against her sensitive skin, the softness of his lips. And when he settled his mouth on her core, his tongue stroking her lazily, her mind emptied.

He let go of her hand to cup her butt, lifting her higher. His mouth was magic, sending spirals of longing through her system, his tongue wreaking havoc on her senses, sensations building. She reached for him, spearing her fingers in his thick hair, holding him to her. He slid his hand around to her hip, slid it lower to brush his thumb over her most sensitive spot. Once. Twice. On the third pass, her body convulsed with pleasure. It coursed through her, pulsating and wild, until she cried out, her fingers tightening on Zach's hair.

Fay wasn't sure how long the tremors continued, but when her body lay heavy and relaxed and still, when she could finally open her eyes, it was to find Zach by her side, watching her. He looked fierce and triumphant and sexy. He was perfect.

He was hers.

The thought had her jerking upright, her elbow ramming into his side.

"Ow." He rubbed the spot. "It couldn't have been that bad."

"What?" She shook her head, panic filtering through her thoughts, clouding her mind. "Oh, no. No, it was..." Her throat clogged. "It was wonderful. I just... I have to go."

She crawled to the side of the bed, almost fell face-first onto the floor in her haste to escape.

"Hey," Zach said, scooting to the side as she yanked on her panties. He touched her lower hip lightly, and she whirled around, arms covering her breasts. He frowned. "Fay. What's wrong?"

She opened her mouth to tell him nothing was wrong, but she couldn't lie to him. "This was a mistake."

"Did I hurt you?"

She wanted to cry, but she held the tears back. "No. It's not that. I'm not hurt, I just..." Hands shaking, she turned her back to him and put on her bra, fastened it before facing him again. "Like I said, this was a mistake. My mistake. I'm sorry."

He reached for his prosthetic and she had to look away. He was so gorgeous, all tanned skin and toned muscles, his hair mussed from her fingers. She wanted to climb back into bed with him, wanted to lay her head on his shoulder and just be held by him. She wanted him to never let her go.

She could love him. Easily. Too easily.

But that was what got her into trouble, wasn't it, she thought, pulling up her shorts and shoving her feet into her shoes. Holding on too tightly. Expecting too much. Wanting too much.

Tonight wasn't supposed to be about true love or forever or happily ever after. She'd lived through the heartache of losing that fantasy once. Now she knew better. She had to protect her heart. Couldn't risk it again.

"Fay," he said, his voice tugging at her, pulling her back to him, making her wish things were different. That she was different. "Let's talk about this."

But she couldn't. Couldn't trust herself to put into words what she was feeling. The panic was rising inside her, the darkness on its heels. She could feel it bearing down on her. It had almost gotten her a few days ago after their fight. If she loved him and lost him, it would consume her. She couldn't take that chance. Wouldn't. Not even for him.

"There's nothing to talk about." She put on her shirt but did make herself face him. She owed him that much. "I'm sorry. I never should have come down here."

His leg on, he yanked on his jeans and stood. "That's it? That's all you have to say? Fay, I care about you. You and the boys. I want to see where this goes."

"I can't," she whispered. "I'm sorry. I'm not what you think I am. I'm not strong enough. I'm not brave like you."

"Don't do this," he said, a note of pleading in his tone, but his mouth was firm. "Don't walk away from this. Fight for this. For us."

But she'd almost lost herself once, had let her feelings for a man take over her life, let them control her. She'd set everything else in her life aside for Shane—her well-being, her sons and family and friends. She couldn't go back. Couldn't trust herself. So she did the only thing she could do.

She walked away.

CHAPTER NINETEEN

THE BOYS WERE waiting for him in the foyer the next morning, Zach saw as he rounded the corner from the dining room, his duffel packed and on his back.

The boys and Fay.

They stood in the sunlight, the rays catching their light hair, bringing out the red in Fay's and Mitchell's. Elijah's school backpack was near the door, and he ran in circles, his arms spread like wings. Mitch sat on the floor, watching the doorway.

Watching for Zach.

It was enough to make him want to turn around and sneak out the back door.

But that was his anger talking, and he wasn't pissed at Elijah or Mitchell. What happened wasn't their fault. It was his. For giving Fay a second chance. For accepting her excuses, for believing her when she'd said she was over Shane.

For falling for her.

"There he is!" Elijah cried as he raced down the hall, Mitchell following suit. Elijah skid to a stop in front of Zach. "We're here to say goodbye."

"How come you can't live here no more?" Mitchell asked.

"Someone else needs the room," Zach told him. "Remember?"

Mitch nodded but didn't seem too happy with the explanation. They'd discussed this already, several times over the past few days. He'd avoided Fay after their first kiss in her apartment but had spent time with the boys in the yard, had let them help him in the kitchen.

And he'd learned that just because you tell a kid something once—or twice or a hundred freaking times—didn't mean the kid understood.

Especially if it was something they didn't want to happen.

"You could live with us," Mitch said, staring up at Zach hopefully.

"Yeah! You can sleep in our room," Elijah added.

Zach couldn't even look at Fay, but he felt her watching them. Listening. "I've already got a new place to stay."

"But you'll still come here every day, right?" Mitchell asked, lower lip starting to quiver.

Aw, hell, if the kid started crying, there was no saying what Zach would do. Including join in. "Not every day," he said.

"He can't come every day," Elijah said, giving Mitch a shove. "He has to work and stuff." He looked up at Zach. "But you're still coming to my soccer game. I told all the guys you were coming."

"Elijah," Fay called, "what have I told you about Zach?"

Elijah rolled his eyes. "He's not a show-and-tell project." He grinned up at Zach. "But the whole team's really excited. I told them you were a hero and everything, 'cuz that's what Mom said you were."

"Sorry, bud," Zach said, his throat tight, "but I probably won't make it this weekend."

Elijah's face fell. "But you promised."

He hadn't. Had been careful not to make any promises to these kids who didn't belong to him. No matter how much he'd wanted to.

No matter how much he wanted them to be his sons.

"Maybe the next one, okay?"

Elijah stomped his foot. "No! It's not okay. Just don't come to any of them."

He raced off toward the kitchen. Zach tipped his head back and exhaled heavily. "Shit."

"It's okay," Mitchell said, patting Zach's hand. "I still love you."

Zach's throat clogged. He had to get out of here. He bent and gave Mitch a quick kiss on the top of his head. "Love you, too, buddy," he said hoarsely.

Eyes straight ahead, he walked toward the door, hating that he'd have to pass Fay before he left, that he'd have to see her one last time. He'd been through worse, he reminded himself. But it didn't feel that way. It felt as if this was the worst thing he'd ever endured. As if she was the most important thing he'd ever lost.

You'd be surprised what you can learn to live without.

When he'd told her that, he'd believed it. Now he wasn't so sure.

He meant to pass her without acknowledgment, meant to punish her in some small, petty way for how she'd hurt him last night. But he couldn't.

Because *she* was the one thing he'd never learn to live without.

He wouldn't survive without her.

"Come outside with me," he said lowly, urgently when he reached her.

"I don't think—"

"Please, Fay. Just for a minute."

She nodded. "Boys," she called down the hall to where the kids were chasing each other. "I'll be out front."

Zach held the door, and she brushed past him. He stepped outside, pulled the door shut behind him. She faced him and he didn't know what to say. How to start.

So he decided to give her the truth. The part of himself he'd held back, the part he'd been too afraid to share. To acknowledge.

"I love you."

She flinched. Not exactly the reaction he'd been hoping for. "Zach—"

"I love you," he repeated, closing the distance between them until she had to tip her head back to hold his gaze. "And I love your boys. I want to be a part of your lives. A permanent, real part, not as a guest of your bed-and-breakfast. Not as a friend you hang out with. I love you, Fay," he repeated, finding that saying it more than once made it easier somehow. "You make me a better man."

"You don't love me," she said, looking wild-eyed, sounding panicked. "You can't. I'm not what you need. Can't you see that?"

"You are everything I need. I was so lost before I came here, going through the motions but not really living. And then I met you. You and the boys made me realize what I want for my future. A family. You helped me see that I'm more than my injuries. You give me hope. You make me feel whole."

"That's not me. That's all you."

"It was you," he insisted, taking her hand in his, hating how limp she kept it, how cool her fingers were, as if she was frightened of him. Of him changing her mind. "I know you're scared, but you don't have to be. Give me your heart, Fay. I promise to cherish it."

She tugged free. Crossed her arms. "I'm sorry. I can't."

He went cold all over. "You mean you won't."

Because she didn't love him. Didn't trust him. And she never would.

Looked like he'd have to learn to live without one more thing after all.

Fay couldn't stand to watch Zach walk away, so she took the cowardly way out and went inside, shutting the door between them, leaning her forehead against it. Wishing she was brave enough to take a chance, to believe in herself. To believe in love again.

"You messed up."

Fay whirled around to see Josie behind her. "You scared me."

Josie nodded, her dark hair parted on the side, a glittery barrette holding back her bangs. "You ask me, you could use someone to scare some sense into you."

Fay pushed away from the door. "I don't know what you mean."

"Let me make it clear then. You're obviously crazy for Zach, yet you let him go. You. Messed. Up."

"I'm not… Zach and I aren't…"

Josie rolled her eyes. "You can't even lie about it. What's that tell you?"

"That I need more practice?"

"Ha-ha. No. Do you really think you're fooling anyone?"

She'd hoped she was. Hadn't wanted anyone

to know how she'd let herself get into this situation again. "I'm not crazy about Zach," she said. "I can't be. We've only known each other a few weeks."

"So?"

Fay blinked. Several times. "It's not long enough." Not nearly long enough to have developed strong feelings for each other, to know whether or not they were a good fit. A perfect match.

I love you.

Yes, he'd said it, but he couldn't mean it.

Her heart thumped heavily. Her throat dried. Could he? No, that wasn't possible.

"I hadn't realized there was a timeline for things like love," Josie said. "Good thing you've set me straight."

Fay frowned. "Not a timeline. It's just… I don't… I can't have feelings for Zach."

"Why not? He's good-looking, likes your kids and is, like, super rich. I'm not seeing a lot of negatives here. Unless he's a closet asshole?"

"He's wonderful."

"Again, I'm not seeing the problem."

"I just got over Shane. It's too soon."

"Another timeline?" Josie stepped toward her, belly leading the way. "Look, so far all you've done is given me a bunch of lame excuses. What are you really afraid of?"

Everything.

No, that wasn't right. She wasn't frightened of everything. Not anymore. Just this one thing.

"I don't want to make another mistake," she admitted.

Josie's eyes flashed. "Seriously? That is the dumbest thing I've ever heard." She paced to the stairs then back to Fay. "Of course you're going to make a mistake—you're going to make multiple mistakes. Everyone does. The only way to avoid it is to either stop living or stop trying."

"You don't understand. I can't risk it."

"So you'd rather give up than ever put yourself out there again? Maybe you think that's what I should do, too, huh? After all, Shane did a number on me, too. Maybe I should never trust another guy, never fall in love. And I should never have another baby, never get the chance to be a mother because I screwed up once before."

"No," Fay said, horrified that she'd hurt Josie, seeing the tears in the girl's eyes. "No. You deserve all those things. You deserve a second chance."

"So do you! Don't you see? Whatever mistakes you've made, whatever you've done that you regret, they're in the past. You need to forgive yourself and move on."

Forgive herself. It was something she'd never thought possible. *Until Zach.*

"Oh, God," Fay gasped on a sob. "You're right. I messed up."

Josie wiped at the tears on her cheeks. "Then make it right."

Fay pulled the girl in for a quick, fierce hug, then yanked open the door, raced across the porch and ran down the sidewalk. But she was too late.

Zach was gone.

ZACH ANSWERED THE door that evening and almost shut it again. Would have if Elijah hadn't done his ninja trick and slipped inside, quick as you please.

"What are you doing here?" he asked Fay, who was holding on to Mitchell's hand.

"We came to see you," Elijah said, checking out the hotel room's TV set.

Mitch nodded as if in full agreement with his brother. "We missed you."

Zach's hand tightened on the door handle. "Now's not a good—"

"Please, Zach," Fay said softly. "Don't turn us away."

Damn it. Damn her. He hadn't turned her away—she'd done that. She didn't love him. Didn't trust him.

What the hell was she doing here now?

"How did you know where to find me?" he asked as Mitch brushed past him to join Elijah in the room.

"Kane told me."

So much for brotherly solidarity.

Then again, after Zach left Bradford House

this morning, he hadn't told Kane that his staying at King's Crossing, a hotel on the river, was a secret—he should have.

He stepped out into the hall, keeping the door open behind him so they could see the boys. "Low blow, Fay," he said, "bringing the boys with you."

She nodded, wide-eyed and nervous and so damn beautiful it made his chest ache. "I figured there was a better chance of you hearing me out if I brought them."

Like he'd said, low blow. Then again, she'd tossed his love back in his face, ripped his heart out and stomped on it, so dragging two little kids across town all so she could have a few minutes of Zach's time wasn't that surprising.

"What do you want?" he asked.

"Can I come in?" she asked, glancing over as a middle-aged man in a suit left his room to the left.

Zach leaned against the doorjamb. "What do you want?"

She flushed and he felt some remorse for being so hard on her, but she hadn't even given him a chance. Hadn't given *them* a chance, and that pissed him off but good. She still didn't trust herself, didn't trust her feelings and wasn't brave enough to go after what she wanted, and he was done being her freaking cheerleader.

"I was wrong," she said, her quiet words blowing through him like a storm, ripping his insides to shreds. "Please give me another chance."

But he wasn't stupid enough to fall for that again. "One more last chance?" he asked. "I'm afraid you've used those up."

He turned to go back inside, but she touched his shoulder. "Zach, please…"

"No," he growled, whirling around. "You don't get to come here acting wounded. You did this. This was your choice."

She nodded. "I know. And it was the wrong choice. I never should have let you go this morning. I never should have walked out on you last night. I was scared."

"Of me?"

"Of my feelings for you," she admitted softly. "I told myself that I couldn't care about you as much as I thought, not after hanging on to the idea of me and Shane for so long. And part of me was afraid to love you, afraid that I'd lose myself again."

"And now?" he asked, hope burning in his chest.

She stepped closer. "Now I realize that my feelings are real and strong. You once told me that when you look at me, you see possibilities, and that is the nicest thing anyone has ever said to me. I wanted to live up to those possibilities. But I couldn't. Not until I forgave myself for everything. For taking those pills and for holding on to a man who didn't deserve me or my sons. You've helped me do that. You've helped me be ready to move on. I love you, Zach. I love you and I want to be with you. Please tell me I'm not too late. That I haven't ruined everything."

"You haven't ruined it," he said, his voice gruff with emotion. He trailed his fingers down her cheek. "I love you, Fay."

She smiled tremulously. "I love you, Zach. I might still get scared sometimes," she warned him, "but I promise to never walk away from you again. I will fight for you. For us. I'm giving you my heart. More than that, I'm giving you my sons."

Humbled and so grateful he could barely see straight, Zach pulled her to him. Kissed her. "I'll cherish them. I promise."

She touched his cheek. "I know you will. How could you not? This, our story, is the right story. And you're my happy ending."

* * * * *

LARGER-PRINT BOOKS!

GET 2 FREE LARGER-PRINT NOVELS PLUS
2 FREE GIFTS!

⊕ HARLEQUIN®

Romance

From the Heart, For the Heart

YES! Please send me 2 FREE LARGER-PRINT Harlequin® Romance novels and my 2 FREE gifts (gifts are worth about $10). After receiving them, if I don't wish to receive any more books, I can return the shipping statement marked "cancel." If I don't cancel, I will receive 4 brand-new novels every month and be billed just $5.09 per book in the U.S. or $5.49 per book in Canada. That's a savings of at least 15% off the cover price! It's quite a bargain! Shipping and handling is just 50¢ per book in the U.S. and 75¢ per book in Canada.* I understand that accepting the 2 free books and gifts places me under no obligation to buy anything. I can always return a shipment and cancel at any time. Even if I never buy another book, the two free books and gifts are mine to keep forever.

119/319 HDN GHWC

Name	(PLEASE PRINT)

Address	Apt. #

City	State/Prov.	Zip/Postal Code

Signature (if under 18, a parent or guardian must sign)

Mail to the **Reader Service:**
IN U.S.A.: P.O. Box 1867, Buffalo, NY 14240-1867
IN CANADA: P.O. Box 609, Fort Erie, Ontario L2A 5X3
Want to try two free books from another line?
Call 1-800-873-8635 or visit www.ReaderService.com.

* Terms and prices subject to change without notice. Prices do not include applicable taxes. Sales tax applicable in N.Y. Canadian residents will be charged applicable taxes. Offer not valid in Quebec. This offer is limited to one order per household. Not valid for current subscribers to Harlequin Romance Larger-Print books. All orders subject to credit approval. Credit or debit balances in a customer's account(s) may be offset by any other outstanding balance owed by or to the customer. Please allow 4 to 6 weeks for delivery. Offer available while quantities last.

Your Privacy—The Reader Service is committed to protecting your privacy. Our Privacy Policy is available online at www.ReaderService.com or upon request from the Reader Service.

We make a portion of our mailing list available to reputable third parties that offer products we believe may interest you. If you prefer that we not exchange your name with third parties, or if you wish to clarify or modify your communication preferences, please visit us at www.ReaderService.com/consumerschoice or write to us at Reader Service Preference Service, P.O. Box 9062, Buffalo, NY 14240-9062. Include your complete name and address.

HRLP15

LARGER-PRINT
BOOKS!

⬥HARLEQUIN

Presents®

GET 2 FREE LARGER-PRINT
NOVELS PLUS 2 FREE GIFTS!

PASSION GUARANTEED SEDUCTION

YES! Please send me 2 FREE LARGER-PRINT Harlequin Presents® novels and my 2 FREE gifts (gifts are worth about $10). After receiving them, if I don't wish to receive any more books, I can return the shipping statement marked "cancel." If I don't cancel, I will receive 6 brand-new novels every month and be billed just $5.30 per book in the U.S. or $5.74 per book in Canada. That's a saving of at least 12% off the cover price! It's quite a bargain! Shipping and handling is just 50¢ per book in the U.S. and 75¢ per book in Canada.* I understand that accepting the 2 free books and gifts places me under no obligation to buy anything. I can always return a shipment and cancel at any time. Even if I never buy another book, the two free books and gifts are mine to keep forever.

176/376 HDN GHVY

Name	(PLEASE PRINT)	
Address		Apt. #
City	State/Prov.	Zip/Postal Code

Signature (if under 18, a parent or guardian must sign)

Mail to the **Reader Service:**
IN U.S.A.: P.O. Box 1867, Buffalo, NY 14240-1867
IN CANADA: P.O. Box 609, Fort Erie, Ontario L2A 5X3

**Are you a subscriber to Harlequin Presents® books
and want to receive the larger-print edition?
Call 1-800-873-8635 today or visit us at www.ReaderService.com.**

* Terms and prices subject to change without notice. Prices do not include applicable taxes. Sales tax applicable in N.Y. Canadian residents will be charged applicable taxes. Offer not valid in Quebec. This offer is limited to one order per household. Not valid for current subscribers to Harlequin Presents Larger-Print books. All orders subject to credit approval. Credit or debit balances in a customer's account(s) may be offset by any other outstanding balance owed by or to the customer. Please allow 4 to 6 weeks for delivery. Offer available while quantities last.

Your Privacy—The Reader Service is committed to protecting your privacy. Our Privacy Policy is available online at www.ReaderService.com or upon request from the Reader Service.

We make a portion of our mailing list available to reputable third parties that offer products we believe may interest you. If you prefer that we not exchange your name with third parties, or if you wish to clarify or modify your communication preferences, please visit us at www.ReaderService.com/consumerchoice or write to us at Reader Service Preference Service, P.O. Box 9062, Buffalo, NY 14240-9062. Include your complete name and address.

HPLP15

LARGER-PRINT BOOKS!
GET 2 FREE LARGER-PRINT NOVELS PLUS
2 FREE GIFTS!

H HARLEQUIN®

INTRIGUE
BREATHTAKING ROMANTIC SUSPENSE

YES! Please send me 2 FREE LARGER-PRINT Harlequin® Intrigue novels and my 2 FREE gifts (gifts are worth about $10). After receiving them, if I don't wish to receive any more books, I can return the shipping statement marked "cancel." If I don't cancel, I will receive 6 brand-new novels every month and be billed just $5.49 per book in the U.S. or $6.24 per book in Canada. That's a saving of at least 11% off the cover price! It's quite a bargain! Shipping and handling is just 50¢ per book in the U.S. and 75¢ per book in Canada.* I understand that accepting the 2 free books and gifts places me under no obligation to buy anything. I can always return a shipment and cancel at any time. Even if I never buy another book, the two free books and gifts are mine to keep forever.

199/399 HDN GHWN

Name _____ (PLEASE PRINT) _____

Address _____ Apt. # _____

City _____ State/Prov. _____ Zip/Postal Code _____

Signature (if under 18, a parent or guardian must sign) _____

Mail to the **Reader Service:**
IN U.S.A.: P.O. Box 1867, Buffalo, NY 14240-1867
IN CANADA: P.O. Box 609, Fort Erie, Ontario L2A 5X3

**Are you a subscriber to Harlequin® Intrigue books
and want to receive the larger-print edition?
Call 1-800-873-8635 today or visit www.ReaderService.com.**

* Terms and prices subject to change without notice. Prices do not include applicable taxes. Sales tax applicable in N.Y. Canadian residents will be charged applicable taxes. Offer not valid in Quebec. This offer is limited to one order per household. Not valid for current subscribers to Harlequin Intrigue Larger-Print books. All orders subject to credit approval. Credit or debit balances in a customer's account(s) may be offset by any other outstanding balance owed by or to the customer. Please allow 4 to 6 weeks for delivery. Offer available while quantities last.

Your Privacy—The Reader Service is committed to protecting your privacy. Our Privacy Policy is available online at www.ReaderService.com or upon request from the Reader Service.

We make a portion of our mailing list available to reputable third parties that offer products we believe may interest you. If you prefer that we not exchange your name with third parties, or if you wish to clarify or modify your communication preferences, please visit us at www.ReaderService.com/consumerschoice or write to us at Reader Service Preference Service, P.O. Box 9062, Buffalo, NY 14240-9062. Include your complete name and address.

HILP15